FIVE HEART

Rebecca A. Sollitto

Bee's Publishing LLC

Content Warning

This story contains explicit sexual content and references to sexual assault. It also explores themes of power, vulnerability, and the ways women—particularly those working in creative and public spaces—can be exposed to exploitation and abuse. My intent is always to handle these subjects with emotional depth, but they may be painful or triggering for some readers. Please take care as you read, and proceed only if you feel safe doing so.

Dedication

To my parents for always believing in me, to Michael for your love and support, and to Nicole for being part of the journey. I love you all.

Chapter 1

Sabrina

What have I gotten myself into?
I flick my hand half-heartedly at yet another yellow cab as it speeds past. "Damn it," I mutter, hiking up the sleeve of my blazer to glance at the face of my Tudor. Five o'clock sharp. I'd promised Jerry, my editor, that I'd drop off the NYPD documents from the drug raid I covered this week. But I also promised *her* I'd be at Luger's steakhouse by 5:45.

I glance back down at my watch. Forty-five minutes. Midtown is buzzing, as always. Cabs, pedicabs, delivery bikes, the human current of 53rd flowing like I'm invisible. I'm as transparent as cellophane.

"Fuck this," I growl, stepping into the crowd and descending the subway steps two at a time. Jerry can get the paperwork tomorrow.

I rarely admit I have a MetroCard, it's one of my many quiet shames, but tonight, I've got no choice. What does *she* want to meet for anyway?

I squeeze onto the train behind a mother and her daughter. Their shopping bags brush my thigh as I grab the overhead bar. The girl grins up at me, the pure joy of a gapped-tooth smile. I smile back and stick out my tongue. She giggles. Her mother spins her around with a glare, shielding her from me like I'm going to kidnap her daughter. Do I have something in my teeth?

I fumble for my phone to check my reflection in the camera when a text flashes across the screen: *See you at 5:45. I got us a table in the private room, back of the restaurant.*

The pit of my stomach drops. Dani.

Dani and I haven't spoken in over a decade. Not since Five Heart exploded.

My chest tightens. The train lurches forward. I scroll through social media, fingers trembling, desperate for distraction, anything to pull me from the undertow of anxiety now crashing in waves. The usual parade of filtered bliss scrolls past. Shiny people, curated joy, another birthday brunch.

I type *Danielle Richmond* into the search bar. Her real name. The old one. Her original Facebook pops up. One hundred twenty friends. No updates in years. The last post? A grainy shot from a solo gig in Milan. The rest, mostly "Happy Birthday" posts from our old high school classmates. There's mine from last year. "Happy birthday queen!"

Fake, but polite. I ex out and type what I should've started with: Dani Rose. The name that turned her into a brand. Pages of fan accounts flood the screen. Album drops, perfume lines, interviews, American Idol Season 40 judge, red carpet photos, endorsement deals.

I click on a fan page. The profile picture makes my breath catch. Us. The five of us. Frozen in time, preserved like pressed flowers from a life that feels like someone else's dream. I haven't seen that photo since the day we shot it. And now? Now I have forty minutes to gather a decade's worth of courage.

I haven't laid eyes on this picture since it originated. Dani's in the center, naturally, dripping in hot pink zebra print and glossy white pleather pants like she was born for the spotlight. Even at sixteen, her body moved like music, and those pants? Magic. It sickens me. Her hair cascaded in thick, bouncy brunette curls, the kind of volume that defied gravity and reason. We were the planets and she was the sun we orbited. I seethe with envy around Dani.

To her left, sprawled on the floor like some brown glowing goddess of glam, is Jonna. Legs for days. She wore a sparkling, silver chrome crop top with a matching mini skirt that caught every beam of light. Jonna never had to try; she just was breathtaking. She could have ruled the runway, but I think she's on baby number four now? She always mentioned wanting a big family like the one she was raised with. She probably gives all the moms in PTA a run for their money.

Clare stands to Dani's right, one arm raised triumphantly with her bejeweled guitar like some glitter-drenched warrior. That tight aquamarine bandage dress hugged her petite frame like it was custom created for her body. Platinum blonde, sweet as sugar, but fiery as hell. The kind of loud-spoken, obnoxious maneater that made boys stammer and girls feel total jealousy. She never fully realized the spell she cast on the world. Last I heard, she passed her bar exam. She got married too. Not that I made the guest list. Long Story.

And there's me. Ugh.

Shimmied in next to Dani the Icon, and behind Jonna's flawless legs, half-swallowed by the spotlight and trying to pretend I belong. My bass hangs awkwardly against me in a red-and-white checkered dress I swear I didn't choose, paired with a torn denim jacket like the ghost of grunge made a Target run. I'd begged to dye my hair for the album cover, but our manager Steve had snapped, "Red hair is your signature!" So, there I was, copper curls that I was born with, spilling over one eye like I was hiding, throwing a half-hearted peace sign that felt more like a white flag. Who was I trying to be?

And then way off to the right, there's Nora. Her long, jet-black hair is sleek and haunting, draped over her shoulders like a curtain. Dressed in a black leather jacket and a dark mini dress, she leaned against Clare, arms folded, expression blank. They branded her as the goth one, like that was all she was.

We all had our roles, right? I was the quirky redhead. Jonna, the exotic beauty. Clare, the glowing pop princess. Dani, our fiery frontwoman, already a legend before she turned twenty. And Nora… Nora was sadness wrapped in silk. You can see it, if you really look. The way her eyes sink instead of shine. Nobody noticed it back then. But I did. Even in this photo, I can feel the weight of it, pressing at the edges.

Funny how we were all just girls playing parts written by strangers. And yet… this photo caught the truth. Or maybe I'm the only one able to see it.

It makes sense now, why she fell so far off the deep end. It started long before the tabloids got wind of it. Back when we were just kids. No one saw it then. But in this photo? The sadness in her eyes is undeniable. I linger on Nora the longest. Maybe because she's the one I remember most vividly.

Nora stayed with me in Hell's Kitchen six years ago, right when I landed my first gig in the *New York Times* mailroom. She had just turned twenty-one and wanted to see if city life was worth the noise. Nora and I always kept in touch after Five Heart's descent, so it was comforting to know a familiar face in the city. I was scraping by on an intern's salary and needed help with rent, so having her crash with me made sense. For a while, anyway. Then the drinking started. She'd sing at sleazy bars for quick cash, and the nights got darker. The crowd she ran with…even worse. And that boyfriend… what was his name again? Covered head to toe in tattoos, piercings like a pincushion. Ah—Dante.

I caught them once, coked out and tangled up in each other nude in our bathtub. I had only gotten up to pee. One glimpse of that chaos, and I knew I couldn't have her in my space anymore. I was straight edge. Focused. I'd just scored the internship of a lifetime, a foot in the door of a world I'd clawed toward for years after the fallout.

Maybe I shouldn't have kicked her out so fast. Maybe I should've helped her. But I was trying to build something for myself. A new name. One I could say with pride. A name that didn't include four other women who always seemed to eclipse me.

I save the photo of our old girl group, Five Heart, to my archives and click over to my Facebook profile. My headshot greets me: smooth blonde hair, professionally highlighted, crimson lips curved in a winning smile. I'm wearing my tailored ebony Armani suit, red-bottomed heels peeking out beneath the desk. The caption below: *Sabrina Daniel — Investigative Reporter, The New York Times.*

The swarm of anxiety begins to ease. In its place: the cool, quiet hum of satisfaction, a feeling of worthiness, and earned self-respect.

"Ninth Ave," the train's polite voice announces. My stop. My nostalgia evaporates in an instant. Snap. Back to reality.

I dart forward, squeezing through the closing doors just in time. I don't usually make the trek to Brooklyn, but I know the backstreets like muscle memory—my ex used to live near the bridge. The sharp clack of my Valentinos echoes against the pavement as I weave through the crowd toward the restaurant.

Approaching the packed entrance, I pause. Phone up. My front-facing camera on. Reflection looks phenomenal. Smile on. I smooth the creases in my blazer, square my shoulders, and brace myself. Time to reunite with our Lord and Savior herself, Dani Rose.

FIVE HEART

Chapter 2

Jonna

"Honey, please get the kids up!" I shout from behind the closed bathroom door.

The only time I get to myself, to actually breathe, is first thing in the morning. I sit on the toilet for forty-five blessed minutes, scrolling through my photo gallery while pretending I'm relieving my bladder. I pray Dexter doesn't notice.

The kids are getting so big. Alissa, my youngest, just two months old, still has my hormones tangled in knots. I swipe through photos, tearing up as I stare at the snapshots of our growing family. Dexter, Jr., aka DJ, our oldest, starts fifth grade today. Harley's just two years behind, heading into third. I love that they're close enough in age to look out for one another at school. Finn, my little shadow, is starting preschool today. Three years old. How did that happen? And then there's Alissa. I stop on a recent picture of her. Rounded cheeks and perfect, sleeping like an angel. She looks exactly like my brother who passed away last year. Every time I see her, I see him. But instead of breaking my heart, it gives me hope. A reminder that he still exists, through her.

I glance at the time on my phone. Only five minutes?

"DEXTER! GET THE KIDS UP!" I yell again, louder this time.

I pause, listening for signs of life in the house. Nothing. Underwear still around my ankles, I kick open the door and bellow, "HUN, THE KIDS—"

Dexter is standing right in front of me, shirtless, in his plaid pajama pants, holding two steaming cups of coffee. Startled, he flinches and spills one of them all over his bare chest.

"SHIT, SHIT, SHIT!" he yelps, bolting to the sink and splashing cold water across his now-flushed skin.

"Oh my God!" I fumble my phone, trying to rush over, but trip over my own underwear and crash onto the tile next to the puddle of lukewarm coffee.

We freeze. Lock eyes. And I burst out laughing.

"What the fuck!" I wheeze through uncontrollable giggles.

A crooked grin creeps onto Dexter's face, and finally, that familiar hearty laugh pours out of him. It's been months since I've heard it. We laugh together until we're breathless. He offers me his hand and pulls me up from the floor.

"What the heck was that?" he says, shaking his head. We stare at our reflection in the mirror. Disheveled, mismatched, half-dressed, stretchmarks galore, and we keep laughing.

"Mommy?" Harley stands in the doorway, her face puzzled. Her eyes land on my bare backside.

"Oh honey, you're up!" I yank my underwear back on and quickly turn to face her.

"Yeah, Daddy got us up," she says, still confused. I glance at Dexter, relief washing over me.

He always comes through. Even when I want to nag him (a trait I unwillingly inherited from my mother), he's our rock.

"Thank you," I mouth. He nods and starts cleaning up the mess while I grab my phone and lead Harley downstairs to the kitchen.

DJ's already dressed in his school uniform, shoveling Fruit Loops into his mouth like Kellogg's is going out of business. Harley joins him, pouring her own bowl. Finn's sprawled on the vinyl floor, coloring green circles outside the lines of his Spider-Man coloring book.

"Finn, Spider-Man's red, remember?" I say as I pour myself a cup of liquid survival.

"I think he thinks it's the Green Goblin," DJ mumbles between mouthfuls.

"No, he just likes the color green," Harley says, admiring Finn's work.

I ruffle Finn's hair on my way to the fridge. "It's beautiful, bud."

Ding. A text.

"I saw Mommy's butt!" Harley squeals to her brothers.

"EWWW!" DJ and Finn scream in unison, making faces.

"Not my proudest moment," I mutter, sipping my coffee, and check my phone. The chaos around me fades when I see the name on my screen.

Dani. Dani Rose. The kids' voices blur into white noise. My gaze locks on the message notification. Do I open it? Are my read receipts on? I panic, rush to Settings, and shut them off, just in case I decide not to respond. But I hesitate. Just her name stirs up a whirlwind.

I must have zoned out because the next thing I hear is Finn crying bloody murder, Harley and DJ fighting over markers, and chaos returning in full force. Dexter strolls in, now dressed for work. Handsome as ever in navy slacks and a pinstriped button-down.

"What's going on?" he asks, scooping up a sobbing Finn.

I set my phone down and switch into Mom Mode. "Let go of those markers! They're your brother's!" I bark.

"I was just showing him the red one and DJ snatched it!" Harley protests.

"No I didn't! She's lying!" DJ yells back.

As they bicker, Dexter glances at me. Really looks at me. He always knows when something's wrong. "What's the matter, babe?"

"Dani." The name falls out before I can stop it.

"The singer?"

I nod.

"What about her?" he asks.

"She messaged me. I haven't opened it yet."

Without a word, Dexter takes my phone and taps it open.

"Wait!" I protest, but it's too late.

He scans it. "She misses you. Wants you to come stay with her in Manhattan this weekend for her birthday."

I blink. "What? That's... so random. I haven't seen her in years."

"Four, right?" he asks.

"Something like that," I mumble, pulling my hair into a messy knot.

"I can't just up and leave. What does she think? I'm a mother of four!" I start angrily unloading clean dishes from the sink to the cabinets, trying to distract myself from the emotional whiplash. "She can't just expect everyone to drop their lives whenever she calls. We're not in high school anymore."

"I think you should go," Dexter says, voice soft.

I pause mid-rant. "...What?!"

"You should go," he says, gently shutting the cabinet and turning me toward him.

Our noses almost touch. We're eye to eye. Always have been. At 6'1", I was the tallest girl in school, and it made finding someone to match me nearly impossible. But Dexter? He matches me in height, strength and heart.

"You deserve a weekend away. Manhattan's only two hours from Locust Valley. My mom's coming to stay this weekend, remember? You don't want to host her anyway." He smirks. He's not wrong.

"But the baby," I say, tearing up. Damn hormones.

"She'll be fine. So will DJ, Harley, and Finn. Go see your friend. Maybe she needs you, like that last time…" His voice trails off.

Yeah. Dani always reaches out when she needs something. Last time, I was a glorified babysitter to her at her grammy afterparty.

"I wonder if she messaged the other girls too… Maybe I'll call Clare? I know they still talk."

"Didn't Clare help her with that copyright infringement case last year?"

"Something like that." I pull up Clare's number in my contacts. She's still my best friend, even after the death of Five Heart. We stayed close. She was my maid of honor, and I was hers, in Palm Springs just last year.

"Call her. Go to the city. We'll be fine," Dexter says, grabbing the lunch I packed him and kissing my forehead. He tilts my chin, looking me square in the eyes. "I love you. Let me know what you decide." He kisses Finn on the head, yells goodbye to the kids and wishes them a great first day at school before heading out the door.

I stare at my phone, debating what to do. The truth is, I already know I'll say yes. I just don't know if I'm ready for the storm that comes with it.

Chapter 3

Clare

It's a scorching August day in Orange County, and I am so done with this heat. Heat from my boss, my clients, my husband, and the actual freakin' weather. I wave a folder full of client documents in front of my face, trying to create a breeze. Sweat trickles down between my breasts, so I unbutton the top two buttons of my blouse, revealing just a hint of cleavage. Thank God for Vic's Coffee. I take a long sip of my iced mocha latte and keep fanning.

"Is there anything else I can get for you, ma'am?" the young waiter asks, eyes glued to my chest.

"Eyes up here, buddy," I say coolly, taking another sip. "No, thank you. Just the check." Before he walks away, I gently grab his wrist. "I'm also not a ma'am. I'm maybe five years older than you," I assure him with a smirk.

He flashes a devilish smile. "You know, you look like someone famous. My older brother had a poster of her on his wall growing up. Clare Devon, ever heard of her?"

I roll my eyes and slurp the last of my watered-down coffee, obnoxiously. "Yeah, who hasn't?" I flick my hand and dismiss him. Just as I'm about to leave, my phone buzzes again for what feels like the hundredth time today.

"What do you want now?" I bark at the phone, ignoring the judging stares around me. Whatever. Let them stare.

Twenty-five missed calls. All from Damien. He's spiraling.

Which… fine, he kind of has a right. I shouldn't have slept with my partner at work. But come on! Tom is so hot. When you spend every waking minute with someone that attractive, how do you not end up sucking their face off? Also, Damien has absolutely zero depth to him. All he talks about are his precious collector vehicles and blow. Tom is more than the surface… he's the Mariana trench.

Ever since I handled Dani's case last year, my career has launched into the stratosphere. Now I'm the go-to reputation attorney for the elite. I stepped away from the spotlight as a kid, but somehow, here I am again. There are perks. Being married just makes those perks harder to fully enjoy.

Damien calls again. I rush outside and press my back against the coffee shop door, unbuttoning a third button to let my lace ebony bustier peek through.

"What?" I snap into the phone, sweat collecting at my hairline.

"Babe, where have you been? Your location either glitched or you turned it off," Damien says, his voice tight.

"Ugh." I sigh hard. "Can't a girl get coffee in peace?"

"I was just worried," he mumbles.

"No. You wanted to see if I was fucking Tom." I hang up. "It's too hot for this nonsense," I mutter, brushing down the frizz on my blown-out blonde hair.

I take a deep breath, push my breasts together, and strut back inside Vic's like I own it. Just like my mother always ingrained in my brain, "Always show confidence, that's how you'll find a wealthy fellow." Now, it has become my mantra.

The women glare. Their husbands wink. I can't help but feel utter satisfaction when the effect of, well me, grabs hold of every person in the room. Eyes follow me all the way to the counter, where my server is waiting with the bill. I hand him my black titanium credit card and twirl my hair around my finger.

"Sorry about that. Just a call from a new prospect," I say smoothly.

"I've never seen a black card before," he says, wide-eyed.

A sharp laugh escapes from my core, loud enough to demand the whole shop's attention. "Oh, honey. You haven't seen anything yet."

Of course, the card's not mine. It's the firm card. My boss is the real powerhouse. I just happen to benefit from working under him. Or on top of him… depending on the day.

I sashay out to my newly-leased pearl Benz C300 and blast the A/C, watching joggers, bikers, rollerbladers, couples holding hands, all soaking in the summer heat while I'm simmering in my own scandal. Ding. Another message.

"What now, Damien?" I groan, rubbing the lines from my forehead. But it's not Damien. It's Dani.

Oh God. What have you gotten yourself into now, Rose? I open the message.

Hey girlfriend! Miss you tons. I have a HUGE client for you. I'm at my Manhattan penthouse this week. Come by this weekend, flights are on me. I know it's inconvenient, but it's also my birthday. I'd love to spend it with you! Also, this client is BIG!

My curiosity spikes. Who is it? Clooney? Jolie? I've always wanted to work with Angelina. If only I had been an attorney when she split from Brad…

I type back quickly: *I'M IN! Here's my CashApp for the flight: ClareBearxoxo.*

Send.

It's probably for the best to get away for a few days. The whole Tom situation is still fresh, and Damien is… unwell. I swear, he's so obsessed with me, I wonder if he'd still stay if I murdered someone.

"I need to be around people who aren't driving me insane," I declare to myself and drive to the firm.

Breaker & Gallagher, Attorneys of Orange County—the sign on the building taunts me.

It should say DEVON & Gallagher. Yes, my name in front of Tom's. I imagine the sign, bright and bold. Clare Devon, in lights. I smirk at my own delusions.

Tom's in the office today. He's wearing that emerald green Gucci suit that hugs every part of him just right. Former Buccaneers player. Total Florida boy turned SoCal powerhouse. Went to Stetson for law school, ditched football, and never looked back. But his body? Still built like a wide receiver. Slick brunette hair. Perfect five o'clock shadow. Sculpted jaw, stubbled chest.   Damien could never. Damien is a Sicilian sliver of the man Tom is.

Being petite and on stage with Five Heart, the other girls always towered over me. I hated it. Always tried to push my way to the front of the stage. But a man that can tower over me? That, I can swing with. I stroll into the building like it's front and center stage and head straight to Tom's office.

"Clare," he says sternly, that tone he uses when he's trying to act like he's in charge.

But there's a softness too, a flicker of surrender. I've got him wrapped around my finger. I shove the folders off his desk and slide onto the edge, legs parted slightly. He leans back in his chair, visibly relaxing.

"Ms. Devon," he smirks, twirling the cap of his pen against my thigh, "what do you think you're doing?"

"Oh, you know," I tease, tracing my stiletto along his groin, "just losing my mind over all the assignments my big, bad boss keeps piling on."

He closes his eyes for a moment, probably imagining me naked on his desk. He reaches for my shirt, ready to rip it open, but I slap a folder between his hand and my cleavage.

"Uh uh uh… not yet," I sing, wagging a finger.

"What?" he groans, loosening his tie.

"I need the rest of the week off. Dani invited me to Manhattan. It's her birthday. She also has a huge celebrity client for me. So technically, it's work."

He rolls his eyes. "Did someone die or something?"

"No! Like I said, birthday. Plus, it's Dani Rose. This could be big. Maybe career-changing."

"You can go," he says finally, "but only if you come here, sugar lips."

He yanks the tie off and pops open my blouse, my lace bustier and curves spilling out. I laugh, letting him lift me onto the desk. We fold into each other like silk and flame. Somewhere in the back of my mind, a whisper of logic chimes in, *Now if only convincing Damien was as easy as undoing Tom's tie.*

Chapter 4

Dani

Outside the plane window, rain pelts the tarmac, blurring Nashville into the same washed-out gray that's been clouding me the last few days. Washed-out and sleepy, exactly how I'm feeling. The seatbelt sign dings above, snapping me out of my daze.

"How you doing, darling?" my mom asks softly, her Southern accent wrapping around the words like a hug. She hands me a can of ginger ale and two Advil, then buckles herself in across from me. I shrug. Pop the pills. Wash them down.

"I'm okay," I lie. But she knows I'm not. She always knows. She looks at me with those gentle, knowing eyes, but doesn't push. Not today. Not yet.

"Death's never easy to navigate," she says quietly. "Especially someone who was like a sister to you. If you want to talk, I'm here, baby." She leans back, pulling a furry sleep mask over her eyes, giving me space. I sigh as the plane lifts off. Up and away.

FIVE HEART

We land a few hours later at Teterboro. Private, quiet. Easier to move unnoticed. Wearing a baggy heather gray hoodie and matching sweats, I sling my Dior bag over my shoulder and head for the nearest restroom in the lounge.

I glance in the mirror and flinch. Hair: a tangled mess in a loose bun. Mascara: smudged beneath my eyes like a bad noir film. Sweatshirt: stained with ketchup, of all things. I strip off the hoodie and stuff it into my duffle. Black tank top and sweats will do. My phone buzzes. Rolf, my driver, has arrived. Outside, my mom waits beside the Range Rover. Rolf rushes out and opens my door like always.

"Good morning, Ms. Rose. I hope your flight was excellent," he says in his broken English.

I manage a small smile and slide into the backseat. My mom responds for me, cheerful as ever. "Oh, it was just divine, as always! We love a good mimosa on a private jet, helps with flying jitters." She's the light, always. Knows when to push and when to pretend.

We pull out of Jersey and into Manhattan. The roads are oddly clear for a Monday. Eerily so. I barely have time to sink into my thoughts before the Range Rover rolls to a stop on Cornelia Street.

Home. Well, one of them. I own the penthouse above one of the historic buildings. I usually live in my Nashville bungalow, but New York felt right for this visit.

My mom gives me a soft hug goodbye. Rolf escorts me unseen through the lobby and into the private elevator.

I open the front door. My penthouse is untouched. Sterile. Exactly how I left it. The cleaning crew is clearly overachieving. Not even a single fingerprint. I toss my bags to the floor and sink into the curved ivory velvet couch in the center of the great room. I grab the remote and flip on the 88-inch mounted TV.

Rambling politics. Good. The news hasn't broken yet. Only two people know the truth. Me. And my mom. Why was I given this responsibility? Anxiety claws its way up from my gut. I pull my knees to my chest and fight the tears rising fast. Then I hear it.

"In other pop culture news, Dani Rose has canceled her upcoming Diaries Tour…"

My head snaps up. I jack up the volume.

"Fans are outraged after already grappling with high ticket prices. Now, a sudden cancellation leaves them confused and disappointed. Rose and her team have yet to confirm whether refunds will be issued."

A teen girl appears on-screen. "I saved all year for this concert. I just bought my ticket a few days ago. I was so excited. Now it's canceled? It's such a slap in the face. I'm really disappointed in Dani."

I turn off the TV. My reflection stares back at me in the black screen. Mascara streaked. Eyes red. Shoulders slumped.

And I break. I fall apart, sobbing into the silence. The kind of cry that pulls from somewhere in the deepest trenches of your being. The feeling that fame can't reach and money can't numb. I stumble to my bag, digging through blindly until I find my phone. My nightly ritual of scrolling through my contacts, hovering my finger over one of the girl's names, almost curating enough courage to press 'call', always made me feel still connected to them all somehow. I needed to feel that more than anything.

Beep beep. A gallery notification popped up instantly. *This day, 10 years ago.*

A photo. Me. The girls. *Five Heart*. All of us, together. Happy. It was that show we did in San Diego. The impromptu concert we put on by the shore for the locals. Just us, raw and real, no PR stunt, no marketing plan. Just heart. Even Nora, in the photo, was grinning ear to ear with her tongue sticking out like a goofball. I can still smell the salt air, and hear the seagulls screaming above the speakers. I cry harder. But I smile, too. God, I miss them.

My fingers hover over the screen. Maybe… Maybe I can bring them together. Just for one weekend. I need to stop being a coward and reach out to them. But, how…

My birthday. I almost forgot I turn 28 this month.

I wipe my face and start crafting texts, each one personalized. Sabrina will want the scoop. It could boost her career. She deserves that. She lives just a few blocks away, I think. I never make time for her when I'm in the city… not that she'd want me to. But maybe this time…

Clare will bite the moment I mention a potential celebrity client. I'll bait her with just enough mystery. She's too curious to say no, and she loves free flights. Free anything, really. I chuckle to myself. Cheap as ever, ClareBear. But Jonna…

Jonna just had her baby. There's no way she'll leave her newborn behind. Still, I have to try. I'll just be honest. With all of them. I just… miss them. I miss us. Five Heart. Who knew that going solo would come with so much silence?

I tap out each message, rewriting them until they're just right. Then I hit send. One by one. And whisper a prayer into the empty apartment. I just need my girls back. Even if only for a weekend.

Chapter 5

Sabrina

I push my way through the revolving doors of the packed steakhouse. Even for an early Friday evening, this place is buzzing. I weave through clusters of people, silently annoyed. If anyone still recognized me, the crowd would part like the Red Sea. But my red hair's gone, and with it, my spotlight. I stumble toward the hostess stand, frustrated.

"Hi, how many in your party?" the hostess greets with a fake smile.

"Um… two, I think?"

"Reservation?"

"Yes, I'm here for the 'private room.'" I air-quote sarcastically.

Her expression changes. She whispers to her co-host, who whispers back. "Yes, Ms. Daniel, right this way."

"How do you know my… name?" I trail off, trying to keep up as she speeds ahead.

We move past elegant diners, wine critics, and foodies, all immersed in their five-star steaks. Eventually, we reach a door marked Wine Cellar.

"The room's in the cellar?" I ask, raising an eyebrow.

"Ms. Rose requested utter and complete privacy, so we created a special setting just for you." Her face is glowing with pride.

"But isn't it, like, freezing in there?"

"We temporarily moved all the wine to a separate storage. It's been repurposed for you and your guests."

Guests? Dani, who else did you invite…?

The hostess descends the stone stairs, and I follow reluctantly. To my surprise, the cellar is stunning, like a private scene out of a Tuscan romance. A long mahogany table stretches down the center, draped in ivory cheesecloth. Taper candles flicker from vintage brass holders, casting golden light onto the rustic wood-paneled walls.

And there she is. Dani Rose. Billboard-charting, perfume-selling, global icon. But in this dim candlelight, sitting nervously in a gold Chiavari chair, she looks less like Dani Rose… and more like Danielle, my best friend.

Long Island high school memories flood me. Carpooling with her mom Stacy, singing in the backseat, scribbling lyrics in the margins of our notebooks. Danielle and I'd had dreams. To write, to sing, to shine, and to overcome anything that came our way. She was always shy about performing, but I lived for the spotlight. We'd been cast in our high school production of *Rent* as Maureen and Joanne. She froze on stage during the first verse… so I took over as Maureen. She regained her confidence as Joanne by verse two. That's what we did. Balanced each other.

Now, in this moment, I see her again, the same terrified expression from that stage. She's frozen. Pleading with her eyes.

"Dani," I say. Her vulnerability is like a shiver in the air, but as soon as I step closer, it vanishes. She straightens her back, flips her auburn waves, flashes the gold Rolex, the Cartier Love bracelets. Dani Rose returns.

"Sabrina?" she squeals, standing up and embracing me tightly. I freeze. My arms hover awkwardly before patting her back. It's been ten years since I've touched her.

"It's me," I say, dryly. She steps back, looking me over.

"You went blonde!"

"Mhm."

She leads me to the table. "Come sit next to me. We have so much to catch up on!" I move like a robot and sit stiffly beside her. She beams. "I'm so proud of you, Sabrina. You always wanted to be Lois Lane, and you did it!"

I smile sheepishly. "Well, yeah… I guess you're right."

"Don't be shy! You're killing it. When you cracked the Evan Peterson case? Mind. Blown." She even does the explosion gesture.

"Thank you," I say, modestly.

"And you, Dani… I mean, come on," I try to return the energy, but it comes out almost monotone. She looks away, her gaze distant. I feel the mood slipping, so I push harder. "You became the Stevie of our generation. I'm proud of you. Truly." Somewhere deep inside, a part of me means what I say. Even though I love my career and always wanted to be an investigative reporter…a part of me still misses that stage. That spotlight. That girl with the guitar. But not the girl who got bossed around. Not the "nerdy redhead" outshined by early-blooming bandmates. Dani grabs my hands and squeezes warmly.

Click, clack, click, clack. Heels echo on the stone stairs.

"Girls!" Dani exclaims, letting go of me to embrace Clare and Jonna in a dramatic group hug. I sit still, watching them. Stunning, all of them. Especially Clare. Did she get her boobs done? They turn to me. Oh god. Here it comes.

"BRINA!" Clare shrieks, nearly launching herself across the table.

"Clarebear!" I try to match her energy.

"Oh my god, Ms. Blondie! Who are you trying to be, me?!" she laughs.

"Maybe you were the inspiration," I reply lightheartedly. Clare sits on Dani's other side.

"Jonna, wow," I say. "You look amazing." Four kids and she looks untouched by motherhood. Especially after just delivering her newest addition, but Jonna was blessed with her parents' genetics. Pure Armenian descent.

"Thank you, Sabrina, so do you!" she replies, glowing.

Jonna takes the seat across from us. A fifth chair sits empty beside her. The waitstaff reenters like clockwork: one fills our water, another uncorks vintage Bordeaux, and the third lays out shrimp cocktail topped with caviar.

"Ladies, what a treat this is." Clare raises her glass. "Salute! To old friends, new places, and good graces."

"Cheers!" Jonna adds.

"Salute!" Dani echoes.

"Yay," I say, clinking glasses with them. Our eyes all slide to the empty chair.

"Did anyone reach out to Nora?" Jonna asks gently.

"I doubt she'd come," Clare blurts. "She's a loser." She downs her wine.

A knot twists in my gut. "She's not a loser. She's just a lost soul."

"She smoked meth at my ex's friend's condo!" Clare thunks her glass down.

"What?" Jonna gasps.

Clare leans in, always the gossip. "Two years ago. Before Damien. I was a paralegal for my ex's buddy, a personal injury lawyer. Nora said she was in LA for a supporting role. I guess she's acting now? I let her crash with me." She topped off her glass, then sipped her wine with a smirk. "Well, my ex throws a pool party, and I walk in on her smoking meth with some weirdos. Maybe it was crack? Who knows. She might've been the dealer."

We all stare, stunned. No one speaks. I swirl my wine, trying to mask the chill crawling down my spine.

Jonna raises her hand. "I have a Nora story, too." Dani winces slightly, I begin to feel the pit of guilt in my gut expand, and Clare perks up, the controversy bringing her to life.

"Do tell!"

"She stayed with me a few years ago," says Jonna. "Said her boyfriend dumped her. She had nowhere to go. So, Dexter and I picked her up and she stayed a month."

"A month?" I ask, shocked.

"Jon, you never told me that!" Clare snaps.

"Yeah, well… she helped with the kids. Especially Finn. She really helped with my post-partum. Eventually she saved some money and left for Colorado. She said she had better chances there. Honestly? I kind of didn't want her to leave."

"Interesting," I whisper. "How'd we get from cocaine with Dante, to mommy's helper, to crackhead in Orange County?"

"Dante?" Clare's eyes widen. "Okay, now you need to share."

I nod. "She stayed with me when I got my internship at the *Times*. She helped out, paid rent. We always vibed. Even with her gloomy, emo energy, she was always a cool girl. But her partying got out of hand. So I…" I hesitated slightly, "…I kicked her out. No warning. Just gone." I stare into my hands, like the answer to Nora's spiral might be hiding in my palms.

"Wow, Sabrina," Dani whispers. I glance up. Her eyes are glassy. Full. Unblinking. "How could you do that?"

Clare and Jonna look at me, confused by the weight in Dani's voice.

"I… I had to." I whisper. "I was building something. I had to protect my future. I just hope she's okay." There's a long pause.

"Well, she's not." Dani's voice is sharper now. She stands. We all look at her. Tears streak down her cheeks, her hands trembling.

"There's a reason I asked you all here tonight." She exhales, trembling. Then, steady, she says it. "Nora is dead."

Chapter 6

Clare

What. The. Fuck. Did she just say what I think she just said? I glance back and forth between Sabrina and Jonna, then back at Dani. Everyone is silent. The girls are too stunned to speak.

"What the hell are you talking about?" I yell.

Dani looks me straight in the eye. "She's. *Dead.*" She begins to sob into her palms, completely defeated. She falls limp in her chair and, like clockwork, the girls and I tend to her in unison.

Jonna begins bawling her eyes out. Snot spilling out onto her dress sleeve. Sabrina firmly presses her hand on Dani's shoulder.

"How do you know?" Nosy Sabrina is the first to ask. It's the reporter in her. We all take a step back from Dani as she wipes the tears from her cheeks with the back of her hand and musters up the courage to tell us.

"Is that why you cancelled your *Diaries* tour so suddenly?" I ask, a slow wave of guilt from my earlier indiscretion creeping down into my chest.

Dani nods. "It's a long story," she mumbles, her voice hoarse. The waitstaff arrives with another bottle of wine, this time an Argentinian Malbec. Dani shoos them away before they can present the bottle.

"Wait." I gesture for the waiter to come back. "We may need the extra alcohol."

The waiter reluctantly pours our empty glasses to the top, draining the bottle, and darts back up the stairs.

"We've got booze and time. Spill the beans," I say, trying to lighten the situation. Maybe I'm being a little too lax.

The girls all turn to me with a dirty look. I shrug and sit back in my chair, taking a sip of peppery Malbec. Everyone leans in, hanging on Dani's next words.

"I was playing a show in Denver. It was a festival, lots of young people on molly and God knows what else. Nora showed up at my set. It was weird, because she'd been trying to reach out to me for a while before showing up. She called a few times, texted, wanted to get together. One of the messages made her sound… scared? I was so busy… I feel awful. I ignored a few messages, but I did call her back. She sounded… well, kind of drunk."

Typical Nora.

"When I spotted her in the crowd, I motioned for her to come backstage after my last song. She did. She hung out with my band. She seemed alright. Quiet. But… a little off. Frantic, maybe. Paranoid?"

"I invited her to grab food with me. I was starving. The only place open was a 24-hour diner around the corner from the festival. It was packed, and I kept getting stopped. I told Nora I'd be right back and just needed to clean up in the restroom. I was only gone five minutes." Dani stares at the floor.

"When I came out… I couldn't find her. The locals were crowding me for selfies and autographs. I couldn't find a waiter, they must have been short-staffed, so I asked the busboy if he'd seen her. He walked me through the empty kitchen. Said he saw her run out the back door. But when I went outside and around the side of the restaurant… Nora was on the ground in the ally. Seizing."

Dani starts to cry again but takes a deep breath and powers through.

"Thank God no one else was back there. But I almost wish there had been. I didn't know what to do. Nora died in my arms."

I'm too stunned to speak. I have so many questions. Just as I open my mouth, Sabrina pipes in. "What did you do? Did you take her to the hospital? Did you call her dad? Why hasn't anyone known about her death until now? This couldn't have just happened." Sabrina, all hard-hitting questions. Classic reporter.

Dani sighs. "It happened last weekend. Her dad hasn't returned any of my calls. He's probably out on a bender like usual. As for the hospital… I didn't want the media attention. She's still a celebrity, in a way. I kind of took matters into my own hands until I could see you girls."

"What do you mean, you 'took matters into your own hands'?" Jonna finally speaks. She sounds concerned.

"Yeah, what does that mean?" I add.

Dani looks at us warily. "Look, I know you're going to judge me, but I have a team of doctors working solely on Nora. They have their own center. We're waiting on the autopsy, but my team believes it was a fentanyl overdose."

Sabrina scoffs. "A team of doctors? Wow. Fame and fortune really do change people. Just because you're rich doesn't mean you can play God."

I kind of agree with Sabrina on this one.

"And what makes you think I won't bring this to *The Times* and write a piece? You can't drop this on me and expect me to stay quiet. Her family and friends deserve to know she's dead!"

Dani's cheeks flush. "Sabrina always needing the scoop. Even if it costs others everything!"

Okay, this is not good. Jonna shrinks into her chair nervously.

I stand up and raise a hand to get their attention. "Look! This is crazy-ass news for everyone. Sabrina has a right to be upset, and Dani, so do you. But Sabrina, just let Dani explain."

Sabrina folds into her chair, arms crossed, fuming.

Dani sighed, stuffing her hands in her lap.

"It was Nora's wish that I get together with you before news broke. So yeah, I'm dodging the press, but I'm also respecting her last request. And respecting you to be the first to know. She wanted us together." Dani's voice cracks.

"How do you know?" Jonna asks quietly.

"Did her ghost tell you?" Sabrina mocks.

Dani shoots daggers at her. "She left a note." She pulls a neatly folded piece of paper from her clutch and drops it in the center of the table. When no one moves, I snatch the note and open it. The print was written in ebony ink. I don't remember Nora's handwriting, but I read it silently taking each word in:

Dani,

You are like a sister to me and know my struggles. I know I could have been a better person and friend to you and the Hearts. I know I don't show it, but I cherish the memories we had together.

I can't go on any longer with this life. I've had too many pains and struggles. My dad being gone, and my mom being dead… I can't find peace anymore.

I came tonight to say goodbye. My last wish is to see you and to ask you to tell Sabrina, Clare, and Jonna to get back together.

I'm sorry I couldn't say it in person. I love you.
See you in another life.

-Nora

I feel like I'm going to throw up. I toss the note onto the table and run to the corner of the cellar. I hurl into the nearest planter. Dani rushes over, wraps an arm around me.

"You okay?" she asks. I nod, but I'm not. Poor Nora. I knew she was in her depressed girl era. I just didn't know how deep the roots went, and I'd just spoken ill of the dead. Of my friend. God, I'm awful!

Behind me, I hear gasps.

"What do you think Nora meant by wanting us to get back together?" Jonna asks softly.

"Maybe she just wanted us to be friends again?" Sabrina offers.

"No," Dani says. "I think I know." She takes a breath. "She wants Five Heart back together."

I glance at Jonna and Sabrina. They're as shocked as I am. "I don't think so…" I laugh nervously.

"Yes," Dani says firmly. "I mean it. I was with her that night. The urgency, the note, showing up to my show.

It all makes sense. She wanted Five Heart back. And honestly, so do I."

Dani looks at us with glassy eyes. "I don't know if I can keep being a solo artist. It's lonely. I'm losing my creative edge. We had something special, all of us. I know you all have your own lives. I'm not asking you to leave them behind. But maybe…
for Nora, we do one last show. A tribute. A goodbye."

Goddamn it. I love the idea. Even with our fallout from the studio… I'm all in. But I wait to speak up. I glance over at

Sabrina. She hesitates, a quiet sigh escaping her. Her gaze lingered on Dani, something wounded flickering in her eyes. I knew all too well how deeply the band's breakup had scarred her.

"Yes. I think, in honor of Nora's memory, we should do one last show." Sabrina exhaled loudly, the weight of her decision pressing down on her.

"I'm in!" I exclaim, solidifying Sabrina's choice. Dani's eyes glimmer with a sparkle of hope. We all look to Jonna. She's silent. Then she breathes out, "I can't."

Dani visibly flinches. "Why not? It's for Nora."

Jonna stands. Eyes full of tears. "You're right, Dani. I can't just drop everything. I have four kids at home, one of them is two months old! She needs her mom. I can't be gallivanting onstage in a mini skirt pretending I'm sixteen again!"

I sink back into my chair.

Jonna keeps going. "You tricked us here for your 'birthday,' which isn't even until next week. You drop this bomb on us, and now you want to restart a band with us? You're insane, Dani. Completely insane."

"You're right!" Dani shouts. "I am insane! I tricked you. I stretched the truth. But a woman who used to be our best friend, in her final moments, wanted this! So yeah, I lied. But I did it for Nora!" Silence.

"Dani… you did the right thing," Sabrina says softly. "You did what Nora wanted. This note proves it. One last show. For Nora, and for us. It'll give us closure. For her… and for the band."

That one stings. The way the band ended… It was never resolved.

Jonna begins to pace back and forth and finally exhales. "One show?"

"One show," Dani promises.

"I will talk to Dexter first, before I can make any promises," Jonna says firmly.

I nod.

We all stand and push past the table, collapsing into each other's arms. We weep.

Chapter 7

Dani

Sabrina left the restaurant afterward to feed her cat. She said she had some files to give her editor too. I think the entire ordeal was too overwhelming for her and she had to absorb it the way she knows best. Alone.

We made a promise, all of us, to not say a word about this until Sabrina could break the story in *The Times* unscathed. She agreed to release the news to the press. She felt guilty about scoring the byline, but it feels right coming from her, not from some media shark.

Jonna and Clare came back to the penthouse with me, and we actually let loose. The buzz from the 1977 Bordeaux wore off, so I broke out some rare añejo I'd been gifted recently, along with three beaded shot glasses. We were all in silk and cotton night attire, lounging on the ivory velvet couch. Clare pointed at the bottle and jumped up and down in excitement.

"Should we make a toast?" I asked, excitement flickering beneath the grief I hadn't yet learned how to set down.

"Yes! That is my *bitch*! The party starts!" She clapped as I set down the glasses and topped each one off with the dark liquid.

Tequila. Grant us the ability to numb our feelings for one night. To enjoy each other's company. It's been so long since I've spent time with friends. Any friends, for that matter. I simmer down my thoughts as each girl reluctantly grabs a shot glass.

"To bringing the band back together, even if it's just for one show," I say with my amber liquid in the air.

We don't even cheers, just nod in agreement and take the shot. Tequila never goes down easy for me, but this was… delectable. "Wow, that's good," I say, wincing at the warm burn lacing my throat. I pour us three more, and this time, the girls take them without hesitation.

We sprawl out on my abstract rug, cracking up over high school memories.

"I remember when I met you and Sabrina!" Jonna snorts, wiping away tears of laughter from Clare's last joke. "You guys were just so iconic! I knew we'd have the best time together."

Clare, slurring just slightly, chimes in, "Yeah, you two were always in a corner with your guitars, scribbling in your composition books and humming so loud I could hear you from Mrs. Scripter's class!" We all giggle. "Remember you made a sign-up sheet for the girl band and held auditions? Oh my God, some of those kids sucked."

We all erupt. It's true. They were terrible. But not Clare and Jonna. Their voices shined. With Jonna's alto and Clare's soprano, and of course Nora's haunting harmony, the five of us created something… magical.

"Do you remember when we fought over that one boy?" I ask, cry-laughing. "He was basically an amateur groupie in the making. What was his name again? The one with the plump lips?"

"Cameron!" Jonna blurts out. We all recite it at once, exploding into laughter. I haven't felt like this in a while. Not since Sam.

"Speaking of boys," Clare teases. "Dani, seems like you've been riding the single train for years now."

I clench up. Buzzkill.

"Well, tell us! We live for the juicy celeb gossip," Clare exclaims. Jonna nods eagerly.

"Nothing to tell. I'm married to my music," I say flatly.

"Boo!" Clare throws a thumbs down in my face. "I don't believe that for one second. You must get lonely on tour. You can't spend every waking second with Stacy!"

"Well… I kind of do spend every day with my mom," I chuckle. "But yes, every now and then I have my occasional fuck."

Jonna's ears perk up. "I wish I could have an occasional fuck. It's been four months! And when I was pregnant with Alissa, Dexter said he could 'feel' her when he was in me, so we couldn't even finish."

"Weird!" Clare makes a face and turns back to me. "Have you slept with any celebrities we know?"

I think back to my time on the road. A few guys in Toronto. One in Delray Beach. No big names. But I let them in on a fun little secret. "You know who tried to sleep with me years ago?"

Their eyes widen.

"Who?!" Jonna shouts.

"Elijah Wood."

"What! I love him!"

Clare looks confused. "Who's that?"

"Wow. You are a terrible millennial, and it shows," I say, throwing a pillow at her.

"What? I really don't know. Is he hot?"

"I think he's cute," Jonna says.

"You know, *The Hobbit*?" I prompt Clare. "*Lord of the Rings…*" Still nothing. Clare shrugs. We just laugh again. Complete fullness.

Clare and Jonna crash in the guest room. I trudge into my bedroom, just as I left it, sheets wrapped around the quilt in a tangled mess. I picture Sam's hourglass silhouette curled between the folds. A shiver runs down my spine. I imagine her lips brushing mine. She used to whisper every night before we fell asleep: "See you in the morning."

I clutch my stomach, aching for her weight beside me. Knowing I won't see her in the morning. I collapse into bed like a log, eyes fixed on the slowly spinning ceiling fan. The room begins to spin with it. I'm lulled to sleep by the gentle hum of añejo.

A few days pass. Clare flies back to Newport Beach. Jonna's back with her family in Long Island. The tour's cancelled. I have all the time in the world.

I search for the most reputable funeral homes in the city. I had Nora's body transported to New York, since her dad lives in Poughkeepsie. I'd hoped having her close would trigger his long-dormant fatherly instinct. But I doubt it. He's always been in and out. You'd think after Nora's mom died in high school, he'd have stepped up, but alcoholics can't be trusted.

Sabrina told me to meet her at a coffee shop on Lexington. I pause my search and throw together a disguise: peach silk Dolce scarf wrapped around my head, the biggest black sunglasses I own. It's August, but there's a breeze. I slide into a white peasant blouse, long denim skirt with a slit, and worn black combat boots. I stare at my reflection. Nobody will recognize Dani Rose in this outfit.

FIVE HEART

I have Rolf drop me a block away, no flashy Rover Sport, no escort out of a car. People notice that stuff. A gust of wind hits as I turn the corner toward Seed & Bean. It's not too crowded. Good. I leave the disguise on and spot Sabrina in the back corner, laptop open, two coffees waiting. She waves awkwardly. I hate that things are weird between us. The way Five Heart ended really changed her. I think she resents me for what I've become. Still, nobody can quite replace a childhood best friend. That's history, and nobody can rewrite our history.

"What's up, Breakfast at Tiffany's?" she smirks, eyeing my outfit.

"I didn't want to get noticed," I whisper.

"Trust me. Nobody in here listens to your bouncy pop music," she deadpans, tugging my sunglasses off.

I let her. But I keep the scarf on just in case. Sabrina takes a deep breath and spins her laptop toward me.

"The final draft," she says. "*The Forgotten Heart: Nora Hayes' Tragic Goodbye,* by Sabrina Daniel."

I scan it up and down. Again. My eyes fixate on a photo, the first one we ever took together. Our debut album cover. Nora looks so sad. That was right after her mom died.

"I archived it from Facebook. Thought it fit," Sabrina says gently.

I force a smile. Trying to hold back the wave rising inside me. Once this gets published, her death becomes real.

"It's perfect," I whisper. "And you're the perfect person to share it. I hope you get a promotion at work."

"That's not why I'm doing this," Sabrina says. "I don't care about money or status. I just want to do right by Nora. Change the narrative. Make people remember the real her. The amazing person she was before the drugs and liquor possessed her. I know how cruel other outlets would've been, but I get to tell our version. The truth."

I reach across the table and take her hands in mine. She clicks *Publish*. Just like that, Nora's death belongs to the world.

Chapter 8

Jonna

"Breaking news! This just in—teen pop sensation Nora Hayes from the girl group Five Heart passed away last week. Autopsy reports are still determining the cause of death, but speculation from multiple toxicology reports indicates an overdose."

I glance up from the kitchen, knife in hand mid-chop. "Turn that shit up!" I shout to Dexter.

"Hayes had a troubled past after the band's split. Unable to secure steady work, she was desperate for stability. Sabrina Daniel, Hayes' former bandmate turned journalist, broke the news yesterday morning. Hayes' father, Walter Hayes, has yet to comment publicly on his daughter's passing."

I slam the knife against the quartz counter. "That's because he's probably drunk in a dive-bar bathroom stall, choking on his own puke!" I yell at the TV.

Dexter turns and shushes me. The kids are all napping, even the baby. These quiet pockets are rare, especially since they smothered me the second I walked in the door. Now… peace. He clicks the television off and slides behind me, wrapping his arms around my waist. His warmth softens the edges of my frustration, almost like he's holding a live grenade that could go off if he loosens his grip. I lean back into him.

"Are you going to be okay?" he asks, voice low. I turn in his arms, my floral apron fanning out with the movement.

"I don't know," I admit flatly. Last night in bed, hardly romantic pillow talk, I'd floated the idea of a tribute concert. He shut it down before I could finish. But I push again.

"About the tribute show…" My tone is cautious. His hands drop from my waist.

"Not this again." He turns, pouring himself a Glencairn of bourbon from the half-full bottle on the counter.

"I know it's asking a lot, but I feel like I have to do this."

"You don't have to do anything."

"I want to do it."

"Well, we don't always get what we want." The glass hits the counter with a sharp clink.

I stiffen. "I don't understand why you're being unreasonable." My voice ricochets off the kitchen walls. "You were the one who told me to meet with Dani in the first place!"

"I'm not being unreasonable." He starts pacing around the island, bourbon in hand. "You want to drag our family into the spotlight for someone who barely made an effort in your adult life."

"That's not fair—"

"I don't want the gossip columns circling us again. I had to deal with that circus when we first started dating. Thank God you became a has-been celebrity so we could finally live in peace." The word has-been lands like a slap.

"Excuse me?" My voice spikes. "I chose to step back, for you, for our family. Don't think for a second I don't have the talent or the ability to do this."

"I never said you didn't have talent, honey. I just don't want the attention. It's not good for the kids."

"They'll survive! It'll be fifteen seconds of fame. They won't even remember." A small tap on my lower back freezes me.

"Mommy. Are you and Daddy fighting?" Finn's voice is tiny.

I crouch down, brushing his cheek with my hand. "No, sweetie, just a discussion."

He grins, wraps himself around my leg. "I missed you so much. Please don't go hang out with Auntie Clare and Auntie Dani again."

Dexter shoots me the *See?* look. I glare back.

"I won't leave that long again, okay?" I say softly. Finn nods, then bounds into the living room toward his toy box.

"Don't make promises you can't keep," Dexter warns. I turn back to the cutting board and ignore him.

The next morning, after dropping the kids at school, I meet Selma for brunch. Selma is… well, Selma. Head-to-toe designer. Luxury car. Only flies first class. The type of woman who can make brushing her teeth look like a Chanel ad. We met years ago at the only runway show I ever walked for Michael Kors. She was working backstage, and we've been inseparable ever since. I pull into The Ranch, the farm-to-table hotspot in town. She's already there, Aperol Spritz in hand, sunglasses perched like she's about to be photographed.

We order our usual. Clink glasses. A few hours of freedom. I spill the recent news, everything except the tribute show.

Selma shakes her head. "Oh my… poor Nora."

"I just wish I could have done more," I murmur, eyes drifting to the wall behind her.

"There's nothing you could've done. If she was suicidal, you wouldn't have known. You can't blame yourself."

"I don't." I pause, picking at my napkin. "I just wish there was a way I could make it up to her."

Her brows lift. "How?"

I take the leap. "Her last note…it was vague, but we believe she wanted us to get the band back together."

Selma bursts into laughter. "You're not serious."

"Why wouldn't I be?" My tone sharpens.

"You were sixteen then. You're almost thirty now. Four kids. How exactly is that supposed to work?"

First Dexter. Now Selma. My jaw locks. She notices. The laughter dies.

"Sorry. That was really bitchy."

I shrug, drain my drink. "It was."

The food arrives. Perfectly plated, steam curling into the air. Selma sets down her fork, dabbing her lips. "What if we did a *Vogue* cover? Comeback of the century spread. I'll put you in the new Hermès drop. You'll get the marketing you need, and I'll save my budget on models. It's a win/win."

My jaw drops. "You want us on the cover of *Vogue?*"

She tilts her head like it's the most obvious thing in the world. "Why not? You're basically a walking supermodel."

I just stare at her. "*Vogue?*"

"Yes, darling." She waves her fork in the air. "Now finish your meal so we can call the girls."

By the time we leave The Ranch, I've already got my phone in my hand, pulling up the group call. One by one, the names light up: Dani, Clare, Sabrina. The second everyone connects, it's instant noise, like backstage before a sold-out show.

"What's going on? Why is this a four-way call? Did someone else die?" Clare asks.

Selma giggles. "Okay, listen. Pack your heels, your hairspray, and your best damn angles. We're shooting the comeback of the century… for the cover of *Vogue*."

Three seconds of silence, and then an explosion.

"SHUT. UP." Dani shrieks.

"You're lying!" Sabrina gasps.

Clare lets out the same squeal she used to do when the crowd chanted *Five Heart!* at meet-and-greets.

Selma's grinning. "I'll style you all in Hermès. Think sharp, iconic, the kind of spread that ends up taped to teenage bedroom walls."

You can hear Sabrina's pacing through the receiver. "I'm calling Marco tonight. These grown out roots are not making it onto *Vogue* paper."

"Oh, so suddenly you care about hair?" Clare teases.

"Excuse me, I cannot be known as the 'Signature Red Head' this time around,"
Sabrina fires back.

"Okay," Dani cuts in, "as long as no one resurrects the White Sparkle Disaster."

I groan. "You mean the one that ripped during 'Runaway Summer' and flashed half the crowd?"

"That was you, Jonna!" Clare laughs so hard she's wheezing.

Everyone's talking over each other. Boots vs. no boots, hair extensions vs. natural, who gets the middle spot in the photo (Clare's already called it). It feels like sixteen again. Loud. Unfiltered. Reckless.

Then Dani's voice softens. "Hey… on a different note. I found the perfect funeral home in New York. Private, quiet. They can handle the service." The chatter dies instantly. "I know it's last minute, but they had an opening next weekend. I just…I want to get it over with. For her. For all of us."

Sabrina's voice is gentle. "That works for me."

"Same," Clare adds. I echo them.

Dani exhales, like she's been holding it all day. "Okay. Next weekend. We'll celebrate her life, and then…"

"And then," I finish, "we bring her back to life in the only way we know how."

Selma clears her throat, a smile in her voice. "And you'll do it looking like goddesses." We all laugh softly and hang up one by one.

Chapter 9

Dani

September 6th, 2025. Nora's funeral. The day has finally arrived. After a frantic week of planning floral arrangements, casket exterior and lining, program design, I'm spent. Mentally, physically, emotionally.

Rolf drives my mother and me to the church an hour early. My assistant Dev and my team have been here since morning, fussing over every detail. We step through the cathedral's heavy arched doors into a room that feels both sacred and suffocating. The funeral is in Nora's hometown of Poughkeepsie. Violet gardenias, her favorite, line the pews. I remember how her mother had planted them all over the backyard. Sheer ivory drapery sweeps across the high ceiling, cascading down toward the mahogany casket where Nora rests. I scan the casket, checking for any imperfection. Everything must look perfect. Nora would have demanded nothing less.

From my purse, I pull the folded eulogy, reading my scribbles again and again until the words start to feel memorized. The cathedral doors fly open, spilling sunlight across the floor. Dev barrels in, out of breath, clipboard in one hand, pen in the other.

"Dani. You're here. Great!" She's panting between sentences. "The French café a block away is all set for the reception. Light bites, mimosas, no hard liquor as requested. Just in case Nora's dad decides to stumble in." I motion for her to breathe. She nods, continues. "Media's covering the funeral. We told them, outside only. No reporters or cameras inside."

I arch a brow.

"Well, except Sabrina," she adds with a nervous laugh.

"What outlet?"

"CNN," she says flatly. Ugh. They'll spin the whole day into their own narrative.

My mom chimes in, "Are there gonna be a lot of celebrities? What kind of lineup? We don't want attention gettin' outta hand."

"Mom." I cut her off. "That's why I picked this town. It's out of the way. Nora's family is here."

"Yeah, but CNN…" she presses.

"We'll tell them not to disclose the location," I snap, rubbing my temples. "They can film arrivals. That's it."

Dev gives me a mock salute. "Got it." She vanishes into the back to fluff the décor.

My phone buzzes. It's our new 'Five Heart Lives' group chat.

Sabrina: *Pulling up early. Looks like rain is on its way. Do we have umbrellas?*

Clare*: Oh shit! Just got my hair blown out. Flight was delayed, I'll be there 10 mins before start :(*

Jonna: *Dropped the kids at Nonna's an hour ago. No traffic, it's a miracle.*

I type back: *No umbrellas. Weather's fine right now. Dev's on it. CNN is covering the funeral…outside only. Please help keep stray reporters out.*

Clare: *I'll ram them with my car if I have to.*

Dani: *They better not piss me off today. Not today, Satan.*

Three laughing-face emojis pop up.

Dev: *guests are arriving.*

The funeral director greets me. She'll run the service, keep it smooth. I thank her, then step outside to meet people. Invitations went to Nora's family, close friends, some high school acquaintances, and a few celebrity connections.

The boy band No Reason is coming. Clare dated their lead singer, Ryan Wood, for a season. The drummer, Eric Snow, dated Nora. They were intense. Dark, and twisty, practically obsessed. She used to talk about tattooing their future wedding rings on.

Selma's coming too, which surprises me—she's not exactly an upstate New York type. I throw open the doors and chatter swells around me. The sky is darkening. Guests with umbrellas already have them out.

Dev materializes at my elbow. "Checked the weather and it's going to pour. Umbrellas are on their way."

"You read my mind," I sigh.

"Go get 'em, tiger." She grins, nudging me forward.

I smooth my long-sleeve black silk dress and greet the first group of people. Nora's cousins, then her uncle, who's half-grinning, half-tearing up. I hand him a program before it gets awkward. A couple girls we went to high school with, Flora and Zara, hug me and offer condolences. We joke about our music theory teacher, Mr. Flounder, who used to snore through exams. We'd launch spitballs, some landing right in his open mouth, and he'd keep sleeping.

Sabrina steps out of a taxi, locks eyes with me, and heads over like backup arriving just in time. She charms guests instantly. Two girls even ask for selfies with her. She is probably eating this up.

A blacked-out Hummer pulls up. Robbie, Ryan, and Eric from No Reason climb out, all in matching suits. Robbie grins wide, his alabaster teeth blinding me.

"Dani Rose!" He engulfs me in a bear hug, still towering over me from our band days. He hugs Sabrina next. Ryan comes over and side-hugs me next, his long auburn hair swishing around, scanning for Clare.

"She's running late," I say.

"Typical," he mutters.

Eric approaches last. He has the same shaggy hair, same eyebrow piercing, and the same heavy eyes. His sadness is palpable.

"Hey, Eric," I say softly, hugging him.

Jonna and Dexter arrive just as Selma's car pulls up. She's in a tight black lace Versace dress, snakeskin stilettos with an actual snake detail curling around her ankle. Fabulous.

"Thank you for coming," I say.

Selma slips off her sunglasses just enough to reveal a sly smile. "Darling, for this? I'd cancel Paris Fashion Week."

Jonna squeezes me. "You okay?" she whispers. I nod.

Dexter hugs me like we're old friends. "We have matters to discuss…later," he says meaningfully. Jonna rolls her eyes and mouths 'the tribute show' to me.

A horn blares and Clare's teal Beetle convertible rental screeches to a stop, half up on the curb. Damien, her husband, trails behind her as she struts toward us in a white dress, hair in perfect bouncing curls, cleavage for days. Ryan's jaw practically hits the pavement. She stops to hug a few guests on her way in, and someone in the crowd raises an eyebrow. "White dress… to a funeral?"

Clare doesn't miss a beat. "I thought you couldn't wear white to a wedding. No one said anything about a funeral."

The guy blinks, speechless, at her response. She hugs Sabrina, Selma, Dexter, Jonna, Eric, Robbie and then me.

"No hug for me, Clarebear?" Ryan teases.

Clare pretends to look around. "Did you hear something?" she says with a faux-innocent shrug. The girls and I giggle. Ryan just smirks, shaking his head.

I turn to Damien. He's a handsome Italian man, slim, not her usual lumberjack type. I extend my hand. "Nice to meet you, finally!"

"You as well," he says warmly. "I've heard many wonderful things."

I glance at Clare, surprised. I'd figured the opposite, since I wasn't invited to their wedding, but I let that go a while ago. Damien turns slightly away, checking the bitcoin trends on his phone. I caught Clare watching him with disgust.

The CNN van pulls up suddenly. Sabrina storms over, jabbing her finger at the reporters. I can't hear her, but I know she's laying down the law. The funeral director finally ushers us inside after what's felt like hours of socializing. We file to the front pew. My chest swells at being with the girls again, even as grief gnaws a hole in me.

Chapter 10

Clare

Damien and I sit with the girls and Dexter. Dani really outdid herself. The gardenias, the drapery, it's all breathtaking. The director welcomes everyone, opening with scripture. I glance behind me, taking in all of the people that came to honor Nora. I catch Ryan staring. Gross. I flip him the bird.

The director raises her voice an octave. "I'd like to introduce Danielle to read her eulogy."

Dani walks to the podium just as the doors creak open. I glance back to see who came late to the show. My stomach drops. Steve, our old manager, and Donovan, our label head, stroll in like they own the place. Donovan's eyes swept the crowd, calculating and predatory. Steve looks unchanged, still bald, still carrying a beer gut like a badge of stagnation. Donovan on the other hand, aged like fine wine. Tall, dark, and devastatingly handsome, with a quiet intensity that follows him like a shadow.

I grab Jonna's hand and point at our unwelcomed newcomers. Her mouth drops open.

"What the fuck!" she hisses under her breath.

Dani starts speaking. Thank God she hasn't noticed them yet.

"When you meet someone like Nora, you don't just remember them. They imprint on you, like a tattoo you never planned, but wouldn't remove for anything. We were just kids when we met. We could sing, sure, but mostly we were scared out of our minds and trying to pretend we weren't. Nora never pretended. She laughed too loud, called people out when they deserved it, stayed up all night writing lyrics that made no sense until suddenly they did. Onstage, she was electric. Offstage, she was the one checking if you'd eaten, if you'd slept, if you were okay when the cameras weren't around. She carried her heart unprotected, loved without armor… and the world didn't treat that kind of heart kindly. Teenage fame looks like a dream on TV, but it can chew you up before you even know you're in its mouth. We were still learning who we were while the world decided for us. And sometimes, it takes the best parts of you before you get the chance to hold onto them. I loved you, Nora. We all did. And I'm so damn sorry the world didn't love you better."

Applause swells and people actually stand. But before the moment can settle, Walter stumbles in, reeking of booze. He lurches toward the podium, pushing past the front pew.

"That was a g-g-good speech!" he slurs. "But I got somethin' to say about my daughter."

Dexter tries to intercept, but Walter jerks free, shoving Dani out of the way and gripping the microphone like it's his lifeline. "She was a pain in the ass sometimes, always too good for her old man! Thought she was some big star and never came home enough, never called enough. Fame does that to ya! You think she was an angel but—"

Eric suddenly barrels forward from the side aisle and lands a clean right hook to Walter's jaw. Gasps erupt as Walter stumbles back into Dexter's arms.

"Don't you dare talk about her like that," Eric snarls, eyes blazing. Dexter uses the moment to drag Walter toward the door, but Walter's still kicking and yelling.

I leap up, desperate to shift the room's attention. What can I do? I start singing softly. Track five on our debut album, written by Nora herself.

"Deep in the trenches, along the ravines,
I travel the world in a soul-flying dream..."
I step forward, voice growing louder.
"I search for the meanings, fight perilous fiends,
I'm chewed up and spit out, but still sparkle and sing."
Walter's still shouting in the background, but I push harder, try to filter out his belligerence. Full on Broadway now, arms wide, voice echoing off the stained glass:
"Never grow up, never be wise,
I choose ignorance every damn time,
Never stand true, never act used,
because in the end, you're left bound and bruised!"

Chapter 11

Sabrina

I shove the CNN crew toward the door. Brian's still filming, face smug. "Brian. OUTSIDE. NOW." I shove him again, harder this time.

He stumbles backward as I push him through the heavy cathedral doors, and he lands outside on his ass. That's when I see it.

Oh. My. God. The street is packed. A massive throng of fans stretches down the block, umbrellas bobbing in the rain. Some are holding posters, others are screaming, *"Five Heart! No Reason! Five Heart! No Reason!"* The sound is deafening.

I spin back to Brian, rain soaking my hair in seconds. "Where the hell did all these people come from? How did they even find out where this funeral was?"

He smirks. "Word travels fast when you've got a scandal, sweetheart. Couple of tweets, a few texts… boom. They're here."

My eyes narrow. "You leaked it."

He doesn't answer, just grins. I want to punch his smug little face. The fans surge forward, pressing toward the door. I try to slam it shut, but they push past me, pouring inside like a wave.

Inside, the pews dissolve into chaos. Dev flapping her arms, the funeral director shouting over everything, Dani darting between guests in panic. Clare is still belting Nora's lyrics like she's trying to hold the world together with her voice. No Reason jumps in to harmonize with Clare. Robbie brings the falsetto and Ryan's slapping his leg, creating a beat.

The crowd loses it. Phones up, flashes popping, someone yelling "Reunion tour!"

Selma's filming, smiling like she's watching dollar signs fall from the ceiling. Brian's back inside, filming like it's the scoop of the year. Then Stacy, Dani's Southern spitfire of a mother, stomps into the center aisle in her kitten heels and points toward the door.

"Alright, y'all. Show's over! Out! OUT! This ain't a damn honky-tonk, it's a funeral!"

Somehow, people start moving toward the exit under her command. That's when I snap.
I storm into the aisle, rip the camera from Brian's hands, and smash it onto the marble beneath our feet. The crack echoes.

"OUT!" I scream, rainwater clinging to my hair, mascara smudged but gaze like steel.

For one suspended beat, everyone stops and all is silent. All that remains is rain hammering the roof of the church. Somewhere, a gardenia slips from the casket and lands on the floor.

Chapter 12

Sabrina

After the fallout of the funeral, we all sit in silence at the reception café. Hair ruffled, mascara streaking our cheeks, and clothes still damp from the rain. We'd announced there wouldn't be a reception, but since we'd already paid for the restaurant to close for the afternoon, no-showing felt wrong. It's just us, the husbands, Selma, Stacy, and the boys from No Reason, gathered around a round table with untouched mimosas practically calling our names.

"That was really… something," Robbie finally says, breaking the silence. We all glance at each other, unsure whether to laugh or cry.

"I thought it was beautiful," Ryan offers.

"You would," Clare mutters, rolling her eyes. Damien takes her hand under the table, a silent plea for her to cool it. The boys snicker.

"I'm just glad I got to read my eulogy. I know Nora heard it," Dani says softly. We give her half-hearted smiles, but my stomach twists tighter with guilt.

"I'm so sorry about Brian," I blurt. "He can be such a *dick* sometimes."

"How was he able to spread the news so fast?" Jonna says, brow furrowed. "All those people wouldn't have made it to Poughkeepsie that quickly from the live filming."

The table buzzes with speculation until I interrupt. "It's my fault."

They all look at me like I've grown twelve heads.

"Oh, darling, don't say that," Stacy says in her Southern drawl. "You laid down the law with them. You did the best you could."

I shake my head. "No, it *is* my fault. I don't want to admit this, but Brian and I have a past. We're rivals in the journalism world, and sometimes that kind of tension needs, relieving. So we relieved each other. Sexual tension," I mumble, staring at my feet. The room shifts; the pieces click for them.

"I wanted to outdo him so badly that I bragged I'd have firsthand access to the funeral. Called him a washed-up reporter who isn't current. And, when we were bantering over text the next day, I accidentally let the location slip. I didn't even realize it until it was too late."

Eric's face hardens. "So you told the reporters where we were."

"It just…it slipped out." My throat tightens.

Dani shoots to her feet, eyes like daggers. "What the fuck, Sabrina." She slams her chair into the table and storms out.

I start to follow, but Stacy's hand pushes me back into my seat as she hurries after her daughter. Eric follows close behind. The rest of us just sit there, stunned.

"Well, this is awkward," Clare says dryly.

"Not as awkward as how I feel," Ryan mutters.

"Excuse me?" Clare swivels toward him. "What are you talking about?"

Ryan stares her down. "Should I tell him, or you?"

Damien's eyes dart between them.

"Oh my God, Ryan, get over it!" Clare snaps. "We dated when we were teenagers. My husband obviously knows that already. Don't start shit just for your own amusement. God, you haven't changed."

Ryan pushes away from the table and stalks to the bar. Jonna bursts into laughter.

"What the hell is this day?" She downs her mimosa in one gulp. The attention shifts off me, and I quietly sip mine.

Soon there are six empty glasses waiting to be refilled. An hour passes. People mingle, hors d'oeuvres circulate, and the tension thins. Dani's at the bar with her mom, venting and drinking hard. I sit alone in the corner, marinating in regret. I fucked up. And Brian's still a dick. Ever since that one-night stand, I've been obsessed with outshining him. His words echo in my head: *You'll be at the top one day, but you'll be there alone.* And maybe he's right. I've clawed my way upward without caring who gets hurt. Now, I finally have my friends back, and I've blown it.

My stomach churns violently. I bolt to the restroom and barely make it into a stall before puking. The door creaks open.

"Brina, you okay? I saw you run in here," Robbie's voice calls gently.

I wipe my mouth on my sleeve. "I don't know," I rasp.

He slips inside, crouching to help me up. Robbie was always the one looking out for us girls back in the day. A few years older, on the same fast-track to fame, the boys in his band were like our brothers. I'd always had a hidden lust for Robbie, but being the 'nerdy one' I never expected him to feel the same about me.

He brushes the hair from my face.

"Don't feel bad. It was an accident. You said it yourself. You didn't try to sabotage the funeral."

"I'd never."

He meets my eyes, and for a heartbeat, I think there's a spark.

The door swings open again. Selma stands there, smirking. "Get a room… anywhere but the powder room."

We shuffle past her back into the café. Dexter and Jonna are saying their goodbyes; Dani and Stacy are already gone. Ugh. I have to fix things with her before Monday's photo shoot. I turn to Robbie.

"Will you help me smooth things over with Dani? I really can't have her mad at me right now."

He smiles and nods. I need to get ahead of this, and damage control at the office before the funeral turns into a salacious headline. I slip out of the restaurant, call an Uber to the city and head to *The Times*. Let's fix this mess.

Chapter 13

Dani

Beep. Beep. Beep. The alarm on my phone shrieks me awake. I slam my hand down on the off button and, like a switch, sit up wide awake and surprisingly alert. My heart is already racing. Today's the *Vogue* photoshoot. I glance at the empty space to my left and sigh. I could really use Sam right now. I unlock my phone and search her name. Our last message, eight months old, stares back at me*: Good luck with that, Dani.* It mocks me.

My chest tightens.

We were driving through Nashville, wind whipping Sam's soft black wolf cut into my face, Chappell Roan blasting from the speakers. She brushed her hand over mine, and I marveled at her profile. The cutest little pixie nose, scattered freckles over her rosy cheeks. She was small but hella fiery. Archangel-made.

We pulled up to a little coffee shop on 12 South. I was in my usual disguise, a knit beanie, aviators, and two space buns. Sam walked a couple steps ahead, but she always did, partly to shield me from curious eyes, partly, I think, because she was still respecting my choice to keep us private. Which, looking back, was the start of the unraveling.

We took our usual table. My standard order, black coffee. The darker the roast the better. Sam's usual, chai tea with a splash of cinnamon. She thrived on chai. I remember buying a kettle so I could make her chai whenever she stayed the night. I slid my aviators off, scanning the room. It seemed to be just the usual rich retirees, no one who'd recognize me. Sam reached across, taking my hands in hers, her eyes locking on mine. Her touch radiated warmth through me, pulling me into an embrace without moving from my seat. I wanted to hold her so tight in that moment. Show the world who I loved.

"Ohmigod, are you Dani Rose?!" The voice cracked through like a cymbal. A young man in a floral shirt stood at our table, clutching his phone. I dropped Sam's hands instantly, tucking mine into my lap. I pasted on a smile.

"Guilty," I said lightly.

He started to hyperventilate. "Can I please get a selfie? My boyfriend Herald and I absolutely LOVE you. Your album *Harlot* was FIRE!"

I glanced at Sam, sitting cross-armed, unamused, already pulling back into herself, and felt the hurt radiating off her. I took the selfie, thanked him, and sent him on his way.

"We better get out of here before he tags me in this coffee shop," I muttered. Sam shook her head, grabbed her tea, and headed for the door. I scrambled after her, nearly tripping over a crack in the pavement.

"Sam, wait!" She didn't. She opened the driver's side door. I reached it just in time to slam it shut, trapping her between me and the side mirror. Our noses grazed.

"What's the matter?" I asked, searching her face.

"I can't do this anymore, Dani." Her voice was calm, too calm.

"Do what?" My stomach dropped.

"This."

Her hands shot up to my face, gripping my cheeks hard enough to force my lips forward. Then she kissed me. Kissed me so hard, so sudden, in full view of the street. The taste of cinnamon lingered on my tongue. I began to panic, floodlights in my brain: the women walking their Yorkies past us, the possibility of a phone camera aimed our way. I broke the kiss, stepping back, wiping my mouth instinctively as if I could erase the moment from public view. Sam's eyes narrowed.

"And there it is. The final test."

"What?"

"I told you when we first met, I don't touch new-found lesbians, but you swore it'd be different with you. I have waited almost a year. I'm done." She yanked her door open and slid in, rolling the window down just enough to deliver the knife twist. "Word of advice. Don't string along the next woman, or man, or whatever you think you want. We're human, Dani. Not your playthings." She drove off, leaving me in the parking lot with my hands over my face, sobbing.

I'm staring at that same message now. My phone flies against the wall. I scream into my pillow.

Clare stayed with Jonna for the weekend of the photoshoot, but Damien flew back home to Cali. The girls plan to meet me at *Vogue*.

Rolf drops me off in front of the building with a bustling crowd. Clare and Jonna pull up at the same time. We linger outside the building and figure it's better to be spotted. It's good for marketing, my publicist says.

Inside, Sabrina's already on a bench, waiting. Her hair is freshly highlighted and looks gorgeous. I give a polite smile, still nursing my irritation while the others hug her.

"You ready for a great day?" she asks, awkward but trying.

"Mhm."

She lowers her voice. "Not looking for anything when I say this, but I need you to know I took care of the media situation. I was able to get the footage from Brian. So, the only footage anyone would have is from fans on their cell phones, which won't make national news. I promise."

"How did you talk him into handing over the footage?" I pry.

She rolls her eyes. "A lot of humiliating pleas and degradation from him. And also—" she motions her closed fist back and forth by her mouth.

"Oh, shit," I say, the frustration leaking out of me.

"So are we good now?" Sabrina asks, eyes glassy.

I nod back, guilt needling me at the price she paid. She really does care. She wants this to work for Five Heart.

We make our way to the fourteenth floor where *Vogue* resides. Selma greets us the second the elevator opens onto a glamorous front desk.

"Oh, darlings!" she sings, corralling us into a group hug.

"Hair and makeup, stat!" We're handed off to a squad of black-clad artists. The hour blurs. curling irons, powder brushes, Moet Chandon and laughter. Gorgeous models float by. Bella Hadid rises from a folding chair close by and stops dead in her tracks when she sees me.

She kisses my cheek. "Dani! My love! How are you?"

"I'm well," I lie with a grin. The girls swivel.

"Hi, Bella!" Clare waves like they're old friends. Bella blinks, trying to figure out Clare's features, then brightens.

"Oh my god—Five Heart! I knew you looked familiar. I had your debut album on repeat!" She half-sings as she struts past, "Freeeee, we are freeee! Get up and seeee, making history!"

Clare and Jonna squeal like fangirls. Sabrina and I share a smirk.

"Oh my god! We look HOT. Like, I would fuck myself," Clare declares at the floor-length mirrors after we are all completely styled.

"Well, you could," Sabrina snarks.

As we all admire our renovations, I just soak in the moment. The girls are back.

The photographers run us through poses. This time, I put the others in the middle. I want them to have their time to shine. Clare and Sabrina jockey for center, while Jonna and I giggle mercilessly behind them. We shoot a little snippet of our anthem, "Just a Daydream." The videographer builds a tiny music video set. We dance and sing our hearts out. At one point we all tarantella in a circle. I haven't laughed genuinely this hard in months. For the first time since Nora's funeral, and since Sam, I'm not thinking about loss, or the ways I've failed. I'm just Dani.

And Five Heart is alive again.

Afterward, we lounge on the edge of the set, still in full hair and makeup, heels kicked off, sipping bottled water while the crew breaks everything down. Clare breaks the spell. "Oh, by the way, I meant to tell you guys! I saw Steve and Donovan at Nora's funeral."

Sabrina's head whips around. "Steve? Our Steve?"

"Steve the manager," Clare confirms, "and Donovan, the label CEO. They were standing in the back for like, five minutes. I almost didn't believe it."

"I saw them, too," Jonna says, pulling her knees up on the low stage platform. "Thought maybe I was imagining it, but no. It was them."

I blink. "Wait. They were there? I didn't see them."

Clare shrugs. "You wouldn't have. It was when Walter was yelling uncontrollably, and those fans started rushing the doors. Total chaos."

Sabrina's brows knit, but it isn't confusion. It's something sharper, like recognition. Her gaze lingers on the floor a beat too long, then flicks up to meet mine. The look makes my stomach dip. It's gone as fast as it came, but the weight of it stays.

If I'm honest with myself, Donovan is one of the reasons I don't look at men the same way anymore. I've never even said that out loud before.

Selma breezes back in, still all sparkle. "Ladies, now that the shoot is wrapped, what's next? This *Vogue* spread hits stands in three weeks. You should be ready to ride the wave."

Clare practically bounces. "That's perfect timing to announce the tribute concert. We drop the date the same day the issue drops. Boom! Instant press explosion."

We toss around ideas until we land on New Year's Eve weekend. Open-air venue, violet and black color scheme in honor of Nora's stage colors. Start the New Year off right.

Then Clare leans forward, eyes glittering. "And speaking of timing, my birthday's in a few weeks. You know what that means? You all fly to California, stay at my place, and we will get our slumber party on! I have unlimited wine, bad rom coms to binge, all that girly crap. And—" she jabs a finger at each of us, "—we turn it into marketing gold. Poolside selfies, behind-the-scenes rehearsal teasers, maybe a sexy TikTok trend that goes viral before we even hit the stage. Free publicity, people! We're talking California-level exposure. I mean, why waste my birthday on just cake when we could be trending?"

We all exchange glances.

"I'm in," I say, no hesitation. I am ready to put my everything for this show.

"Me too," Sabrina adds with a smirk. "As long as I don't have to be in a bikini for this TikTok trend you're already planning in your head."

Jonna laughs but hedges. "I have to check with Dexter. Things are kind of hectic at home right now. But I'll see what I can do."

Clare leans back, smug. "Girl, please. Dexter loves me. He'll pack your bags himself when I call."

By the time we change back into street clothes, the late afternoon sun is slanting across the city. A gust of wind greets us as we step out of the *Vogue* building together, the crowd outside buzzing with curiosity. A few fans call our names, phones lifted for photos. We linger on the sidewalk in a loose circle, talking over each other about California, the concert, and the spread. So much excitement, we can't contain it.

Clare loops her arm through Jonna's, steering her toward their waiting car. "Alright, ladies, start hydrating now. I expect glowing skin, scandalous pajamas, and at least two of you to make out with each other when we get wasted off of rosé. California doesn't do low energy."

Sabrina snorts.

"So, a normal trip to your house?" Jonna adds.

"Exactly." Clare winks. "And if we don't go viral, we're doing it wrong." Clare and Jonna peel off together.

Sabrina and I stand side by side a beat longer. She gives me a quick smile, but there's something in her eyes. That same shadow from earlier, the one she tried to mask.

We hug and she heads for the subway. I stay on the sidewalk and watch my girls disappear into the city's current, my chest warm with something I haven't felt in years. Five Heart is back.

Chapter 14

Clare

Blown-up flamingos. Endless bottles of Veuve Clicquot. A crime scene sequin/glitter explosion. It took me all of Friday night after my deposition to get it perfect. Damien helped hang mirrored disco balls from the living room ceiling and blew up every single pool floatie until his cheeks turned red.

Our modern villa sits directly on Newport Beach, pool spilling over into the Pacific horizon. Even though I can drop a paycheck (or three) at Saint Laurent without blinking, I'm a saver at heart. Not because I'm timid or afraid to live, but because I learned early that money meant power. It meant escape.

I grew up poor in a house ruled by an abusive father and a mother who saw me as her second chance. She didn't want a daughter. She wanted a legacy. Every choice I made was supposed to prove something about her, to finish the life she never had the courage to live herself. But I refused to be her projection. When the band broke up, I didn't just walk away from the spotlight. I walked away from her. I needed distance from the manipulation, the expectations, and from the endless cycle of her reinvention. Last I heard she's on boyfriend number seven since leaving my father. Always chasing something new. Always unsatisfied.

I built my life carefully, deliberately, brick by brick, because no one ever handed me anything. I earned my independence. Between Damien's trust fund, my high-profile clients, and the occasional Five Heart royalty checks, I bought this California oasis for *me*.

Walking through the fur-and-sparkle living room, I feel my inner girly girl's satisfaction. Outside on the lanai, the curved pool is lined with neon floaties and bottles chilling in tubs of ice. Damien's old DJ setup hums in the corner, waiting to set the night on fire.

I hope the girls won't freak out when they learn I invited more than just them tonight. What they don't know won't kill them. Twenty-eight isn't technically a milestone, but with the band back together? This is history. Sure, I wish Jonna could come, but Dexter's got her on lockdown lately. Dani and Sabrina took the private jet out from the East Coast and should be here within the hour. God only knows how they're doing together one-on-one.

Upstairs in my bedroom, I shimmy into my lavender sparkle cowl-neck dress. This morning's blowout is still perfect, and my gold shimmer face card is worthy of a magazine cover.

"Fabulouuuusss," I sing to myself, twirling at my reflection.

Damien comes up behind me, his mouth dropped open, breath hot against my ear, and his cock hard as a rock, pressing into me through his joggers.

"You look sexy as hell," he growls, lips grazing my skin before fastening to the side of my neck. His tongue is slow, deliberate, like he's staking a claim. I want to roll my eyes, but I've been out of the office so much this month I haven't been able to enjoy my daily orgasms from Tom's tongue. So, I let myself lean back into Damien instead.

I spin to face my husband, my hand finding his thick, straining length through the fabric. With my other hand, I grab the back of his neck and drag his mouth to mine. Our tongues crash together, twisting and sliding like they've been starved. His fingers slip under my thong, brushing my clit in a teasing circle. Finally, after two years, he's found it. My breath catches, my hips instinctively pressing forward, chasing more.

He keeps stroking me, slow and steady, while our mouths stay locked, heat building between us until my knees threaten to give out. I moan into him as he pushes two fingers inside me, curling them just right. My grip on him tightens; I stroke him in the same rhythm he's using on me, feeling the tension coil tighter in both of us. The pressure snaps. I'm coming hard, my body trembling against his. His groan vibrates through my mouth, and he finishes in my hand, hot and pulsing.

"Oh my," I gasp when it's over, still catching my breath. He pulls his fingers from me, grinning that devilish grin. For a moment, I remember why I married him. I smile and kiss him lightly in thanks.

"Bet Tom can't do *that*," he smirks. And just like that, moment over.

I roll my eyes, rinse off, and call from the bathroom, "My friends will be here soon, why don't you go out for the night?"

"No way," Damien says, suddenly in the doorway. "I wouldn't miss your birthday for the world. Also, I pulled out my old turntable, I wanted to dust off my skills."

I roll my eyes, and I try to protest that this is supposed to be my night, but he's already rummaging through the closet. The doorbell rings, and I practically launch myself down the stairs, my heels clicking against marble.

"Birthday baby!" Dani shouts the moment I swing the door open, holding a giant floral-wrapped present.

"Oh my god, hi!" I squeal, throwing my arms around her. She smells like champagne and jet fuel.

"Happy birthday, Clarebear!" Sabrina glides in right behind her, flashing a grin and hoisting two bottles of Dom Pérignon like a trophy.

"You absolute angel," I say, hugging her, my eyes already locked on the gold foil.

"It's not a party without me," a voice chimes from behind them.

I nearly trip over my own feet. "*Selma?*"

She's there in head-to-toe cream silk, looking like she stepped straight out of an editorial.

"In the flesh," she says with a mock curtsy. "Do you think I'd miss your birthday and the launch of Five Heart's comeback?" Her alabaster smile could light up the entire Pacific coast.

And then, over her shoulder, Jonna appears, shy smile and all.

"You came?" I shriek, throwing my arms around her like I might never let go. "Dexter actually let you loose?" I tease, my voice muffled in her curls.

"I actually did!" a deep voice answers before Jonna can, and I realize Dexter's right there behind her, looking mildly offended.

"Oh, kidding, obviously," I say, giving him a quick side-hug.

"It's fine," he says, but his smile is half amusement, half *you're lucky I like you.*

"Happy birthday, Clare." The whole crew floods into my glitter-bomb living room, voices bouncing off glass and chrome.

Dani spins in a slow circle, taking it all in. "Wow, you decorated so…" She trails off, scanning the space, from the sequined throw pillows to the mirrored bar cart. "So you, ClareBear," she finishes with a laugh.

FIVE HEART

I strike a pose in the middle of the room, glistening in my dress.

"I know. It's fabulous." Damien swaggers downstairs and meets us wearing the paisley Tom Ford button-up I bought him for Christmas last year that I always beg him to wear.

Selma pops open one of the bottles of Dom, and we all toast to new beginnings, old memories, my birthday, and Nora.

"To Nora!" we all sing in unison. Glasses clink.

An hour later, Damien's in full DJ mode, rolled up sleeves, weaving beats together like his life depends on it. We're all sprawled across the deck chairs, the pool lights shimmering just enough to make us look like some chic resort ad. The music's low, conversation's easy, and for once, no one's on their phone. It's bliss.

Ding-dong.

I grin into my champagne flute. Nine P.M., right on schedule. I set my glass down and push up from my chair, already feeling Dani's eyes on me.

"Who is that?" she asks, suspicious.

"Oh… nothing," I say innocently. "Just a little surprise."

The doorbell rings again, louder this time, and the sound of voices carries in from the front. Jonna sits up. "Clare."

I shrug, trying not to burst out laughing. "I might have invited a few more people."

Sabrina narrows her eyes. "Define a few."

I jolt inside and open the door, and my definition arrives in stilettos and designer sneakers. A herd of them. Champagne bottles in hand, music already playing from portable speakers. They flood through my house and out to the backyard like I just opened a dam.

Within seconds, the air smells like perfume, weed, and someone's expensive cologne. The music jumps from background volume and mixes with Damien's concoction, creating a wave of beats filling our ears on max volume. The deck chairs that were ours a minute ago are now occupied by a group of attorneys from the office. Some random man in leather walks out trying to light a cigar.

I glance at the girls. Dani's staring at me like I've lost my mind, Jonna's already laughing, and Sabrina's shaking her head, but not moving.

"Relax," I tell them, grabbing a fresh bottle of Dom. "If we're going to market this tribute concert, we need the right kind of exposure. Consider this a photo op." They all exchange looks. "It's mostly people from the office, and a few other old friends of mine I invited. I don't know who that guy is, though." I point at cigar guy.

Time flies by, drinks are flowing, music is jamming, and we were able to make a cute TikTok of us dancing to an old Five Heart song by the pool in our mini dresses. I post the reel to my social media and tag the girls. Hashtag: *Birthday Girl, Five Heart, The Band is Back!*

I'm stretched out on the lanai furniture with a few people from the office when Yarrick, my paralegal, grins and holds out a lit blunt. "Puff, puff, pass?"

I take it between my fingers, bring it to my lips, and inhale deep. The smoke floods my lungs, earthy and sweet, heat curling down into my chest. As I hold it in, the night air feels suddenly warmer, heavier. My skin tingles under the sequins of my dress, my head lightening just enough to soften the pool lights' shimmer. I exhale in a slow, perfect ring that drifts upward into the string lights. That's when the gate from the side yard clicks open, and three familiar silhouettes step into the glow of the pool lights. Robbie. Ryan. Eric. No Reason in the flesh.

"You came!" I squeal, hopping up and hugging each of them in turn. Robbie smells faintly like cedar and leather.

"Wouldn't miss it," he says with that half-smile that's gotten him out of more bar fights than I can count. I hand him the blunt, and he takes a long drag before passing it to Ryan. As

Robbie exhales, his gaze locks on someone behind me. I turn to see Sabrina laughing with Dexter near the edge of the deck.

He hands the blunt off and says, "Excuse me," with a grin, striding toward her like the rest of the party just disappeared. And then, like a bad plot twist, the front door swings open. I look through the opened lanai door from across the distance. It's Tom.

"Tom," I gasp, my heart jerking into my throat. I jolt up and dart to the front door.
"Happy birthday, my love," he says smoothly, holding a dozen roses in one hand and a small jewelry box in the other.

Panic flashes hot through me. I grab his arm, whirl around, and push him back out onto the front porch before anyone inside can see. The door clicks shut behind us.

"What are you doing here?" I hiss, glancing over my shoulder like someone might be watching. "You know my husband is home."

He smirks, stepping in close, the scent of his cologne wrapping around me like a secret I'm not supposed to have. "Everyone else from the office is here. I'm still your boss. Can't I celebrate my number one employee?" His laugh is low, teasing, dangerous.

"I told Damien about us," I blurt, words tumbling fast. "I thought if I told him, the fucker would finally leave me. But he didn't. He's still here."

"I'm not intimidated by your husband," Tom says, voice low and certain. And he shouldn't be. Damien's half his size, all trust fund and no fight.

"Clare, this is for you." He extends the jewelry box, tied with a wide red bow. I can't help the smile that slips out. I untie the bow, pop the lid, and there on a velvet pillow glimmers a diamond tennis bracelet, each stone catching the porch light like it's alive.

"Oh my, Tom. It's gorgeous."

He takes it from the box and clasps it around my wrist, his fingers brushing my skin.

"Now, whenever you look down, you can think of me."

I grab his cheeks and kiss him, tasting tobacco and vanilla. When he pulls back, his eyes burn into mine. "The next jewelry box you open from me will be a ring."

The words hit hard. Sweet and dizzying. I step back.

"Tom, I—" I rub my arm, trying to steady myself. "I'm married."

His jaw tightens. "When are you going to leave him, Clare? I love you. He won't take care of you like I would."

He loves me. He's never mentioned that little tidbit before. I think I love him too.

"Please enjoy the party," I whisper, motioning him inside, because I can't fall apart on the porch with my never-ending thoughts. The door opens onto chaos that swallows us whole. Music pounding, voices spilling from every corner. We weave toward the lanai.

Out back, it's full-on debauchery: girls topless on flamingo floaties, couples making out in the shadows. Dani's dancing with Carmine from my office, Sabrina's perched on a deck chair with Robbie hovering close, Jonna and Dexter are arguing near the grill, words sharp and low. Damien's at the turntable, body hunched over the mixer like he's summoning the music Gods.

Then a sight snaps me out of my hypnotic state. Tom, dancing with a young woman in a tight crop top and leather mini skirt, her midriff bare, her boobs practically in his face.

A flash of heat explodes in my chest, sharp and reckless. The alcohol is coursing through my veins, loosening something I usually keep locked down tight. This isn't me. I know that even as I move. I stalk across the stone before I can stop myself, fingers fisting into her hair and I yank her backward hard. She stumbles, shrieking, the sound cutting through the haze for half a second before it's swallowed by the burn in my blood.

FIVE HEART

For a beat, I'm watching myself from the outside, shocked at my own hands, my own fury, wondering when restraint slipped away.

Before anyone can react, my hands are on Tom's hips, dragging him into me, an unspoken, primal declaration.

The music screeches to a stop. Damien is at the turntable, staring at us with murder in his eyes. My girls clock it too. All the guests have their phones up, recording.

He lets out a sound I've never heard before, somewhere between a roar and a battle cry, and barrels toward Tom, fist raised. The first punch misses by a hair. He swings again, knuckles skimming Tom's cheek. Tom fires back with an uppercut that connects with Damien's nose. Blood spurts like a horror movie, spraying the air, speckling my lavender dress.

"What the fuck!" I scream, shoving myself between them, arms out. Damien's nose is crooked, his eye already swelling. Tom's fists are still up, his expression fierce and hurt. Looking at them both, two men I think I love, both ready to tear each other apart for me, something in me buckles. I push through the drunken crowd, stumble up the stairs and down the hall, and lock myself in the master bedroom.

I slide down the back of the door, knees to my chest, shaking. For once in my life, I've never felt smaller. Three loud knocks.

"Leave me alone!" I yell, pure teenage me reincarnated.

"It's Jon," comes the muffled reply.

I crack the door and she slips in and locks it behind her. We drop to the floor together, breaths syncing in the silence. She takes my hands, flips my wrist over revealing the bracelet.

"You know I love you," she says, soft but firm. "But… what the hell are you doing?"

Tears sting. "I think I love Tom." We sit in it. Let the words hang like smoke.

"What about Damien?" she asks finally.

"It's a marriage of convenience," I say, eyes on the carpet. "Every man I've been with has been to benefit myself, as awful as that is. Tom is the first man I think I've ever truly felt love for." She exhales and pulls me into a hug.

"Oh, Clare. What a mess. I'll support you. But you can't do this to Damien."

I nod. "I know."

"You don't need to decide tonight," she says. "Tomorrow, we'll figure it out together." She glances around, searching. "Tomorrow… What time is it?"

I check the clock on my nightstand. "12:01 a.m."

We whip our heads toward each other and yell in unison: "The release!"

I yank my laptop from the drawer and pull up *Vogue* online. There we are, our faces blazing on the homepage.

Four girls. Five Hearts. The comeback of a century.

We squeal like teenagers, flipping through the spread, trading compliments and insults the way only best friends can.

"You look so hot," she says.

"Are you kidding? That dress was made for you."

We keep going until laughter dissolves the last of the panic in my chest. We decide to head back out. When we emerge, the crowd has thinned into pools of conversation and half-empty glasses. The music's down to a heartbeat. I spot Tom sitting on a deck chair by the lanai door, a bag of frozen peas pressed to his knuckles. He looks up the second he senses me.

Dexter runs up to Jonna and me. "Are you guys okay?" he asks, concern etched across his face.

"Yes, love, just went to comfort Clare," Jonna says, resting her hand on Dexter's arm to ease his worry.

"I'm okay, my life's just spiraling is all," I say sarcastically.

"Where are Dani and Sabrina?" I glance around, half-expecting them to have come to check on me by now. Rude.

"Well, last I checked, Dani was smoking a joint with that girl from your work, and Sabrina and Robbie locked themselves in one of your guest rooms," Dexter says.

Jonna and I exchange the same wide-eyed look of surprise. Selma floats over, practically glowing.

"What a party," she says extravagantly. "Oh, and congratulations again on going live! Can't wait to pick up a magazine at the stand by my apartment tomorrow morning. I better get going, though. I have brunch with my editor early." She kisses us both on the cheek before sashaying toward the door, Chanel No. 5 trailing behind her.

As soon as she's gone, I feel it. The burn of eyes on me. I turn slightly, and Tom still sits on the deck chair, consuming me with his whole being. He's not blinking.

Jonna leans close, her voice just for me. "Go," she says, nudging me toward him. The champagne seems to take control of my legs. I weave through the thinning crowd, heel catching on the edge of the rug. I stumble forward, and Tom's arms shoot out, catching me before I can face-plant into the pavement. He steadies me, his grip warm and solid.

"Careful, birthday girl," he murmurs, eyes glinting. It's then that I notice his gaze drop to my wrist, the diamond tennis bracelet he gave me blazing under the pool lights, then to my left hand, where Damien's wedding ring sits. One sparkles with possibility, the other, with history.

"Every time you look at that bracelet," he says quietly, still holding me, "I want you to remember you deserve more than what you've settled for. You deserve to be wanted, every second of every day." My pulse spikes. "You think Damien's going to give you that?" His eyes flick to the ring again. "That ring is from a man who keeps you because it's convenient. I'd keep you because you're everything."

"Tom…" My voice is barely there.

He leans in, his breath brushing my ear. "You wouldn't have to hide anymore. No pretending in front of your friends.

With me, there's only you." His hand slides lightly over my hip, thumb tracing idle circles. "Say the word and I'll handle it all. The divorce, the settlement. You'll keep your half. I'm a damn good lawyer, Clare. And I'm yours." I glance down. The diamonds catch the light like they're winking at me, but so does Damien's marquise solitaire. Two different lives glittering side by side on my skin.

For one dizzy second, I imagine slipping the wedding band off and handing it back, but my voice stalls in my throat. "I…"

Tom's eyes search mine, fierce and unwavering. "Clare. Don't walk back into that house wearing his ring. Come with me tonight. Start over."

The thought terrifies me almost as much as it thrills me. For the first time in years, I'm not sure of myself, and that's the most dangerous feeling of all. And maybe that's exactly why I'm tempted to burn everything down and choose him.

Chapter 15

Dani

The sun's rays slip through the slanted blinds, slicing across my face and dragging me out of a deep, drunken sleep. My eyes sting as I rub them, slowly taking in Clare's guest room.

For a second, I forget where I am. Then it hits me—I stayed the night.

I roll over and my breath catches at the lump of a person beside me. Carmine. One of the attorneys from Clare's firm. And, apparently, my late-night mistake. Or was it a mistake? The memory comes in flashes, like Polaroids dropped on the floor.

Two mimosas on the flight. Endless flutes of Dom at the party. Two slow, heady drags off a blunt. I haven't been that fucked up in years.

Carmine sleeps soundly now, her dark hair spilling like ink across the pillow. Her snakeskin skirt is still twisted around her hips, but she's topless, one supple breast peeking out from beneath the sheet like a secret I'm not supposed to see. And I remember exactly how that felt in my hands. She was a goddess from the moment she introduced herself. Soft black hair woven into two French braids, big gold hoops catching the light, a cropped brown top that hugged her curves, and that skirt brushing against me even now.

We'd met on the lanai, Zedd blasting from Damien's DJ setup, our mutual favorite. It was all laughter and refilled glasses until Ryan strolled over, passing us the last of a blunt. I should have said no. Mixing was a bad idea. But I hadn't truly let go in so long… so I said fuck it.

That's when the night began to dissolve into sensation instead of sequence. Carmine's hand on my arm pulling me inside to the guest bathroom. The heat in her eyes when she leaned in. The bathroom door clicking shut. Her mouth on my neck, slow, exploratory, like she was learning me one inch at a time. She brushed her lips against my cheek, slowly dragging her way to my lips. Hers were as soft as velvet. I froze for a heartbeat, Sam flashing through my mind like a warning. But Carmine tipped my chin back and held my gaze, silently telling me it was okay. Between the haze of champagne and smoke, Sam's ghost slipped away. I gave in.

Our tongues tangled, greedy, reckless. My hands found her breasts. Full, warm, and perfect for my grip. I pinched one nipple just to hear the muffled moan she spilled into my mouth. Outside, the bass dropped, vibrating the walls.

She pulled back with a wicked smile and whispered, "Let's take this upstairs." I nodded, too far gone to care about the consequences. We cracked open the guest room door and Sabrina and Robbie spun their heads toward us. Half-naked and tangled up together on the bed. Sabrina's eyes went wide, horrified that I'd caught her. I just giggled, shut the door, and let her have fun.

Carmine laced her fingers through mine and led me to the next bedroom. The second the door shut, she pushed me onto the bed, climbing over me with an urgency that made my pulse race. Her kisses turned frantic, our mouths colliding like we'd been holding back for years instead of minutes. I didn't fight her lead. Not once. She slid my hipster panties down, lifted my dress, and teased her tongue along the inside of my thigh. Every nerve in my body went taut. She dragged the tip lower, hovering, teasing, making me beg without a word. She made a slow circle around my clit that made me gasp so hard my chest ached. Warmth spread like liquid lightning, shooting through my core. My hips rocked toward her mouth, chasing that rhythm. But I wanted more.

I pulled her up and kissed her hard, tasting myself on her tongue. Something in me snapped. I flipped her beneath me, slid my fingers inside her, feeling her arch up into my touch. I ground myself against her thigh, riding her in sync with my hand. We broke at the same moment. Two sharp, breathless releases that left us collapsing together, the room spinning.

Somewhere between the aftershocks and the quiet, we passed out. Now, in the stark light of morning, sober and very aware, panic starts to curl in my chest.

I glimpse at the robe hanging from the door. Slipping quietly out of bed, totally naked, I wrap myself in the white cotton robe. Padding downstairs, I spot Clare on her couch, clutching her morning coffee and staring blankly at the wall like she's in a trance. In the kitchen, I pour myself a cup before joining her.

"You good?" I ask, studying her face. She doesn't move, frozen, like a statue. Finally, she blurts, "Damien left." I blink, unsure of what she means.

"Like… left to go pick up bagels?" I laugh, taking a sip of my liquid energy.

"No," she mumbles. "He left me." She shoves her phone at me, revealing a 2 A.M. text from Damien: WE ARE OVER!

"Oh my god, are you okay?" I sit up straight, fully grasping the gravity of the situation.

"I think," she says slowly. "I'm just scared what happens next."

I place a gentle hand on her back, rubbing small circles. "Didn't you kind of want this to happen? I thought you were unhappy with Damien."

She turns to me, tears brimming. "I did! I prayed for this day. But I knew he'd never leave me! I'm the best he'll ever have, and he knew it. I thought I was safe. Now he's going to take the estate, drain my bank account, and I'll have nothing!" Clare's voice rises, panic spilling over.

I set both our coffees on the table and turn her to face me. "You don't know that. And you can make this right. Tell him you made a mistake. I'm sure he'll forgive you for whatever happened. He loves you."

"Dani, you don't get it. I don't love him. I love Tom."

The words hit me like a slap. Clare's never mentioned an affair before; apparently, she kept this from all of us.

"But I also love my life. I mean, look at this house!" She spreads her arms wide, gesturing at its perfection. "And look at my face! This isn't just good genes. I go to the best med spa in Orange County! How will I afford to keep up my lifestyle if Damien divorces me?"

Footsteps creak on the stairs. Sabrina and Robbie appear, trying to pretend they're not eavesdropping.

"We see you," Clare says sharply.

They relax and walk into the room.

"Don't mind us. We were literally catching up all night and just passed out mid-conversation," Sabrina says, trying to spin a cover story.

"Oh yeah, catching up," I wink. "It's okay, guys, we're all adults here."

They ignore the jab and drift into the kitchen to start a fresh pot.

"Look, don't be hasty," I say to Clare. "Take some time. Figure out what you really want. I'm here for you. Do you want to come stay with me for a few days? I'm heading back to Nashville for a week after I drop the girls in New York." I imagine Clare in cowboy boots and flannel, ridiculous, but charming.

She shakes her head. "No. I need to go see Tom." Without another word, she disappears upstairs into the abyss.

Sabrina and Robbie rejoin me on the couch. "I know you know," she says, smirking at Robbie. He sips his coffee and grins.

"Hey, good for you guys," I laugh.

"And who did you go to bed with last night? Don't think I didn't see who was pulling you upstairs," Sabrina teases. Mortified, I scramble.

"Oh, we weren't. Her and I just connected over our Italian background. Her family's from Bari, same as my grandmother." I force the story together quickly. "We talked about Italy for hours."

They shrug, apparently buying it. Safe again. That's when Carmine trudges down the stairs, a casualty of champagne. She's still in her brown top and snakeskin skirt, her braids now undone into soft waves that bounce with each step.

"Morning." She smiles. We lift our coffee cups in return.

"I'm going to get dressed and go for a run," I blurt, part escape plan, part prevention, making sure there's no chance of an awkward conversation with Carmine in front of Sabrina and Robbie.

"Oh my god!" Sabrina shrieks, looking at her phone. She spins it toward me. Our *Vogue* cover is online. I snatch the phone, eyes wide. Holy shit.

"Wow… it looks amazing. It's… real," I breathe.

Carmine slips behind me, resting her hand on my ass. "Let me see," she says, peering over my shoulder. I quickly step out of her reach and show the image half-heartedly. She catches the shift in my body language and immediately withdraws. "That's really cool," she says flatly. "I'm going to head out. Tell Clare thank you for letting me crash. I'll see her first thing tomorrow." The front door slams behind her.

Sabrina, Robbie, and I exchange glances.

"Well… that was weird," Sabrina says. I wipe sweat from my forehead and head upstairs to change into my athleisure.

The street is still quiet from the night before, the air carrying that faint smell of dew. My legs burn pleasantly from the last mile I ran, and I tug my ponytail tighter, earbuds thumping in my ears as I round the corner toward Clare's driveway. That's when I see it, a black Escalade idling at the curb, windows tinted dark enough to swallow your reflection. The driver's door opens, and out steps Donovan.

The morning light glances off his deep mahogany skin and the sharp line of his charcoal suit. Gold cufflinks wink at his wrists as he closes the door with deliberate precision. He carries himself with that same unshakable cool demeanor. The kind of presence that turns heads even when no one wants to look. My feet slow. I hadn't laid eyes on him in years, but Clare and Jonna told me he and Steve were both at Nora's funeral, standing in the back like ghosts. That image alone has been enough to unsettle me ever since. And now here he is, unannounced, on Clare's doorstep. Is he following us?

I tug one earbud out. "What the hell are you doing here?" I say, trying to catch my breath.

Donovan smiles like I've just made his day. "I heard there was a reunion in the works." His eyes flick toward Clare's house, then back to me. "And *Vogue* confirmed it for me." From under his arm, he slides out a rolled magazine, holding it like a secret weapon. He takes his time unfurling it, smoothing the glossy page until the cover of our shiny group stares back at me. His eyes flick down my body once, and his hand brushes too close when he holds out the magazine.

"Congratulations," he says lightly, tapping a finger against the image. "It's a beautiful shot. I especially like the part where you forgot to tell me about it."

I cross my arms. "We don't need your permission to take a picture."

"Maybe not for the picture," he says, tucking the magazine under his arm again. "But for the concert this picture is selling? That's another matter."

My pulse kicks hard. Every time he talks, my body remembers things my mind refuses to fully admit. The faint scent of aftershave in hotel corridors. The weight of a hand on my shoulder, that lingered too long. My voice catching in my throat when I was younger. I lock those memories away, shoving the door closed.

"You're not involved in this," I say flatly.

He steps closer, voice dipping into that calm, careful register he always used when he wanted control. "See, I still own the Five Heart trademark. Name, logo, the whole package. And the label, my label, still owns the master's to all those hits you're planning to dust off for your big night."

I yank out the other earbud. "We can change the name. Play other songs."

Donovan chuckles, shaking his head. "You could. But the fans don't want other songs, Dani. They want 'Runaway Summer,' 'City Lights,' all those little anthems that made them fall in love with you girls. And without my blessing? Off-limits."

"That's blackmail."

He shrugs. "Call it what you want."

I square my shoulders. "Then we'll promote it through my current label. My deal. They have the muscle to push a Five Heart show without you."

That makes him grin wider.

"Except you don't own Five Heart. I do. And your label can't market something you don't have the rights to. They can promote you, as Dani Rose the solo artist, performing your current songs." His gaze sharpens. "But the group's old work? Those belong to me. Which means unless this concert is just you, the girls can't sing a note from our past without my approval."

A wave of anxiety splashes down my spine. "You're unbelievable."

"It's business," he corrects smoothly. "Here's my offer: we do this through the label. You get full use of the name and the catalogue for the tribute show, and maybe more. You get your nostalgia. I get—a seat at the table. Everyone wins."

And suddenly Clare's voice from the other night comes back to me…*He and Steve were there. Just standing there. Watching.*

Why? Why show up then? Why show up now? I take a step back, my skin crawling. "And if we don't?"

His smile sharpens. "Then you'll have a very intimate concert in someone's backyard, singing songs no one came to hear, or a heavy lawsuit that will destroy each and every one of you on your hands. The choice is yours."

He tips his head in a mock bow, slips back into the Escalade, and drives off, the magazine still under his arm, like a trophy. I stand there in the driveway long after he's gone, my chest tight. The run didn't leave me breathless, he did. And I can't shake the feeling that whatever happened to Nora… his shadow was somewhere in it.

Chapter 16

Jonna

The house smells like Eggo waffles, syrup, and baby powder. The signature scent of my life right now. DJ's at the counter drumming with two wooden spoons, Harley's screaming that Finn erased her Netflix kids profile, Finn's yelling back that Harley "looked" at his juice box wrong, and Alissa's in her bouncer cooing sweetly while kicking like she's prepping for a toddler triathlon.

Dexter's already at the office, which leaves me as referee, chef, and crisis negotiator. I'm halfway through wiping peanut butter off the fridge door when my phone buzzes. Dani's name lights up the screen.

"Hey, Jon," she says quickly, and before I can even answer, "I'm patching in Sabrina and Clare." Three beeps later, the four of us are on.

"What's going on?" I ask, pinning the phone between my shoulder and ear as I grab a crayon out of Alissa's mouth.

Dani doesn't waste a second. "I ran into Donovan. At Clare's house."

I freeze. "You what?"

"I didn't tell you sooner because…" She exhales. "I couldn't even process it. And I've been dealing with other stuff."

Sabrina pounces. "Other stuff?"

"Not important," Dani snaps. "What matters is Donovan's moving to block the tribute concert unless we go through his label. He claims he still owns Five Heart and the master's. If we want the name or the old songs, it's his way or the highway."

Clare's voice is crisp. "Translation: he wants creative control and a cut of everything."

"That's blackmail," I say flatly.

"It's business," Dani mutters.

"The worst kind. We need a plan before he locks us in."

Finn barrels through the kitchen yelling that the cat is in his room again, Harley chasing after him with a Barbie shoe like it's a weapon.

My chest tightens. "I can't meet in the city. I can't keep ditching the kids. Alissa's growing so fast, and I'm missing it." My throat catches. "Feels like she's growing without me."

Silence.

Then Dani says softly, "We'll come to you."

Sabrina's reply is immediate. "Locust Valley it is."

Clare sighs. "Fine. Dani's riding with me from the airport."

When they arrive, it's pure chaos, in the best way. Harley's showing Sabrina her glitter nail polish collection— "This one's called Mermaid Scale!"—Finn's asking Clare if she knows Iron Man personally, and DJ's cornered Dani in the kitchen to sing her the theme song he wrote for Fortnite "but on the piano."

FIVE HEART

Alissa's gurgling happily in Dani's lap, chewing on the strings of her hoodie, when Dexter gets home mid-chaos. Tall, still in his suit, with the calm of a man who's learned to live with background noise.

"Ladies," he says, kissing my temple. "Dani. Clare. Sabrina." He eyes the table piled with coloring books and coffee mugs. "Band practice or takeover?"

"Bit of both," I tell him. He grins, heads upstairs to change, and calls over his shoulder, "Give me ten minutes and I'll take the kids so you can talk business."

We settle around the dining room table. Dexter's in the living room with the kids, their laughter mixing with Alissa's baby babble.

"So," Dani starts, "what's the play?"

Sabrina leans forward. "We ditch the Five Heart name. New branding."

"That kills the nostalgia," Clare cuts in. "And he still owns the trademark on the original group name. Even close variations could be argued as infringement."

"What about rerecording the hits?" I ask. "Taylor Swift style?"

Clare shakes her head. "Different situation. We could re-record, sure, but the publishing is still controlled by the label. The compositions are owned. The melodies, the lyrics. We'd need to change them enough to be considered derivative works, and that opens us to a different kind of legal fight."

Look at Clare being all lawyer-like. Sabrina taps the table. "Okay, so full re-records aren't safe in time for this show. What about live performance rights? Don't venues handle that with ASCAP or BMI for performance royalties?"

"Yes and no," Dani says.

"That covers general performance licenses, but not when you market the event as Five Heart. That's trademark territory, and Donovan owns it. We could sing the songs at a bar tomorrow, but not in a major, ticketed event tied to the brand."

"So we strip the brand out of the show," I say. "Market it as a solo artist festival. Dani, Clare, Sabrina, and me… whatever I am now."

Clare smirks. "You're bass and the legs, babe."

We all laugh, but Sabrina's already thinking. "Then we license one song, just one, from Donovan. The hit no one will forgive us for skipping."

"'Runaway Summer,'" Clare says immediately. "It's the cornerstone. Pay him for that one track and keep him off the rest."

Dani nods. "We fill the rest of the setlist with solo work, unreleased tracks we own outright, and deep cuts where the rights reverted to us."

"Plus," I add, "we can rework certain songs into legally distinct arrangements, change the key, alter the lyrics, restructure the bridge. If it's transformative enough, we can argue fair use in a live setting. It's risky, but it's leverage."

Sabrina grins. "And we keep an all-original acoustic encore ready, so if he tries to pull the license last-minute, we end on something he can't touch."

"Let's keep brainstorming, but these are really great ideas," Dani says and then glances at Clare.

"What about you? How are you doing with everything?" Clare's diamond bracelet glints under the light, but her wedding ring is gone.

"You didn't tell us," Sabrina says quietly.

"I made a decision," Clare says, her voice even but eyes tired. "I haven't told either man yet."

We reach for her, a hand on her arm, a squeeze at her shoulder. She gives a small smile. "Don't worry about me. Let's get back to this."

Dexter appears in the doorway, tie off, Alissa in one arm, Finn hanging from the other. "How's the master plan coming?"

"We think we got it," I tell him.

He grins. "Let's hear it."

Dani ticks it off on her fingers: "Rebrand the event to Five Heart: The Last Dance to sidestep direct trademark infringement, license exactly one hit, most likely Runaway Summer to give fans their nostalgia without giving Donovan a cut of the full show, fill the rest with solo work, deep cuts, and reimagined arrangements altered enough to argue derivative originality, and keep an original-only acoustic encore ready in case he tries to sabotage the license."

Dexter nods. "Smart. If you need someone to read over those agreements before you sign, I know a guy."

"You mean you," Clare says.

He smirks. "Maybe." Then he kisses the top of my head. "Alright, back to the kids. You four save the music industry, I'll save the carpet from apple juice."

Chapter 17

Sabrina

It's a breezy October morning as I clack my way to the revolving doors of *The New York Times* for what I know will be a hectic workday. I'm wrapped in a maroon trench coat with my signature Burberry scarf stuffed snugly around my neck, freshly highlighted waves bouncing with every step.

It's been a few weeks since our emergency debrief over Donovan in Long Island, and we've kept everything strictly under the radar. Jerry, my editor, has started to question me about my "effort" lately, and he's right. I've been distracted. Between the Five Heart rebrand, Nora's death, and my new romance with Robbie, my investigative sharpness has dulled.

I take the elevator up to the eleventh floor, greeted by a few interns who already have my coffee waiting. Ever since the magazine drop, I've become a minor celebrity around here. Men swooning when I pass, interns offering their metaphorical organs if I needed one. Even Brian from CNN is suddenly begging for forgiveness. This attention? I could get used to it.

FIVE HEART

Being shoved to the back behind the girls when we were younger left me starving for the spotlight.

Now, I'm feasting. I grab my coffee and take a sip.

"You remembered my order. Great job, Shannon," I say with a half-smile.

"It's Rhiannon," she corrects with an eager grin. "And I could never forget your order, Ms. Daniel." I'm already halfway down the hall before she can find another reason to keep me talking.

Another intern, Tyler pulls out my chair and hands me a folder. The files I asked him to dig up yesterday on the pedophile principal at PS 115. The story just dropped without my byline, but I knew something was missing. My own digging revealed he wasn't even certified to be a principal. He'd smooth-talked his way into the role. A real *Catch Me If You Can* act, and worse, he'd been molesting third graders the entire time. "Does no one do background checks anymore?" I mutter aloud.

"You would think!" Tyler says, lingering too long behind me. I wave him away so I can start typing. Then Jerry slams a newspaper down over my keyboard. I look up into his angry, mustached face.

"Good morning, Jerry," I say cautiously.

"Daniel, what the hell is this?" He points at the cover of *The Wall Street Journal*. A photo of me and Robbie locked in a kiss at Seed and Bean. Oh lord. I squint at it, pretending not to see what's obviously plastered across the front page.

"Your newfound celebrity status is going to spit all over our credibility," he says in disgust.

"Well, technically, I was always a celebrity, Jerry. Just not as prominently recognized as I am now," I reply.

He shakes his head. "I'm taking you off the principal story."

Panic surges through me. "What? I worked so hard to find his background!"

"You can be listed as assistance in the back," he says flatly.

"In the back? By the obituaries?" I shout, floored. Everyone in the cubicles stops to watch as our argument unfolds. Jerry walks away, head high.

"Ugh!" I storm into the bathroom and slam the door.

I scroll through social media to calm my rage, and it sadly doesn't work. So, I pull up my contacts and call Robbie. He's been in the city these past few weeks, working at the studio with the other boys from No Reason on a new single. They claim they were "inspired by us" to become relevant again.

"Hey, beautiful," he answers on the second ring.

"Hey, handsome. What are you up to?"

"The boys and I just wrapped at the studio. We've been here all night. I was going to grab breakfast, then crash at the hotel."

"Well, I'd love to join you for breakfast, if you'd have me," I say innocently.

"Aren't you working today? I thought you had that big case."

"No, it's a slow day at the office. Pin me your location, I'll meet you!" I flush the toilet for cover, grab my maroon trench coat, and head out into the metropolis.

Robbie and I decide to skip the public breakfast and go straight to his room at the Marriott Marquis, avoiding another tabloid moment. We order an obscene amount of room service and a bottle of Moët. Our legs tangle under the covers as we feed each other syrup-drenched pancakes.

"You know, this is all I ever wanted," he says, chewing happily.

I lick a drip of syrup from his lip. "Oh yeah?"

He sets down his fork, tilting my chin up until our faces are almost touching. "Just you, me, a bed, and the best pancakes in the world."

"These *are* the best pancakes in the world," I laugh, breaking the gaze nervously. I've never felt this way about a man.

He stabs the last bite and pops it in his mouth. "So… the show's at the end of December tentatively. It's October now. What are you doing the next two months?"

"Well, the girls and I are each working on our own songs to perform. I haven't even started yet," I admit.

"I have a pitch," he says. "What if I was featured in one of your songs? It might even help your legal case with Donovan. I'm not under his license. It would be completely original."

I touch his cheek, thrilled he wants to be part of this. "I don't know, the other girls might not go for it."

"I don't think Ryan or Eric would love it either," he admits. "But it could be our song. You and me."

"Our song?" My heart warms. "We don't even know what we are, let alone have a song." I try to joke, but there's truth beneath it. Robbie and I have never defined whatever this is. Boyfriend? Fling? Future husband? That last thought sneaks in like a spark.

"Well, what do you want us to be?" he asks. For once, I don't want to lead.

"Whatever you want us to be," I say.

"Well… Ms. Daniel," he says, taking my hand. "I'd love the honor of being your boyfriend, if you'll have me."

I pretend to think, counting on my fingers. "Duh!" I throw myself on him and kiss him deeply.

"You're my girlfriend," he says, almost like he's convincing himself.

"Uh-huh," I murmur against his lips before our tongues twist together like ocean currents. I grind over him, feeling him harden through his cargos. The kissing deepens; his hands grip my hips, and soon he tosses me under him, stripping his slim-fit tee to reveal sculpted abs and just the right amount of chest hair.

I shed my white button-up and skirt until I'm in my red lace bra and panties.

"You know I love red on you," he growls. His pants hit the floor, revealing him, and then my panties hit the window. He flips me over and slides into me without hesitation, and I gasp at the size. The thrusts come hard and fast, my back pressed to his ribs. Time stops and nothing else exists but the sweat, the tangled limbs, and the perfect, obliterating rhythm of us.

Later, I come home after ditching work and spending the afternoon on Robbie's mattress. My tuxedo cat, Max, chirps when he sees me. I pet him until his tail shoots up, then pour food into his bowl. I slide open the balcony door and sink into my rattan chair, gazing at the cityscape bathed in orange and fuchsia from the setting sun. For a moment, I breathe in pure peace. Five Heart is back. I have a boyfriend, Robbie, lead singer of No Reason. Life feels full. Then the air shifts. A faint familiarity of stale coffee, humming amps, then Donovan's face floods my mind. Intrusive thoughts taking the wheel.

A memory I haven't remembered until now, maybe I subconsciously chose not to. I'm pulled back to a day over a decade ago, Nora and I at the studio, working on a single. We arrived before Dani and Jonna. The air was thick with the smell of stale coffee and the faint buzz of the amps warming up. Donovan was already there. He called Nora into the sound room, his voice just low enough that I couldn't make out the words. They were arguing. Sharp movements, clipped gestures. Then I saw it.

He gripped her chin, jerking her face up toward him. It wasn't gentle. The horror in her eyes said more than I ever could. Nora's shoulders rose, tense, her lips parting as if to speak, but nothing came out. Then his hands slid to her shoulders, holding her in place, leaning in close enough that her back brushed against the console. His fingers moved, slow and deliberate, down the front of her shirt.

The hum of the amp seemed louder. She froze, every muscle locked, until she noticed me watching through the glass. Her eyes flicked to mine, a flash of something between panic and warning. She jerked back, stepping away from him. Donovan stepped back too, adjusting his stance like he'd just been talking shop the whole time. His mouth kept moving, tone casual, as if nothing had happened. I stayed where I was, pretending to check my phone, pretending I hadn't seen. But I had. And I knew.

A shiver crawls down my spine as the city shifts from sunset to night, the lights glittering against the darkness, a constant reminder that New York never sleeps.

The next day, I can't shake the look on Nora's face in my flashbacks. That flash of raw, unfiltered horror in her eyes. It's been haunting me all night, dragging me through one fevered half-dream after another until my sheets felt like restraints. Every time I closed my eyes, I saw her again. Not the Nora in the stage lights, but the Nora who seemed to know something the rest of us didn't.

The spiral began there, but it didn't stop. My mind kept replaying the greatest hits of our history together, except now every memory came with a shadow. The first red flag. The sound room at the studio, that initial incident we brushed off because we didn't want to fracture our dream. Then, the night Five Heart split for good.

Nora had said that night that she felt like she was carrying the world on her shoulders. That she was always protecting us. That she didn't feel seen. Didn't feel valued. At the time, I filed it under "band drama" or ego, exhaustion, maybe a bad night. But now? Now it feels like a confession I didn't understand.

When she stayed with me years ago, in my cramped one-bedroom, grinding away as an intern at *The Times*, she'd let little barbed comments slip whenever I brought up the band. Things like, "If only you knew how lucky we are to be out." I always thought she was being ungrateful, bitter about the past. I never considered she might be warning me.

She'd come home from some dive bar gig around the corner, clutching a bottle of cheap chardonnay like it was the only thing keeping her upright. Her voice was ever changing back then. Turning into this deep, smoky rasp from endless nights of drinking and singing over the static hum of bar smokers. She'd drop crumpled notebook pages on my coffee table, lyrics scrawled like they'd been clawed out of her brain, and she'd sing them for me, half-tipsy, half-reverent. One night, she handed me a song she wrote and said it was written for me, a thank-you for our friendship.

We'd been inseparable once. I was the first of us to really know her, back before Clare and Jonna joined, before the record deal.

It was sophomore year. Dani and I had made a "Band Sign-Up" sheet, tacking it to the school bulletin board. Nora didn't sign it. She just sat next to me in homeroom, doodling lyrics in the margins of her binder and humming these haunting melodies under her breath. I asked her one day if she'd audition for our upcoming band. She said no. Her mom had just died that week. She looked so hollow I almost dropped it. But something told me to push.

She showed. And, she didn't just sing, she detonated. Dani and I sat there in my parents' garage, wide-eyed, as this quiet, grief-wrecked girl opened her mouth and knocked the air out of us. She was our first recruit. Our glue before we even knew we'd need glue. The memory is still warm in my chest when it hits me. Hard.

I bolt upright, adrenaline snapping me awake. There's something I need to see. Something I know is still here. I tear through my room, drawers yanked out, closet baskets dumped onto the floor, papers flying. It looks like a break-in, but I don't care. Then I remember. Under the bed.

I drop to my knees and drag out the shoebox. The one I painted back in high school with "Five Heart" scrawled across the lid, doodles of butterflies and hearts crowding the edges. My hands tremble as I pop it open. It's all here.

Photo booth strips from the mall, right after Clare and Jonna officially joined. We look impossibly young, like we could outrun time itself. Even Nora's smiling, like she'd finally found her people. Our debut CD. VIP passes still on the hot pink lanyard. Guitar picks. There, tucked between a Polaroid and a folded gig flyer was the song. The one she wrote for me. The one she sang the night before I walked into that bathroom and found her and Dante wrecked beyond repair. I must have stuffed it in this box during my move to my current residence. I hold it up to the light, eyes skimming over her crooked lines, the way her letters always seemed to lean toward each other like they were whispering. Something clicks. My pulse starts hammering.

Even though it's dusk, I snatch my phone and dial Dani. Straight to voicemail. I call again. Two rings this time before she picks up, groggy. "Hello?"

"Dani!" My voice is too loud, too fast.

"Can you send me a screenshot of Nora's suicide note?" A beat.

"Um… why?" she asks, almost zombie-like.

"I don't have time to explain, just send it to me!"

"Okay, okay… Can I go back to sleep if I do?" she mumbles.

"Yes. Thank you." I hang up before she can protest. I'm vibrating as I sit at the edge of my bed, heel bouncing, heart in my throat. My phone finally chimes after what seems like an hour. The image fills my screen. I zoom in until the words blur. My gaze flicks between the note and the song, back and forth, over and over.

There it is. "Just as I suspected," I whisper. The handwriting is wrong. Nora typically wrote with her letters slanted. But this… this was too bubbly, too rounded to be true. I instantly bolt upwards and shove my feet into black leather knee-high boots, throw my tan Burberry trench over my flannel pajamas, grab my bag, and hurry out the door. I need to make copies of both handwriting samples, and unfortunately, I didn't own a scanner or printer. To the office.

By the time I reach *The Times*, the building is still mostly asleep. The lobby security guard barely glances up. The elevator hums softly as it carries me to the eleventh floor. The newsroom is dark except for a few scattered desk lamps. My desk sits in its usual spot, but I detect there's something new. A manila envelope in the dead center. No name. No post-it. Not sealed. I open it.

Inside there's a copy of Nora's suicide note, old clippings from our early days, paparazzi photos of Nora, and a single typed sheet:

You're looking in the wrong place. Ask who benefits. Start with the manager.

My skin prickles. A floorboard creaks behind me and I turn, startled. Jerry, my editor, is leaning in the doorway of his office, coffee in hand, watching me.

"You're in early," he says.

I sigh in relief. "Couldn't sleep."

His eyes flick to the envelope. "Well. Try not to get yourself fired before breakfast." He disappears into his office, the door clicking shut.

I stare at the envelope a second longer before pulling out my phone and calling Robbie. I shove the copy of the suicide note and the typed message back into the envelope and toss it in my tote. My head is spinning. What are the chances I have a revelation about the handwriting, and now this? The newsroom feels too quiet, too empty, and the fact that someone was here before me, leaving this… makes my skin crawl.

I push through the revolving doors of *The Times* and step outside into the chilly morning. The streets are dead, the kind of early hour where you can hear a car from six blocks away. My trenchcoat is cinched tight over my flannel pajamas, and my leather boots click against the wet pavement. I'm half-dressed for bed, half-dressed for war. I pull out my phone and dial Robbie. He picks up on the second ring, voice still warm and sleepy. "Morning, babe. What's going on?"

"Robbie, the note isn't her handwriting. It's not even close. And someone left this envelope on my desk with a copy of the note, old articles, photos, and a typed message that says 'start with the manager.'"

There's a pause on his end. I hear faint studio noise, someone laughing, a guitar chord being tuned. His voice changes, sharper now.

"Where are you?"

"*The Times*."

"Come to the studio. Now. We'll talk where no one can overhear. And don't say anything else on the phone."

I don't argue, just wave down a cab and slide in, clutching the envelope in my lap like it might disappear if I let go. The ride feels longer than it is. My brain is racing, trying to piece together who could've left the envelope, what it means, and why the hell someone is pushing me toward Steve. The city is just starting to wake up, light breaking between buildings. When we pull up to the studio, I toss the driver some cash and head inside.

The hallways smell like stale coffee and equipment that's been running all night. A guitar case is propping one of the doors open. I spot Robbie in Control Room A, leaning over the mixing board. The second he sees me, his whole face changes, worry instantly replacing whatever he was working on.

He pushes away from the board, strides over, and pulls me into his arms like he's been waiting for this all morning.

"You're freezing," he murmurs into my hair, his hand sliding down my back, keeping me there. His heartbeat is steady under my cheek, and for a second, I let myself just stay pressed against him.

"I'm losing it, babe," I finally say, my voice muffled against his chest. "The note's fake. And this—" I pull the envelope from my tote, "—just shows up on my desk. No return address, no nothing. Just, this."

He eases back just enough to take it from me, but he keeps his free hand resting on my hip like he's not ready to let me go yet. He flips through the contents with a frown, his brows knitting together.

That's when I spot Eric, leaning against the wall in the corner with a coffee in his hand, watching us. The second his eyes land on the envelope, something flashes across his face. His jaw tightens, and he looks away too quickly.

That's all I need, to realize he knows something. I pull away from Robbie, his fingers trailing reluctantly off my arm, and head straight toward Eric.

"What do you know?" I demand.

Eric blinks, acting clueless. "About what?"

"The envelope. The note. You recognized it. Don't play dumb."

Robbie moves like he's about to step in, but I hold up my hand without looking at him. Eric glances toward the hallway. "Your reputation as an investigative reporter precedes you," he mutters. "But not here."

He motions me outside the control room and into the cooler hallway. "You're right," Eric says. "The note's fake. I didn't write it, but I've known for a while it wasn't hers." My heart kicks up.

"Then why haven't you said anything, and how did you get a copy of the note?"

He shifts against the wall. "I have a buddy at the NYPD, and Steve doesn't just end someone's career if they cross him. He erases it. I can't risk the band. I've seen it happen. Couple years ago, we met this kid, he blew up on TikTok. Young, stupid talented. Steve signed him, told him he'd make him the next big thing. At his single release party, I caught him and Steve in a screaming match. Didn't hear everything, but I heard the kid tell him he 'crossed a line.' Three days later, he was gone. No posts. No shows. His account deleted. Friends stopped talking about him. Just… gone."

I fold my arms. "So you leave me an anonymous envelope and hope I do something with it?"

"Call it a push in the right direction. If you're starting anywhere, start with Steve. He's the one who made sure Nora's story never came out."

"What story was that?" I press.

Eric hesitates. "The one she couldn't tell without blowing up everything. The band, the label, the industry. The one she kept to herself because she thought she was protecting you."

The words punch me. I think back to Nora sitting on my apartment floor years ago.

If only you knew how lucky we are to be out. Back then, I thought she was being bitter. Now I'm not so sure.

"Protecting me from what?"

"That's not mine to tell," he says.

"But Steve made sure no one else could tell it either." I stare at him. "The funeral. You hitting Walter. That wasn't about Walter, was it?"

He shakes his head. "Donovan and Steve walked in together. They weren't there to pay respects. They were watching Dani, trying to figure out what she knows. I didn't like the way it looked, so I made a scene big enough to get them out of there."

A chill runs through me. "Why Dani?"

"Maybe they think Nora told her something. Wasn't Dani the last to see Nora alive? Maybe they're right. Just keep her close, Sabrina. And keep your eyes open. You're not the only one they're watching."

With that, he walks away, leaving me standing there with my head spinning. Robbie's already waiting just outside the hallway, and without a word, he threads his fingers through mine and leads me into the lounge. He sits first, pulling me down beside him so my knees brush his. His arm hooks over the back of the couch, his hand absently playing with my hair while he studies my face. "What did he say?"

I tell him everything. About the fake note, Steve, and that Eric thinks Donovan and Steve were watching Dani at the funeral, absolute word vomit.

Robbie shakes his head, his thumb brushing across my knee. "That's crazy… Eric's never mentioned any of this to me or Ryan. Not a single word. But now that I think about it, since Nora died, he's been off. Jumpy. Like he's hiding something."

"Maybe because he is," I say quietly.

Robbie catches my chin between his fingers, tilting my face toward his. "Babe… be careful with him. If he's hidden this from us this long, I don't know what else he might be keeping." I nod, but the thought sticks. Eric might be helping me, or he might be holding back the most important pieces. Robbie leans in and kisses me slow, and lingering, like he's trying to anchor me in place. When we break, he presses his forehead to mine. "Whatever you find, we face it together. Deal?"

"Deal," I nodded, but deep down, I knew I wasn't built to wait. Not when Nora's ghost was still asking me to listen

Chapter 18

Clare

I haven't heard from Damien in weeks. I assume he's holed up with his parents in their mansion on Lake Tahoe. I haven't heard much from the girls either, just the occasional meme in our Five Heart Lives group chat.

I haven't worn my wedding ring in a while, but the bracelet? That's still on every day. I told Tom I wanted to date before moving full force into anything. I also don't want to make rash moves until I can talk to Damien. At least he's left me alone in my house in my peace, rather than trying to pull it out from under me. I scroll through my socials as I sip my morning espresso before work. My Instagram followers just hit one million. Damn. I've been posting daily reels, secretly hoping Damien views them.

I hold my phone out and hit record. "Good morning, Clarettes! I'm off to work, I have a meeting with a major client today. Going to need two more of these," I say sensually, then down the rest of my espresso. Post. Done.

I slide into my Benz, windows down, Britney blaring "I'm a Slave 4 U." It's a surprisingly nice November morning, and I've got a potential big-money client to prepare for. In the rearview mirror, my plump, glossy lips curl into a smile.

"Breaker and Gallagher, where we serve the people the way they deserve. That's why you should choose our firm to get you through this extraordinary time," I rehearse in my sexiest voice. I pull into the lot and park beside Tom's brand-new Dodge Ram.

His truck is a monster next to my sedan, just like us, side by side. Lately, we've been getting to the office an hour before opening to have a little… one-on-one time. I push open the glass doors and walk briskly down the empty hallway toward his office. He's not there.

"Tom?" I call, rounding the corner into the breakroom, only to feel his arms slide around my waist from behind. I spin around, acting more startled than I am. He runs his fingers through my blonde curls, pulling me closer.

"You get a promotion, for being early to work four days in a row this week," he whispers, his breath warm against my ear.

"I guess I'll be making eight figures at this rate, because I'll be coming early every day," I murmur, resting my hand against his groin.

"Yes, you will," he says wickedly. I giggle at the pun, and he lifts me onto the kitchenette counter. My legs lock around his waist, and I tug him closer by his tie. He stares at me like a predator sizing up prey.

"Well, come here already," I say, hungry for him. He kisses me hard. Like oxygen is optional. His hand slides under my silk blouse, massaging my breast, his thumb tracing my nipple until I ache for more. His other hand slips down my slacks, fingers working magic. I push into him, desperate. He pulls my pants down, shifts my panties aside, and lowers his head, our weekly ritual. His tongue moves in perfect rhythm, building a perfect crescendo with the tip.

Cough. Cough.

My eyes fly open. Carmine is standing in the doorway, frozen.

"Oh my god!" I gasp, just as I climax. Tom hasn't noticed her yet, still lost in his performance. Carmine remains still, voyeuristic. When he finally stands, wiping his mouth with pride, I point behind him. His head whips around, and Carmine gives an awkward laugh.

"You're here early," I say, fluffing my hair. She scoffs in disgust before walking out, shaking her head. Tom looks horrified.

"It's fine, Carmine's chill," I assure him with a playful shove.

"I can't have gossip spreading around the office, Clare," Tom says with a glint of authority.

"I promise, nothing will come of it." I flutter my lashes in his direction and his expression shifts. He grabs my hand, eyes on the missing wedding ring. "Still haven't heard from Damien?" I shake my head. "When can we talk about moving forward?" he presses.

"I don't know, Tom. There's just a lot going on."

He grips my shoulders, dead serious. "If we could really be together, we wouldn't have to sneak around. We could fuck in our home."

The thought sends a shiver through me, us christening every inch of a house we own together, multiple times a day. I look down at my feet, unable to give him the answer he yearns for. He smooths his pants, adjusts his tie, and flips his hair back, aware that his questions would be left unanswered. "How do I look?" He gives me a half-hearted smile, depleting the heaviness in the room.

"Sexy," I grin. We split to our separate offices and play lawyer.

I'm replying to emails when Sabrina texts: *Are you at work today?*

Me: Now that I'm a potential divorcee, yes, I have to be.

She replies with a shake-my-head emoji. *I've been following a lead, and they're in your town. Can I open up to you about it when you have a free moment?*

Me: Just text me quick. My client's about to arrive.

Before she can answer, a bald man appears in my doorway, the buttons of his shirt straining against his stomach. His familiarity hits me like a flash. Steve. My phone pings.

Sabrina: I've been following Steve's whereabouts the last couple of weeks, and he's in Newport Beach!

My stomach drops.

"H-hello," I stutter, standing. Steve strolls in and sits across from me.

"Hello again, Clare," he says, slow and menacing.

"What are you doing here?" I get right to it. "And be quick, I have a 10 a.m. client."

"Marty McFly?" he smirks. I glance at my calendar. Marty McFly is, in fact, my 10 a.m. "Yeah, that's me. Can't believe you fell for it," he chuckles.

My pulse spikes.

"What do you want?" I try to steady my voice.

"I know you saw me at Nora's funeral. Thought you'd reach out to ask why I was there."

"You were her manager at a pivotal point in her life. You had every right to be there," I reply coolly.

He laughs. "I appreciate that. We were sorry to hear what happened to her. Mental illness… Nora was a very troubled girl."

My jaw tightens. "Yeah. The note she left was strange…almost like she didn't write it."

His smile fades. "I'm sure Dani told you we'll sue if you move forward with the tribute concert."

"That, she did."

"I'm sure she also told you Nora's last words to her," he adds. My eyes narrow.

"No, actually. Nora didn't get the chance to talk to Dani before she overdosed and died."

Out in the hallway, I see Tom pass by. I shoot him a help me look. He steps inside.

"How's it going in here?" he asks casually.

"My client *Marty McFly* and I are just wrapping up," I say pointedly.

Tom instantly clocks the situation. "Sometimes Breaker and Gallagher isn't the right fit for everyone. We can refer you to other attorneys in the area."

Steve looks thrown but stands, giving me one last unsettling glare before Tom escorts him out. The moment they're gone, I grab my phone and call Sabrina.

"What the actual fuck, Sabrina!" I snap.

"What happened?" she asks, but I can hear the guilt in her tone.

"He was just here, I booked him in my calendar as Marty McFly!"

Sabrina laughs. "Rookie mistake. You've never seen a movie before?"

"Not the point." I rub my forehead. "He said they'll sue if we do the concert, and he brought up if I knew Nora's last words to Dani."

Sabrina's voice drops.

"I just had a feeling he was coming to pay you a visit. Eric told me something about Steve. He's part of Nora's death. I don't know how yet, but I can feel it. I've been tracking him for weeks. Hacked his credit card, saw he bought tickets to California. Tracked down his credit card transaction to a southwest flight into LAX. I knew he was coming."

"Don't quit your day job," I mutter. Tom reappears. "Look, Brina, I'll call you later." I hang up and practically fall into Tom's arms.

"What was that about?" he asks.

"Take me to Vic's for a latte and I'll tell you everything."

At Vic's, my usual table is waiting. The baristas wave enthusiastically and start making my drink before I even order.

"Wow, you're popular here," Tom says, sliding into the seat beside me.

"This is my happy place," I reply. Two iced mocha lattes appear instantly.

"You okay?" he asks, thumb rubbing my hand.

I nod, then spill everything: Five Heart's reunion, the tribute concert, the lawsuit threat, Steve and Donovan, the strange suicide note, my prenup, the fear of losing my house, my lifestyle, and him.

Tom listens, then grips my hand. "I'll protect you." Simple. Perfect. Exactly what I needed for comfort. We sit there, hand in hand, in my favorite coffee shop, and I realize this is technically our very first date.

I needed a breather from the drama that exploded at the office today. I texted Yarrick—the gayest, most fabulous Indian man and my work BFF—to meet me for drinks at the hottest spot in town, The Den. Every celebrity in the area has been spotted there this month, and now that I have reclaimed my own celeb status, I figured I could make an appearance. If I post a story from there, my followers will spike. Maybe Damien will finally stop being a coward and come talk to me.

I change at home into a black sequin cocktail dress with a dangerously high leg slit, paired with glossy black peep-toe Louboutins. When I pull up to valet, the attendant opens my door and I step out with a deliberately dramatic leg reveal, the flash of my red sole making a statement against the pavers. The crowd outside is dressed to the nines, either waiting for their cars or for a chance to get inside the Michelin-starred restaurant.

I catch a few whispers and gasps as I toss my loose blonde curls over my shoulder and smile for an imaginary paparazzi lens.

"Clare Devon!" someone shouts. Another voice chimes in, "Oh my God, it's Clare from Five Heart!"

I giggle, covering my mouth in mock modesty, then wave at my face like I am overheating from all the attention. Slowly, I climb the colossal glass steps to the entrance, then turn toward my "fans" and blow them a kiss. Phones go up, staggered flashes catching my every move.

Inside, I spot Yarrick perched at the bar. He is almost as fabulous as Selma, basically her male counterpart. When we see each other, we squeal. "Oh babe, that dress! OKURRR," he hollers, spinning me around like a prize. I hop onto the barstool, still buzzing from the attention.

"I finally did it, Yarrick," I say, fanning my flushed cheeks. "I am a celebrity again."

"Girl, you were always a celebrity," he says, snapping for the bartender. The bartender has a chiseled jaw, a tight black button-down with rolled sleeves, and a matching bow tie.

Yarrick's eyes light up. "Why hello," he flirts. The bartender flutters his lashes back. "I will take a cosmo," Yarrick says. "It is girls' night out." He grabs my hand.

"And what can I get for you, Ms. Devon?" the bartender asks. I try not to look shocked that he knows me on sight.

"I would absolutely adore a porn star martini," I say, my voice dipped in devilry.

"Speaking of porn star," Yarrick says, grinning, "Carmie told us about your Scarlett Letter A act today."

"Well, a girl's got needs," I pout, half-joking. We laugh, drink, and gossip the night away. Just what I needed. A couple hours and four cocktails later, I am nursing the last sip of my espresso martini when something in my peripheral turns my stomach inside out. Yarrick is mid-flirt with the bartender when I whip around and see the back of Steve's head heading toward the restroom.

I'm so rattled, I tip my glass, and it shatters on the floor. "Oh my!" I blurt, hand over my heart. "I guess that is my cue to be cut off." I laugh nervously, bend to pick up the shards, and nick my finger. "Ouch."

"Don't worry about that, Ms. Devon," the bartender says quickly. "Go clean up in the bathroom. We'll handle this."

I glance toward the hallway where Steve disappeared. I don't see him. Maybe I'll just avoid the whole thing. The hallway feels quieter than the rest of the restaurant. The music and chatter fade behind me until there's only the faint hum of the overhead lights. I push open the women's restroom door and feel a sudden grip around my wrist, yanking me back so hard that I stumble.

Steve. For a split second, my brain refuses to process it. His face is too close, his grip too tight. The smell of his cologne turns my stomach. My heart spikes and my legs feel watery.

Blood from my cut finger slides down my arm and pools at the bend of my elbow. "Let go of me!" My voice is sharper than I expect, but it doesn't shake him.

He shoves me inside the restroom, slamming the door behind us. The sound echoes against the tile. It's empty.

Before I can twist away, his other hand clamps over my mouth. The pressure of his palm makes it hard to breathe. I bite down hard enough to taste the metallic tang of blood. When he flinches, I wrench my head to the side and smear my bloody fingertip across his cheek. If he kills me, my DNA is on him. His grip tightens.

"You know what Nora told Dani," he growls, the words vibrating against my skin.

I shake my head violently. "I don't!" It comes out muffled but desperate. "Please, let me go!"

"What do you know?" His voice is rising, sharp and jagged.

"Nothing!" My voice cracks, but my eyes never leave his.

"Tell me, Clare. What do you know about the note Nora wrote?" His teeth grit so hard I can see the muscles in his jaw.

I think back to earlier today when I said the note didn't sound like her. I had only meant it as a jab. I didn't think it was actually true. "What did you do to Nora?" My voice breaks on the question.

His stare pins me like a specimen under glass.

"Please don't hurt me," I whisper. My survival instinct roars to life. I know my best weapon is my mouth. I soften my face, lower my lashes, and let my voice go small and trembling. "Steve, you were like a father to me. Please, don't do this. I always looked up to you. Can we just talk? I promise I don't know anything."

The sharpness in his brow eases. His breathing slows. For one heartbeat, I think I might have bought myself a way out. The door swings open.

Yarrick stands there, wide-eyed. "Ohmygawd! GET AWAY FROM HER!"

The sound shocks Steve just enough for me to act. I slam the point of my stiletto straight into his groin. His body folds in on itself as he lets out a guttural scream. I dart into Yarrick's arms as the bartender steps into the doorway, blocking Steve from following us.

Management rushes us into the back office, draping a blanket over my shoulders and pressing a glass of water into my hands. "The police are on their way," the manager says.

I take a sip, staring at the blood streaking my skin. The weight of it all crashes down at once, and tears spill freely. Yarrick crouches to meet my eyes. "Are you okay?"

"I don't know," I choke out. "Can you call Tom?"

He nods without hesitation, already dialing.

Tom picks me up from the restaurant after the police take Steve into custody and get my statement. My car is left behind. The image of Steve being locked in handcuffs plays over in my mind. The way he glared at me through the back window of the cop car was unlike anything I've seen before. His eyes were full of something dark, as if he were silently casting a curse over me. I shudder, my stomach tightening.

We turn down a quiet, tree-lined street before pulling up to Tom's estate. The sight sobers me a little. Burgundy bricks climb high into a structure that looks more like a private monument than a home. White marble pillars line the front porch like a Roman colonnade, holding up a grand overhang with perfect symmetry. The front door is a massive slab of antique carved wood, weathered in just the right places, with an ornate iron knocker the size of my face. Soft golden light glows through tall windows, making the entire façade feel like something out of a vintage fairy tale.

In my drunken, trauma-soaked haze, the words slip out before I can stop them. "Oh… you're *rich* rich."

He chuckles, the sound low and steady, as we pull into the wide circular driveway paved in polished cobblestone. A tiered fountain in the center throws arcs of water into the air, catching the porch lights like liquid diamonds.

Tom gets out first. Like a perfect gentleman, he opens my door and lifts me down from the truck. His hands are steady, his movements easy, as if I weigh nothing. "Chivalry isn't dead," I say with a faint smile, trying to lighten the mood.

I have never been to his house before. I know he won the estate in the divorce from his first wife, though he still pays her alimony. From the looks of this place, I think he will be fine for quite a while.

Inside, it feels like stepping into a cathedral. The air smells faintly of polished wood and old books. The ceilings soar upward into high vaults, their edges trimmed with intricate plasterwork. Gleaming marble floors stretch out in all directions, the surface so reflective it almost looks like still water. Famous artwork, the kind you only see in museums, hangs in heavy gilded frames along the walls. Between them stand statues in pristine white stone, lit from beneath to cast dramatic shadows. A sweeping staircase commands the center of the entryway, curving upward with a carved mahogany banister.

"How many bedrooms is this?" I ask, my eyes moving from one hallway to the next.

"Eight," he replies simply.

"Who even needs eight bedrooms?" My voice echoes faintly in the massive space.

He smirks, taking my hand as we walk toward the stairs. "Us. For the seven children we will have."

I laugh softly, rolling my eyes, but follow his lead. The master bedroom feels like its own wing. Rich rugs spread across the polished floors. A fireplace flickers at one end, casting a soft, uneven glow on the dark wood furniture. From there, he leads me into the bathroom, and my breath catches. It is bigger than my living room, with two vanities, a glass walk-in shower that could fit a football team, and an oversized garden tub tucked under a bay window.

He starts the water of the tub, steam curling upward, and begins to undress me. One by one, each piece of clothing falls away until I am standing bare in front of him, my skin chilled, my body still marked by blood and the weight of the night.

I let him guide me into the bath. I pull my knees up against my chest and, without warning, the sobs come. My breath catches in uneven bursts, my body shaking. Tom moves quietly, filling a glass from the faucet and pouring it gently over me. Then another. And another. The warm water slides down my skin, carrying away the grime, the fear, the traces of what happened. He doesn't rush. He doesn't speak. It's the most intimate, non-sexual moment I have ever had with someone.

There is a weight to it, a quiet depth that feels like real, unconditional love.

I watch him through glassy eyes as he continues, his expression calm, almost reverent. By the time he is finished, I am clean and trembling from more than the cooling temperature of the water. He wraps me in a bamboo towel so soft it feels unreal, lifting me into his arms and carrying me to his bed. I'm still wrapped like a swaddled child as he lies down beside me fully clothed. We face each other, saying nothing. The silence is thick, but not uncomfortable. It feels like time has stopped, as if the house itself is holding its breath for us.

"Do you want to talk about it?" he whispers. I shake my head. I don't want to give shape to the night by putting it into words. Not yet. I just want to stay here, wrapped in warmth and stillness. Reality can come in the morning. For now, I let my eyelids grow heavy as his hand moves slowly through my hair, the steady movements pulling me into darkness.

Chapter 19

Jonna

I'm at the kitchen island chopping strawberries on the pearly quartz countertop for the kids' snack, each slice landing in the glass bowl with a soft plop. The sweet scent fills the air, mixing with the warm drift of coffee from the pot Dexter brewed earlier. My mind keeps circling back to the ticket sale going live today. I can't wait to see the numbers roll in. I probably need to coordinate with the girls soon. Maybe once the kids are in school next week, we can start rehearsals of some kind. Dani's already pulled a miracle, convincing her solo label to team up with us despite the looming Donovan lawsuit. Somehow, they scored Madison Square Garden for January 1st. We were rejected for New Year's Eve because of the ball drop, but it's probably for the best.

Alissa is in her high chair next to me, cooing at each strawberry I toss into the bowl. "You can't have one yet sweetie," I say, popping one in my mouth.

In the living room, DJ and Harley are tearing around in old Halloween costumes two sizes too small. "Kneel to the almighty king!" DJ bellows, his crown tilting off of his head, chasing Harley with a plastic sword. She's shrieking with laughter, sprinting in circles around the L-shaped couch. Dexter is on the couch watching them, Finn sound asleep on his lap, his big hand gently supporting our son's back. The late morning feels so full, loud, chaotic, but in the best way. In our house, if there's no chaos, something's wrong. The doorbell rings, cutting through the noise. I wipe my hands on the dish towel.

"You expecting a package?" Dexter calls, anchored with Finn still nestled against him.

"No, but I'll get it." I head down the hall, half expecting our UPS guy. He's been here constantly this week with all the online shopping I've been doing for gowns for future press tours. But when I open the door, I stop cold. It's Clare. She's wearing an oversized hoodie, white sneakers, her hair scraped into a messy bun. She looks pale under her makeup, her eyes heavy and rimmed like she hasn't slept. Behind her, Tom is in a fitted white T-shirt that stretches over his shoulders, dark jeans, holding two Louis Vuitton carry-on bags.

"Clare?" I say, surprised but instantly relieved to see her. She doesn't answer. She steps forward and hugs me hard. The kind of hug where you feel someone's weight in your arms.

Dexter appears at my shoulder. "Clare, what are you doing here? Did you just come from the airport?"

"Clare needed to see her best friend," Tom says, his voice warm but serious. "I wasn't letting her travel alone."

Dexter blinks, then grins as recognition hits. "You're Tom Gallagher. I saw you at Clare's birthday last month but didn't realize you were *that* Tom. Now you're in my house… oh, man."

"It's nice to officially meet you," Tom says, shaking his hand. Within moments, Dexter is rattling off questions about famous plays from Tom's Buccaneers days, and Tom answers each one with an easy smile.

"Clare, do you realize the greatness standing next to you?" Dexter says.

Clare giggles, "I'm starting to."

The kids rush in, now wearing Pokémon costumes. "I choose you!" DJ points at Tom.

Tom drops to the floor like he's been shot and lets them climb all over him, laughing with them as though they've been friends forever.

Once they're distracted, I guide Clare into the kitchen. She takes a seat at the island. I lift Alissa from her chair and place her in Clare's arms. Clare presses her cheek to the baby's hair, inhaling deeply.

"What's going on?" I ask gently. "You never just drop in… especially looking like this."

Clare half smiles but doesn't meet my eyes. "You remember how Steve and Donovan just showed up to Nora's funeral?"

"Of course." I say.

"And how Donovan cornered Dani at my house, basically blackmailing her?"

"Yes," I say, impatient for the point.

"There's something going on, Jon. Something bad." She lowers her gaze, and that's when I see it, a jagged gash on her finger accompanied by bruises down her wrist.

"What happened to your hand?"

She exhales, steadying herself. "Sabrina texted me yesterday. She's been tracking Steve. She said Eric told her Steve might be behind what happened to Nora… and maybe others in the industry too. Eric thinks Dani could be in danger. He saw Steve and Donovan at the funeral, watching her. Then there was the blackmail. And then." She stops and pulls back the edge of her hoodie. There's a bruise blooming across her neck, another along her cheekbone. My stomach drops.

"Clare…"

She swallows. "Yesterday afternoon he came to my office. Tom got him to leave before it went further. But later that night, I went to dinner with a work friend. Steve was there. He followed me to the bathroom, and shoved me inside. He pushed me against the wall and demanded to know what Nora told Dani the night she died. I told him I didn't know anything. He didn't believe me. Thank God, Yarrick thought I passed out in the bathroom, he came in and saw the entire encounter. Steve got taken into custody." Her hand trembles as she wipes her cheek. "That's why I had to come. I stayed with Tom last night. This morning, he asked what I wanted to do, and all I could think was, I need to see Jonna."

I'm gripping the counter so hard my knuckles ache.

"I also might have made it worse," she admits, her voice cracking. "When he was at the office, I told him, just to needle him, that Nora's suicide note didn't sound like something she'd write. After last night and his reaction! I think he wrote it."

I stare at her. "Clare, are you saying…"

"I don't think Nora killed herself. Neither does Sabrina. Eric doesn't either. Eric knows someone who worked with Steve, and that person disappeared after an argument with him." The air feels heavier.

"If Dani's in danger, do you think she's next?"

"I don't know. But we can't tell her. Not yet. The tickets went live today. I don't want her distracted or afraid until we have more. Plus Steve's probably spending the next few days in jail. It buys us some time. I'm not pressing charges, I don't want this to blow up. Promise me you won't say anything to her." She's asking for the impossible. "Promise me, Jon."

I nod slowly. "I promise."

From the other room, Dexter's laugh booms over the TV. The kids squeal as Tom plays along with whatever game they've invented. My phone buzzes on the counter. Dani's name lights the screen. Clare's eyes lock on mine. She makes a tiny pinching motion. Don't say a word.

I answer it. "Hey."

"Hey! Sabrina and I are at lunch. We're watching ticket sales online. Almost sold out and it's not even noon!" Dani's voice is bubbling with excitement. "Rehearsals start next week. I'm setting up a full PR push: morning shows, meet and greets, podcasts, the works. We're going all in."

In the background, Sabrina calls out, "Tell them the map is glowing!"

Dani laughs. "The map is glowing. Get your butts in gear. We're calling Clare next."

The call ends. Clare exhales. "She only knows about Donovan."

I nod. "And she's already frustrated with him."

I mime zipping my lips. She squeezes my hand, her shoulders loosening slightly. The rest of the afternoon drifts by in a strange, comfortable rhythm. The kids keep Tom busy. Dexter grins like he's known him for years. I order Chinese from around the corner. We laugh over old high school stories, and I notice the way Tom's eyes stay fixed on Clare when she talks. Damien never looked at her that way. I don't condone adultery, but if this is her real happiness, I can't pretend I don't see it.

After the baby is down, Harley and DJ beg Tom to read them a bedtime story. He happily agrees. Dexter and I walk them to the guest room, as they drop their bags and shut the door, we retreat to ours.

I change into my powder blue silk nightgown. Dexter strips to his briefs, his body warm and familiar. I move closer, tracing my hand over his chest and down toward his lower stomach.

His eyes brighten, but he cups my face gently. "Would you hate me if I said I'm too exhausted?" he asks, looking almost guilty.

"Not at all," I admit. "I'm tired too. That was a lot. Clare thinks… Nora didn't kill herself," I say, testing the words.

Dexter sits up. "Why?"

I hesitate. She only told me not to tell Dani, and he's my husband. I tell him everything, including the attack.

His expression hardens. "I can't believe this! This is why I didn't want you wrapped up in all of it. If this comes back on us and our family, I will pull the plug, Jonna."

"Just keep it quiet for now," I plead. "It won't affect us."

"If this bastard comes near our kids, Jon, I won't hold back," Dexter raises his voice.

"I promise, it will be okay. Just don't say anything." I'm not sure it's a promise I can keep. If Nora didn't write that note… then someone wanted us to believe she did. I grab my phone and start a group chat titled "Top Secret Takedown" and add only Sabrina and Clare.

Chapter 20

Dani

The show is sold out. My label is taking us on under their wing. No more threats from Donovan. Maybe he's finally backed off. Life feels good. Nora would be so proud.

Mom and I are at my Nashville bungalow clearing out all the bedrooms towered with clothes and costumes from over the years to make room for everyone. We have our first rehearsal tomorrow morning at the Pilates studio I go to. They're letting us use the space all day. It's the weekend before Thanksgiving—what better way to celebrate than to spend it with my best friends by preparing a Friendsgiving feast tonight?

My bungalow has five bedrooms, perfect for each girl and their significant other. I have never actually had guests stay here before. The beds are perfectly made with no wear on them. I smile knowing my house will be a loud, rambunctious, loving mess in a matter of hours.

"Are you sure you want to have everyone stay?" my mom asks, vacuum sealing a pile of clothes into a bag.

"Of course. Do you know how long it's been since we've all had a slumber party together as Five Heart?" My body feels like it could burst from excitement. She shakes her head and keeps folding.

The girls arrive in staggered waves, duffles and hard-shell carry-ons rolling in, their men trailing with heavier suitcases. I gather them all into a group hug. "How was the flight?" I ask, beaming.

Their energy doesn't match mine, probably jet lag. The only one as enthusiastic is Tom. I hope I get to know him better this weekend, knowing he stole my Clare Bear from her husband. Not that I was ever fond of Damien. Tom scoops me up in a huge bear hug, my face lost in his chest, his muscles stretching the sleeves of his shirt.

"Dani! Thank you so much for having Clare and I this weekend," he says with a grin.

Dexter suddenly perks up. "Yes, thank you for having Jonna and I!" He looks to Tom for recognition.

Sabrina and Robbie roll in last. "Can't wait for rehearsal tomorrow, I have so many ideas," she says, hugging me. Robbie is the last one in, shutting the door behind us like we're all sardines in the entryway.

"Hey, Robbie." I smile, giving him a side hug. He smiles half-heartedly and then quickly looks away.

We break off and I play hostess and show each couple their bedrooms. While they unpack, and decompress, I start setting the ten-person dining table for Friendsgiving. Sheer rust orange tablecloth over blonde teak, folded ivory napkins, matte brass utensils, fern leaves scattered down the center with tea light candles tucked between. Name cards already made written with my best calligraphy.

The oven is on, everything from the caterer heating. I head to my bedroom and change into my most festive fall dress, a Zimmerman long sleeve mini with ruffles and burgundy and brown leaves printed across the fabric. I spin in the mirror, soaking in the feeling of Friendsgiving bliss.

FIVE HEART

When I come back out, the boys are on the couch yelling at the Patriots game. "That was a pass!" Tom shouts, hand on his head.

"That was bullshit, ref!" Dexter echoes.

Robbie is typing quickly on his phone. I stroll over and tap him on the shoulder. "Hey."

He jumps and flips his phone face down. Strange.

"When will Ryan and Eric be here? Dinner's starting soon," I ask.

"They're picking Selma up from her hotel. They'll be here soon," he says, giving a smile that feels just a little too easy.

I head back to the kitchen, the air thick with the scent of turkey and casseroles. The girls still haven't come out of their rooms.

I walk down the hallway to see what they are up to. Clare's room is empty. Jonna's too. I reach the farthest guest room and open the door. All three of them are sitting on the bed, their heads close together. They jerk upright when they see me, like I've caught them in the middle of something top secret.

"Hi." I wave, forcing cheer. My irritation spikes. Nobody has offered to help, and I'm clearly not part of whatever secret meeting this is.

Jonna jumps up. "Can I help you with setting the table?" she asks softly.

"Sure, that would be helpful," I say flatly.

She follows me into the kitchen. I shove oven mitts into her hands. "If you can just set the trivets down and we'll start putting these platters on the table." We carry the hot dishes to the table. "Dinner's ready," I call out.

The front door opens and Ryan and Eric walk in, Selma strutting behind. "The party's here, darlings," she announces, holding a bottle of Caymus, as she's wrapped in cashmere and dripping with diamonds. Everyone drifts to the dining room. Wine is poured. Chatter is polite but thin. Clare suggests we take a moment to honor Nora. We do, and the quiet is heavy before we start eating.

An hour later, three bottles of red are gone and only scraps of food are left. Sabrina and Robbie are feeding each other bites of turkey. Clare, Tom, Jonna, and Dexter are in a heated debate about state taxes. Selma and Ryan are deep in pop culture gossip. Eric and I sit across from each other in awkward silence. He fiddles with his fingers as I glare at him.

"What's going on?" I blurt. The whole table stills. "Why are you guys acting so weird toward me? You've been ignoring me, whispering, sneaking off. Did I do something to piss you off?" My voice wavers but I try to hide it.

"Oh honey," Jonna says, shooting a pleading look at Clare and Sabrina.

"Just tell me," I say flatly. There's a silent long pause, and I clock their nervous glances between one another.

Clare stands suddenly. "Dani, you're in danger."

"What?" I look at Eric, who fidgets and glances away. Sabrina opens her mouth to speak but is cut off by a loud knock at the front door. I push my chair out and go check who's at the door. Jonna comes over with me, almost guarding me. She peeks out the peephole. "Oh god," she says her voice wavering. I check the peephole next. Two tall men in black suits and sunglasses stand outside.

"Dani, move," Jonna says, motioning me back. "Dexter, Tom, over here."

Tom opens the door, towering over them. "We have a cease-and-desist order for Danielle Richmond, Clare Devon, and Sabrina Daniel," one says, handing over an envelope.

Tom's jaw tightens. "Under whose order?"

"Donovan Blake," the other replies.

Tom snatches the documents, mutters, "Goodnight gentlemen" and shuts the door.

Clare grabs the envelope, scanning quickly with Sabrina over her shoulder. "He's accusing Sabrina of hacking Steve's credit card account, me of defaming Steve and assaulting him when I had him arrested, and you of interfering with his business because we're moving forward with the tribute concert."

Sabrina shifts nervously. "He's trying to shut us down," she says, her hands trembling. "If we keep going, he'll sue us all individually. And the kicker—he's demanding we halt all public appearances together until further notice."

"Coward," Clare spits. "Can't even face us himself, sends his watch dogs instead."

I look around the table at all of them, heat rising in my chest. "Then I guess we'd better give him something worth suing over."

We make sure the next day at rehearsal to post our entire day on socials. We know Donovan and his minions are watching. The girls and I have been up all night. They debriefed me on all things Steve, on Nora's presumed suicide being a façade. I didn't realize he was still Donovan's lapdog after all these years.

Back when we were kids, he would practically tremble in Donovan's presence. He would've kissed Donovan's shoe if given the chance. That's why he was always so brutal with us. If we weren't hitting Donovan's impossible standards, we'd hear it from Steve. Endless nights in the recording booth until we nailed a take "just right." Grueling rehearsals where we drilled choreography until our arches screamed, our calves seized, and our toes went numb. Thinking back now, it wasn't normal. It might have even been abusive. We have a plan though. The kind of plan that could either make us legends or get us killed, but at this point it is all or nothing.

Now that I know what Steve and Donovan have been up to, watching us, following us, breathing down our necks, it's clear they want us crushed, maybe even dead. That is not going to happen. The more I think about it, the more I realize I might be in danger just for knowing too much, even if most of it is still pieces of a puzzle I can't yet see.

Sabrina's handwriting find was the match that lit the fire. Two notes. Two different people. Two different agendas. That was before Donovan decided to send those pathetic cease-and-desist letters, like that would scare us. If anything, he gave us the perfect excuse to go bigger.

We are moving forward with the concert. No backing down. We are going to blast the marketing so loud they will hear us from space. Nonstop social media posts. Behind the scenes footage. Hashtags trending for weeks. We want them to see us and know they can't stop us. We decided the Grammys will be our opening shot. We are walking that red carpet like it is ours. Selma is going to style us so hard people will think we fell out of a fashion campaign. Hair, makeup, one-of-a-kind gowns so gorgeous they could cause fainting spells. We are making a statement that night.

It's not just about the clothes. We are going official with the men in our lives. Clare and Tom, America's golden couple. Sabrina and Robbie, the teenage dream all grown up and still somehow sweeter. And me. I'm going to apologize to Sam prior. The girls don't know it yet, but I'm going to win her back, and I'm ready to go public with her. Out of the closet and unapologetic. These constant threats, Nora's death, Clare and Sabrina's newfound love… it's given me the strength to at least talk to Sam. To see if she still wants to know me.
Dating a fan is the kind of headline that will make the internet melt as well. Everyone loves a fairytale where the fan ends up with the celebrity. It gives them hope. Hope was what we needed to make our plan work, and to have Sam by my side during every step.

Once the Grammys have the world watching, we'll have one month to the show. Hardcore rehearsals every single day. We will lock down choreography that feels like Broadway collided with pop heaven. Lighting cues so sharp people will swear they blacked out from the brilliance. This is going to be the show of the century. The kind of night that burns itself into history and makes the rest of the industry wish they had thought of it first.

We are going to give them something so unforgettable that even Donovan will have to choke on it.

And in the meantime, Sabrina will be putting on her Lois Lane mask of excellence and digging deeper into how Donovan and Steve could be tied to Nora's death. She is going to go undercover in Nora's hometown of Poughkeepsie and track down Walter. If she can get her hands on any journals, documents, or photos, anything at all that could help us, she will.

She also plans to hunt down a few old employees who worked with us back at Kaleidoscope Records in New York City. People who were there in the thick of it, who might have seen or heard things they never spoke about. She has access to a database at *The Times* that can make finding them easy, and once she does, she'll get their personal stories. Their truth.

And then there's Eric. Sabrina swears he knows more than he has let on. She says it every time his name comes up, like a warning. After rehearsals today, we are going to corner him. All of us together. He's still in Nashville with the boys staying at a hotel a block away from my house. He will have nowhere to run, nowhere to hide. We are going to get answers.

We resume rehearsal, and for the concert, we decide on a coordinated opening that will be a visual and an emotional punch.

"I'll make my entrance first. Center stage rising up through a trap door lift. Then Clare, Jonna, and finally Sabrina will ascend on their own pedestals, each staggered across the stage for maximum sightline impact. On the massive LED screen, an AI-generated video of Nora will appear, seated gracefully on her pedestal. We'll all turn our heads in unison to look toward her. A subtle but powerful nod that she's watching over us from Heaven." The girls eyes widened, and they all nodded in agreement.

After rehearsals are done for the day, we head back to my Nashville bungalow to shower and get ready for the Eric interrogation. Sabrina already looped Robbie in on the plan, and he is more than willing to help us get answers.

I'll make sure he doesn't leave before you get here, Robbie texted her. *Text me when you're on the way.* She hearts the message without hesitation. We all throw on hoodies and ball caps so we're harder to recognize.

"We ready, girls?" Sabrina asks, her phone in hand, thumb hovering over Robbie's name. We all nod from the entryway of my front door. Tom and Dexter stay behind, unaware of our plans. They are glued to the television watching Sports Center.

She sends the text that we're a go, and we pile into my Maserati. The engine growls as I pull out of the driveway, headed straight for the Graduate Hotel where Ryan and Eric are staying.

The drive is only fifteen minutes, but it feels like we are creeping toward a crime scene. No one says much. The hum of the engine and the faint bass from the stereo are the only sounds filling the car. Every red light feels like it's mocking me.

Sabrina keeps scrolling through her phone, checking and rechecking Robbie's texts. Clare's knee bounces like she's trying to burn off nervous energy, and Jonna stares out the window, jaw tight. The sky is a deep indigo now, the streetlights giving the wet pavement a slick, glassy sheen.

We pull into the side lot of the hotel, far from the front entrance so no one notices us. Sabrina checks her phone again. They're at the bar in the lobby. Eric has no clue.

We walk in through a side door, the air smelling faintly of cedar and bourbon. The lobby lighting is dim and golden, the kind that makes shadows cling to corners. Abstract artwork and sculptures are staggered throughout the building. My heart kicks into overdrive. We spot Robbie instantly, leaning casually at the bar, playing the part like it's second nature.

His eyes flick to us and he gives the smallest nod toward a booth in the back where Eric is seated, drink in hand, scrolling his phone like he hasn't got a care in the world. He has no idea we are about to change that.

We weave through the tables like sharks in slow motion. The hotel bar hums with low chatter and the clink of glassware, but all I hear is the thump of my own pulse. Eric is halfway through his drink when we slide into the booth across from him, cutting off his escape route.

He stiffens, eyes flicking between us. "Let me guess… this isn't a social call."

"No," Sabrina says, sliding in across from him. "We've already covered the manila envelope. I know you sent it. Now we need the rest of the truth."

His jaw works, but he doesn't answer. "You told me weeks ago you didn't think Nora killed herself," Sabrina continues. "And you said that note wasn't her handwriting. You know that because you dated her."

Eric's eyes drop to the table, shoulders curling inward. "Yeah. I know." His voice is heavy, almost breaking. "That's not something you forget."

"And what about that new artist?" Sabrina presses, leaning forward. "The one you saw at the single release party. You told me he was fighting with Steve. Then the next day, he was just… gone. Like he never existed. No questions asked."

Eric rubs his face, looking ten years older than the last time we saw him. "Yeah. I remember. And I remember thinking at the time that I'd seen that pattern before."

I lean in. "From Steve?" His silence is answer enough. "You saw Nora before I did," I guess. "You can see it written all over your face. What did she tell you?"

Eric's expression shifts into something I can't quite read, grief mixed with fear. "She told me things I wish I could unhear. About Donovan. About Steve. About, other people. What they've done. What they're capable of."

Clare's voice is sharp. "So tell us."

"I can't," he says quickly, shaking his head. "It's not about protecting myself. If I tell you, it puts every single one of you in danger. And I don't… I don't want to be the reason something happens to you."

"We're already in danger," Sabrina shoots back.

"Not like this," Eric says, looking up at us for the first time, eyes glassy. "I'm not keeping this from you to be an asshole. I'm keeping it from you because I can't process it myself. It's that bad. And if you knew, it would change everything. And not in a good way." There's a long silence. Finally, he takes a deep breath. "There's someone else you can talk to. Marlene. She used to work at Kaleidoscope. She saw things. She might be able to tell you some of it without… putting you in the crosshairs." Sabrina's voice softens but stays firm. "Full name. Where to find her."

He scribbles it on a napkin with a shaking hand and slides it over. Clare tucks it into her hoodie pocket. "If you're lying to us, Eric, you'll regret it."

We stand to leave, and Eric stays hunched over his drink, looking like a man buried alive. Sabrina turns and says one last thing. "If we don't get the answers we are looking for from this, Marlene, we are expecting some real answers."

He gave us something to chase, but my gut says whatever Nora told him before she died is the one truth that could set this whole thing on fire, and he's terrified of what will happen when it does.

We get back to my bungalow after getting some answers from Eric. The four of us sink cross-legged into the couch cushions, our bodies curling inward as if bracing against the weight of what we just learned. The air feels heavy, pressing down on my chest until I have to say something.

My heart thuds in my throat. I can feel the moment building inside me, inevitable.   "Well," I begin, my voice low, reluctant to drop another bomb after the day we have had. "I have something to confess." Three pairs of eyes turn to me instantly, their postures tightening with unease.

"It's nothing bad," I add quickly, trying to calm them. Their shoulders loosen a little. I take in a deep breath that almost hurts my ribs. "I'm in love with a woman."

The words hover in the air before settling between us. Then, without a trace of judgment, they all scoot closer.

"Wow, that's wonderful," Jonna says softly, patting my back as if to steady me. "What's her name?" Clare asks, her fingers sliding around mine.

"Is she cute?" Sabrina says, reaching over Jonna to grab my other hand. Warmth spills through me, wrapping around the ache in my chest. I never thought I would receive this kind of acceptance.

"Yes," I say, smiling through the lump in my throat. "She's very cute. Her name is Sam. And I completely ruined it." I look down at the floor.

"What happened?" Clare's voice sharpens, full of disappointment and concern.

I draw in a shaky breath. "We were in love. Completely. All she wanted was to be wanted without limits. She wanted to hold hands in public without hiding, to go on dates without pretending to be friends. She wanted our love to be seen. And I couldn't give her that. I was too afraid of what people would think, of what they would say." My eyes fill. "She gave me an ultimatum, and I couldn't give her what she needed." Tears burn down my cheeks. "But I want to now. Especially with everything happening. I don't care anymore what anyone says. I need her beside me through this mess. She doesn't even know about Nora. I have so much to tell her." Jonna takes my hand in hers, firm and warm. "Then tell her." I nod and wipe at my cheeks.

"Do you want us there?" Clare asks.

"Yes," I whisper. "I need you with me."

We wrap ourselves in a tangled hug.

We never made it to bed. The couch became our safe little cocoon for the night. The exhaustion in our bodies from rehearsal mixed with the emotional drain of the day kept us in place.

When I wake, the scent of coffee curls under my nose. Jonna walks in from the kitchen with three mugs and the pot, her hair messy and soft.

"Morning, girls," she says, setting the mugs on the table and filling them full. We all stretch and groan. "Oh god, my back," Sabrina mutters, pressing into her spine.

"We must have passed out right here," Clare says, rolling her neck. "I woke up on the floor," Jonna adds flatly.

We sip coffee, speaking softly about yesterday's chaos until the nervous energy in my stomach becomes too much. I set my mug down and pick up my phone. "Okay. I'm calling her."

We move to the dining table like it's a mission. My phone sits in the center on speaker. We link hands, holding the silence together.

Ring. Ring. Ring. Voicemail. "Hey, Sam. It's me, Dani. I won't spill everything on your voicemail, but I messed up. I love you. I am willing to do whatever it takes. I would do anything for you. Please call me." I end the call before I can lose my courage.

The silence afterward is loud. "Do you think I said too much?" I ask.

My phone vibrates instantly. Sam's photo flashes on the screen. "Oh my god, she's calling back. What do I do?" My voice jumps.

"Answer it!" Clare shouts, pressing the green button for me.

"Hello?" Sam's voice comes through, steady and familiar. I freeze until Sabrina kicks me under the table. "Ow. I mean, how are you?"

"Dani?" she says, puzzled.

"Yes, it is me. I am flustered hearing your voice again," I admit.

"I got your voicemail," she says in a tone I cannot read. I take a leap. "I still love you. I told my friends about you."

There is a pause. "Oh yeah?"

"Yes. They want to meet you." I glance at the girls. Her voice softens but cuts at the same time. "You really hurt me, Rose."

My heart stirs at the nickname. She only called me Rose when we were flirting or in moments that belonged to just us. "I'm only human," I say. "Not a great one, but I know I fucked up. You are the only person I have ever wanted and will want, forever."

Clare covers her mouth, her eyes wide.

"I'll be over in twenty," Sam says, then hangs up.

My eyes fill. "Oh my god, I think it worked."

We scream together, all at once, the way we used to when a school crush would look our way, and scatter like kids before a first date. Clare runs to the kitchen and starts shoving empty wine glasses into the dishwasher. Jonna straightens the throw pillows on the couch, then immediately pulls them apart and restacks them like they might somehow make the place more welcoming. Sabrina hovers near me, reading my face like she's bracing for me to faint.

FIVE HEART

I can barely focus. My hands won't stop shaking as I fix my hair in the hallway mirror, then undo it, then fix it again. Every time I think about the sound of her voice saying *Rose*, my heart skips and crashes against my ribs. Headlights sweep across the front window, washing the room in pale gold. Tires crunch on the gravel of my driveway. For a moment, the only sound is my pulse in my ears.

"She's here," Jonna whispers. I stand frozen by the door, my fingers gripping the edge of the frame like it's the only thing keeping me upright. The girls watch from a distance, half curious, half protective. I open the door.

Sam stands there, framed by the porch light. Her hair is pulled back, a few loose strands catching the wind. She's wearing a dark wool coat over jeans and boots, simple and perfect, like she always was without even trying. Her eyes find mine instantly. "Hi," she says, her voice low but steady. Every word I rehearsed disappears. All I can do is step aside and let her in.

The door clicks shut behind her. The girls are still in the living room, but no one says a word. The air is so thick I can almost taste it. Sam takes one slow step toward me, her eyes never leaving mine.

"You said you love me," she says softly, like she's testing if the words still hold weight.

"I meant it," I reply, my voice just above a whisper.

Her lips press into a thin line, her gaze searching mine for something she hasn't decided if she wants to find. She nods once, like she's filing the moment away, then glances toward the girls. "We should talk," she says. It's not forgiveness, not yet. But it's a start. And for the first time in months, hope doesn't feel like a dangerous thing.

Chapter 21

Sabrina

After an eventful weekend, I'm nestled back in my midtown apartment. Max swirls his tail around my arm, circling me and purring, happy that I'm back. Eric gave me a lead—Marlene, who used to work with us when we were kids at Kaleidoscope Records. I vaguely remember her. She was Donovan's personal assistant and scheduled all our fittings, rehearsals, studio sessions, and pretty much any event we had to attend. Marlene was the organizer for everything. I tracked her down and, luckily, she's still in the city, working on the Upper West Side. She's no longer in the music industry but now works in management for an elite law firm.

Instead of going into *The Times* tomorrow morning, my Monday will be spent tracking her down and getting some intel. After that, I'm taking a rideshare to Poughkeepsie. I'm hoping Walter will be home, but I plan to surprise him by just dropping in. I know for a fact all of Nora's old high school journals are still at her dad's house because they were shipped there after her mom died, and he's a total hoarder. Nora always lived with her mom since her dad was in and out of her life, usually shacked up in a bar, shackled by liquor. Her therapist always told her to get her feelings down on paper. I remember her scribbling away each day during class in those journals. I know they can't be gone.

There's a knock at my door. I jolt up and crack it slightly open through the deadbolt. It's that familiar, handsome mug, my boyfriend. I unlatch the deadbolt and fly into his arms. It's been years since I've had a relationship like I do with Robbie. Every time I'm with him, I just want to scream to the heavens that I love him, but we haven't said those three little words yet. I hate to admit I'm waiting for him to initiate it, but maybe he's waiting for me too.

He's been such a rock during all of this, even while recording his own studio album and trying to reignite his band from the dead.

"Baby!" he exclaims. We hold each other tightly in the doorway. Even though we spent the weekend together in Nashville, it was such a whirlwind. We didn't really get much time alone.

"Come on in," I say flirtatiously, motioning him inside with my index finger. My cat walks over to Robbie and greets him with his loudest meow. Poor Robbie is allergic, but he always pops a Benadryl before coming over. He's a trooper.

He drops onto the couch and switches on the television. I grab us two rocks glasses and a bottle of Belvedere, pouring it straight.

"That was the craziest weekend," he says, rubbing his elbows.

"It was. Tomorrow I'm getting all the answers. I don't care how long it takes me. I won't come back until I know what happened to Nora."

Robbie nods in agreement. "Let me come with you."

"Don't you have to work in the studio tomorrow? You're so close to finishing the album," I ask, flattered he'd rather be my sidekick in journalism.

"I'll go in the evening. I want to help you figure this out. Also, just in case Walter has a complete meltdown like at the funeral, I need to protect you," he smiles.

"My hero," I laugh, grabbing his stubbled chin.

He gazes at me with such profoundness. "You know, Sabrina, there's something I've been meaning to tell you."

My heart skips a beat. "Yeah? What's that?" I ask, holding back the urge to grab his face.

"I've been trying to tell you all week, but every time I try, it's never the right time." He shifts, laces his fingers through mine. "I am in love with you, Sabrina Daniel."

My mouth drops. "I… I am absolutely madly in love with you!"

I throw myself on top of him and press my lips to his. It's a slow, steady kiss. I swirl my tongue over his, and he wraps his around mine like we're playing tag with our mouths. I'm mounted against him, feeling him through the layers of clothing. I move my hips slowly, creating friction. He grasps my waist, moving me faster, and our lips still locked. He pulls off his sweater, then tugs me out of my thermal top. He unzips his jeans, and I slide my panties over under my skirt, lowering myself onto him. I keep the same pace, moving to the beat of his rhythm. He moans into my mouth. "I love you so much, Sabrina," he whispers with each thrust.

The next morning, Robbie and I start early. I call the Upper West Side law firm to make sure Marlene is there so the trip isn't wasted. I pretend to be a potential client, praising her skills.
We take a cab and walk through the glass doors into the modern lobby. Up to the 20th floor, where two receptionists greet us.

"Hi, I'm Diane. We spoke earlier. I was referred to Marlene for my case. If I could speak with her directly, that would be great," I say with my best fake smile. Robbie smiles too.

The receptionist calls her up. "She'll be right with you," she says, motioning us to sit. I bounce my foot impatiently until Robbie rests a hand on my knee to stop me.

"Hello, Diane!" Marlene greets cheerfully, then her face changes. "What are you doing here?"

"That's no way to treat a new client. Two minutes of your time and I swear I'll be gone."

She turns to walk away, but I grab her wrist. "If you don't, I'll blast this firm on social media for being prejudiced about which clients you take."

She hesitates. "Right this way," she says, irritated.

Robbie and I follow her to her office. She shuts the door and closes the blinds. "What do you want?"

"Wow, is that any way to treat an old coworker?" I laugh, but she's not amused. "Look, Marlene, I know you know things. Things that happened at Kaleidoscope behind closed doors. This is off the record. Something happened to Nora Hayes when we were kids. What happened? What do you know?"

She hesitates. "Donovan will kill me if he finds out I said anything. You have to promise I'm safe."

"I promise. I just need to know what happened to my friend."

"Nora came to the office one evening. I was finishing paperwork when I heard Donovan shouting at her. I heard thumps and movement for ten minutes. I wasn't sure what was going on, but something told me not to go in. She stumbled out later, walking like she was hurt. You could tell she'd been crying. Mascara streaks all over her face."

My fists clench. "So he pushed her? Hit her?"

"I don't know," Marlene says. "Her boyfriend at the time came to pick her up. I watched from my window. He looked worried, but she kept shaking her head. I don't think she told him, but he knew something was wrong. He looked right at my window, and his expression… it was like he wanted to burn the place down."

I turn to Robbie. "We need to get Eric to talk."

"Let's still go see Walter and try to find the journals," he says, rubbing my thigh.

"That's all you remember?"

"There was one other time… but it wasn't with Nora. It was with Dani."

"With Dani?" I ask, puzzled.

"Yeah. I walked in on Donovan and her kissing. She didn't look like she enjoyed it. If she hadn't just turned eighteen, I would have reported it. But she wasn't a minor anymore, and I couldn't risk my job."

I shudder in disgust. "Thank you for your time," I say, motioning Robbie to leave. Outside, my head spins. "Dani and Donovan? Why hasn't she ever mentioned that?"

"That is strange," Robbie says.

"Maybe she was doing the boss to stay lead singer. I was meant to be the lead!" I start pacing. The thought disgusted me the second it crossed my mind. But envy is a poison I've never learned to control.

"Sabrina, focus," Robbie says sternly.

I sigh. "I'm sorry. I've always compared myself to her."

"I always saw you, your talent and beauty," he says softly. I smile and snap out of my fit of rage.

A couple hours later, the rideshare drops us off outside Nora's dad's place in Poughkeepsie. The grass is knee-high, shingles are peeling and curling along the roofline, and one of the front windows has a long crack running down the center like a fault line.

"Just like I remember it," I mutter, half-smiling, half-cringing. We walk up the creaking porch steps and knock. A few moments later, the door swings open to reveal Walter, a cigarette smoldering between two nicotine-stained fingers.

"Sabrina," he says, his voice rough from years of smoke.

"Can we come in?" I ask with a smile.

Walter always seemed fond of me back in the day, when we'd come over as kids during the rare times he was actually around. "Anything for one of Nora's friends," he says, stepping aside.

The smell of ash and stale liquor hits us instantly. Empty pizza boxes are stacked like leaning towers on the dining table. A deck of cards is scattered across the surface, some on the floor.

"Taking up poker?" I ask, pointing to the cards.

He glances over, then lets out a raspy smoker's laugh. "I always liked you," he says, jabbing his cigarette toward me.

"What can I do for you, sweetheart?" His smile reveals a missing tooth on top.

"I was hoping to go through some of Nora's old things. We're putting together a scrapbook for the group, and we wanted to include something of hers to make it complete," I say, cobbling the lie together on the spot.

"And you came all the way here for that?" he asks.

"It wasn't far. We just live in the city," Robbie adds casually.

Walter nods toward the hallway. "Her room's the last one on the left."

We follow him down the narrow hall until we step into Nora's room. It's like popping open a time capsule. Violet-painted walls, black curtains, a snakeskin-print quilt still stretched neatly over the bed. There's a faint layer of dust, but everything is exactly as it must have been the day she left. The nostalgia, unsettling and comforting all at once.

"Have yourselves a grand old time. I'll be in my recliner if you need me," Walter says, shuffling away.

Robbie and I exchange a glance, the kind that says, *Let's get to work.*

We start searching slowly, carefully. I pull open the dresser drawers one by one, finding nothing but folded shirts and dust. Robbie checks the closet, pushing hangers aside to reveal old coats and a pair of worn sneakers. We drop to our knees and peer under the bed—nothing but dust bunnies and a long-forgotten hair tie. I glance up at the wall and catch a poster of Winona in her Beetlejuice costume staring back at me. The sight hits harder than I expect. Every Halloween, Nora and I watched Beetlejuice on repeat, reciting the lines like scripture. Clare and Jonna always rolled their eyes at us, but Nora and I would collapse into hysterics, proud of ourselves for memorizing an entire movie while still completely incapable of basic algebra. Dani was always entertained watching us.

A smile falters across my lips before I can stop it, fragile and fleeting, as memories of our Halloween slumber parties replay in my head. Sleeping bags on the floor. Candy wrappers everywhere. Laughing until our stomachs hurt.

I scan the rest of the room, and the warmth drains out of me just as quickly. The past feels louder than the present. And suddenly, the space feels empty in a way I can't ignore.

I'm about to call it when Robbie suddenly grips the corner of the mattress. "Wait," he says. He lifts it up, and there they are. Three journals scattered and stacked, each with a year written on the cover in Nora's handwriting.

"Jackpot," he says, passing them to me. I tuck them into my tote bag, my pulse quickening.

We head back out to the living room. Walter is in his recliner, beer now in hand, eyes on the muted TV. "Find anything useful?"

"Um… no, nothing really, but thank you for letting us look. It was great to see you. Please don't be a stranger," I say politely. Robbie's already called the rideshare. It pulls up as we step outside, the cool air hitting my face as I clutch the bag holding Nora's words.

We slide into the back seat. The driver greets us, but my mind is already gone, locked on the weight of those journals in my lap. I run my hand over the worn covers, feeling every little crease and corner, as if I'm touching a piece of her. I can't wait any longer.

I pull out the first one, the spine cracked from use, the edges fraying. The ink on the cover is a little smudged, but the year is still clear. I flip to the first page.

September 14

Mom died three days ago.

It still feels wrong to even write that down.

The house smells like flowers. Not the good kind of sweet. The kind that makes your stomach hurt. Dad hasn't really looked at me since it happened. I don't know if that's because he doesn't know what to say or because he just doesn't want to say it.

Today Dani called and told me to meet her and Sabrina at Sabrina's house after school. I almost said no. I didn't want to be around anyone. I didn't want to talk. But something in her voice made it sound like I should go.

They had me sing. Just one song, a cover I've done a hundred times in my room. The second I started, the walls of the room felt closer, warmer, and I could almost forget that my chest has been aching since Sunday morning.

Dani grinned. Sabrina nodded like she already knew I could do it. They said they wanted me in their band.

It feels strange, saying yes to anything right now. But I said it. Maybe because I need something to fill the hours that feel so long and heavy. Maybe because when I sang, I felt lighter for two minutes.

I'm not thinking about what this means. I don't care if it lasts a week or a year. Right now, it's just something to hold onto.

Day by day.

—Nora

My heart drops. Her voice is here in my ears, clear as the day I first met her. I swallow hard, my eyes already stinging. I skip ahead a few pages, unable to stop myself.

December 28

A few months ago I was just some girl who sang in the shower.

Today we signed a record deal with Kaleidoscope Records.

The building is huge and smells like expensive perfume and new carpet. Donovan, the

CEO, shook all our hands and told us we were the future. He said he was honored to have us. His smile was the kind that makes you believe every word. For a minute I felt like maybe I was standing where I was supposed to be.

We also met our new manager, Steve. He is going to "handle all our affairs"—his words. He had this fast way of talking, like he already had our lives mapped out. He said we're going to be stars. I believe him, too.

After the meeting, we went to the studio and met another band signed to the label, No Reason. All guys. Loud. Funny. Kind of intimidating. The drummer, Eric, kept looking at me. Not in a creepy way. More like he was studying me, trying to figure out my deal. I tried not to notice, but I did. He has that messy hair, quiet eyes thing going on. I bet he writes in a notebook when no one's looking.

Everything feels like it is moving fast. I don't know where it will go, but for the first time in a long time, I am excited to wake up tomorrow.

—Nora

I close the first journal, my pulse quickening, and reach for the second one. A different year is scribbled on the cover. I flip it open.

October 3

Seventeen feels weird.

Not old, not young. Just somewhere in the middle where everything is too big and too heavy.

Eric took me out last night after rehearsal. Just the two of us. We drove around the city until the sun started to come up, talking about nothing and everything. He kissed me like it meant something, and I think I'm in love with him. Or maybe I just want to be. I don't know if I would even recognize love if it was staring me in the face. But with him, I want to try.

Our first album came out last week. I held the CD in my hands today and stared at my own face in the cover photo, like it belonged to someone else. People are actually listening to my voice. Singing my words back to me. It should feel perfect.

But Donovan keeps telling me I'm slipping. He waits until the others leave and then shuts the door. His voice is sharp and low, like he's trying not to wake the neighbors, but the words still cut. He says I'm not focused enough. That I'm too distracted. That I'm not doing enough for the band. I keep trying to do better. I keep trying to give him what he wants, but the target keeps moving.

I don't want to ruin what we've built. I don't want the others to think I'm the weak link. I don't even know if they've seen this side of him, or if it's just me. Maybe I'm doing something wrong.

Whatever it takes to make him happy, I'll do it. I have to.

— Nora

A cold heaviness settles in my stomach. I glance at Robbie. His eyes are fixed on the page like he's reading over my shoulder. I turn another one.

January 17

Today was bad.

Donovan lost it on me in the studio. Said I was pitchy, that I was dragging everyone else down, that I was going to sink the whole ship if I didn't get it together.

I froze. Couldn't even defend myself. I just kept apologizing until my voice cracked. I told him I wanted to be better. That I needed him to teach me.

He said he would show me some techniques to help with control. Told me to stand up straight and breathe from my diaphragm. I did exactly what he said. He came up behind me, put his hands on my stomach, and told me to breathe in and out.

At first it made sense. I could feel my breaths getting deeper, fuller. Then his hand moved lower, past my abdomen. I kept breathing, because I didn't want him to think I was failing at the exercise. My heart was pounding but I stayed still. I told myself he was helping me. That this was just part of the process. That this is what professionals do when they're trying to make you better.

I need to be better. I can't mess this up.

—Nora

I glance at Robbie. His jaw is clenched, a muscle ticking in his cheek. I flip again, my hands trembling.

May 12

We got the news today. Album two is happening. The first one did better than anyone thought. Donovan said we are "on track to be legends" and the girls screamed and hugged each other. For a second, it felt like a dream.

When everyone was leaving, he told me to stay. Coaching meeting. Same as always.

He locked the door and closed the blinds.

He stood behind me and told me to breathe from my diaphragm. His hands were there like always. He called out notes for me to sing. E minor. D flat. Over and over.

It always ends the same way. His fingers feel like knives.

He says the sensation will help me hit the higher octave. And I do. Or maybe I'm just screaming internally.

— Nora

My hand flies to my mouth. Robbie's eyes are glassy, his fists clenched so tight his knuckles are white.

"Let's get the third one over with," Robbie says, his voice thick. I open the final journal.

May 28

Eric and I are barely speaking. When we do, it turns into a fight. He keeps asking why I'm so distant, what I'm hiding. I want to tell him everything but the words get stuck somewhere in my throat and won't come out.

The girls aren't any better. We can't agree on anything for the second album. The release deadline is in a month and we only have five tracks that are halfway finished. Every time we get in the studio, it's like walking into a storm. Sabrina and Dani are locked in some kind of power struggle. Clare and Jonna whisper to each other and roll their eyes at everyone else.

And me... I'm just here. Alone. Like always.

I wish I could tell someone how heavy this all feels. How keeping secrets has started to feel like swallowing glass. How every day I wake up wondering if I can still do this, or if the weight of it will finally make me crumble.

Some days I think I'm going to wither up and drift away like the last pieces of mom's ashes.

—Nora

I can barely bring myself to turn to the last page, but I do.

November 2

Eric and I are done.

It happened so fast I'm still trying to catch up to it. We haven't been close in months. My fuse was shorter every day. I still love him, but I've been too distracted, too buried in everything else to show it.

The album came out last week. The reviews were bad. Not just bad... humiliating.

Every interview, every number, every headline felt like a countdown clock to the end. We started blaming each other. Every single fight we've ever had got dragged back up. Sabrina threatened to quit. Then Dani. Then Clare. Then Jonna. And then it wasn't a threat anymore.

Just like that, it was over. The only thing I've been working for these last two years, gone.

Donovan tried to pull us back together. Said we needed to "stick it out" for the sake of the label. But Dani and Sabrina couldn't stop screaming at each other. Finally, he told them to leave and "cool off." One by one, they walked out.

Then it was just me and him.

He started yelling, saying it was my fault the band fell apart. That I'd cost him everything. He threw a chair and it crashed against the wall. Marlene heard it, and glanced in, but kept going.

He came up to me. Grabbed me by the front of my shirt. His face was so close I could smell the coffee and smoke on his breath. He said I was costing him his whole company. Then he shoved me back onto the couch.

Before I could even react, he was holding me down. I couldn't move. My chest ached from the pressure. My eyes were burning but I wouldn't cry in front of him.

It hurt so bad.

I wish my first time had been with Eric.

—Nora

I close the journal with shaking hands. My stomach twists so hard I feel like I might be sick.

The driver brakes suddenly and glances back. "Everything alright?"

Robbie shakes his head. "Yeah, we're fine."

But we weren't. Not even close.

Chapter 22

Dani

The sun pries its way through the slats of my linen curtains, strips of gold falling across the hardwood floor. Nashville feels quieter now. Too quiet. The girls have all gone back to their lives, and I'm left here to figure out mine with Sam. This weekend was chaos in its purest form. The cease-and-desist, the interrogation with Eric, the truth spilling out of me about who I really am. And now, the shadow of Donovan's threats hanging over our tribute show like a storm cloud.

I try to convince myself I'm steady enough to lead. I was the one who pulled the girls back together in the first place. But in the silence, when there's no one to be brave for, I feel the eeriness seep in. Seeing Donovan again at Clare's house, the endless threats, it all churned up the small, terrified part of me I thought I'd buried years ago. The part of me that remembers exactly how powerless I felt in his orbit.

I was sixteen when Kaleidoscope Records signed us. Sixteen, and splitting myself between being someone's daughter and being the so-called face of a band. My mom had custody after the divorce, and she moved us from Knoxville up to Riverhead, Long Island. That's where I met Sabrina. She lived a few houses down, and from the very first day on the bus we bonded over theatrics and music. We were the kind of girls who stayed up all night, scribbling lyrics into notebooks, strumming untuned guitars until our fingers ached, laughing about how we'd take over the world.

High school brought the idea of a band. At first, it was just for fun, until we pulled in Nora. She didn't want it at all, but her grief was still raw after her mother died. We practically adopted her. She needed us as much as we needed her, and little by little, she found her place. Jonna and Clare were already best friends, both beauties on the cheerleading squad, always turning stunts into half-sung chants. Their soprano and alto slipped into our harmonies like they'd been waiting for it all along.

By junior year, we were performing at football, basketball, and baseball games. Crowds stuck to us like magnets, not just for the music but for the way each of us was so different. It was chaos wrapped in glitter, and people couldn't look away. Steve discovered us during a homecoming game. He was there for his nephew, but somehow the timing worked in our favor.

Long Island wasn't far from the city, so soon we were commuting three days a week to Kaleidoscope's offices. Most of the time it was my mom driving us. Poor Stacy. She got stuck mediating fights about boys and eyeliner, reminding us that we were about to record our first album and couldn't let some silly drama tear us apart. I can still hear her southern drawl in the car when we were at each other's throats over Cameron.

"You girls are going to be together for a while now," she'd yell over our bickering, one hand clutching the steering wheel. "You're signed and working on your first record! Don't let some stupid boy come between y'all!" She was right. We didn't understand then, but she saw what was coming for us before we did.

The studio nearly broke us. Hours on end locked in, our teenage energy bucking against the walls. We were overworked, exhausted, too young to understand that what we were giving up wasn't normal. But we finished that first album: Our Summer. Indie pop perfection. Gold-certified. Singles like "Just a Daydream," "Runaway Summer," "The Boy Next Door," and "Free for the Season" spun us into orbit. Nora's song, "Never," was darker, moodier, and never charted. But I still think it was the most honest piece of music we ever recorded.

The pressure to follow up was immediate. Seventeen years old, hormones raging, attention scattered. Everyone else had boyfriends, even Nora with Eric from No Reason. I was the only one who didn't, and it made me feel... wrong. That's when Donovan stepped in. He told me he could help me figure it out. I push the thought away, refusing to let it take root. Not now. Not yet.

What I can't shake is the night we broke apart. The second album was killing us. Sabrina and I were at each other's throats, fighting over unfinished lyrics. Clare and Jonna rolled their eyes from the sidelines, mocking us instead of helping. Nora tried to glue the pieces together, but it was too much weight for one girl. We released *Behind the Ivy*, a slower, acoustic mess. Ten tracks dripping with teenage rage, and fans hated it. The reviews gutted us.

Sabrina was always threatening to quit. Every argument, every review she didn't like, her go-to line was, "I'm done. I'm out." But she never walked away. She just wanted the power in saying it.

I was the one who finally broke. I can still feel her breath hot against my face, her nose pressed to mine as she screamed, "This is your fault! If you'd given me the reins, this wouldn't have happened!"

And me, shoving her back, my voice ragged from screaming, "Then take them! I'm done!"

The words hung in the air, heavy as stone.

And just like that, it was over.

The relief was instant. I didn't have to keep pretending. I didn't have to keep standing in the dark with Donovan's shadow creeping behind me. Clare and Jonna threw in their resignations for the drama of it, and Nora was left alone at the label. We didn't even let her try to fix it.

Remembering it now makes my stomach turn. We can't let that happen again. Not this time, not with Nora gone.

I sit up, reaching for my phone. I text Sam, testing the waters.

Coffee?

When she came over this weekend and met the girls, she listened as I told her about my fears. About how terrifying it was to come out, but how after Nora's death, I couldn't keep hiding anymore. Life was too short.

She'd smiled then, her little pixie nose wrinkling, and kissed me, the familiar taste of cinnamon sugar lips, reminding me of freedom.

I press a finger to my mouth, remembering the softness and taste, just as my phone lights up.

Pick you up in thirty minutes.

I breathe out, long and heavy, a whisper of relief carried on it. "We're back," I murmur to myself.

Then I fling off the sheets and start rifling through my closet. Today deserves my best retribution outfit.

Chapter 23

Clare

"So, how's life with Sam?" I ask, balancing my phone between my shoulder and ear while my other arm struggles under the weight of a wicker laundry basket piled high with clothes.

"Really great, actually. Check this out," Dani says, her voice bubbling with excitement.

A ping vibrates against my cheek. I set the basket down on the dining table, the wooden surface creaking under its weight, and tap the notification. A screenshot opens, paparazzi catching Dani and Sam strolling down Broadway, hands intertwined, faces lit with unguarded smiles. They're waving, framed by a halo of city lights. The MSNBC caption reads: *Love is in the air*.

My chest warms, an involuntary smile stretching across my face. "That's so amazing, Dani," I say, picturing her in that moment, basking in something pure. The sound of my front door opening echoes through the quiet house. My stomach tightens. "Let me let you go. Someone just walked into my house."

I hang up and take a slow step toward the entryway, my bare feet whispering against the hardwood. Every sense sharpens, heart rate quickening, breath shallow, as I turn the corner bracing myself for my love or my murderer.

It's Damien. "Oh," I manage.

"Not expecting me?" he says, rubbing the back of his neck as though he is unsure if he belongs here.

"Well, actually no. I haven't heard from you in over two months," I mutter, planting my hands on my hips to ground myself.

"I know," he says, voice low.

"That was such a coward move," I fire back, the words hanging sharp in the air.

He nods once, gaze fixed on the floor. "It was. But I had every right to be upset." His tone shifts, firm now, deliberate. "You know that I love you, Clare. You are my prized possession." His eyes lock on mine with a flash of something territorial.

"I'm not just a possession, or a trophy wife, Damien. I'm a real person," I state, each word a stone I place between us.

"I know you are." He takes a slow step forward. "I've realized you made a mistake. That you only cheated on me because I didn't make you feel seen or heard."

Interesting. I wonder who fed him that revelation.

"You're too precious to me to lose. I understand now that you had an affair because of how poor of a husband I have been," he admits, the shame curling into his voice.

He's not wrong. But what he does not know, what he cannot know, is that I am in love with Tom. Images of the last few weeks with Tom rush into my mind like a tide. Our quiet mornings, whispered plans, the way we have mapped out a future beyond the chaos.

Once the concert wraps and I sell my home in the spring, I'll be financially set. Tom, with his generational wealth, doesn't need to work another day in his life. He is selling his share of the firm, ready to start fresh. He wants me to move into his estate. We've already talked about eloping in Tuscany, vows exchanged under a gold sunset spilling over the vineyards. The thought swells in my chest, making Damien's presence feel even more misplaced. Still, a flicker of guilt tugs at me.

"Let's sit." I gesture toward the couch, ease into it, soft and careful, and tell him everything. That I'm in love with Tom. That we have plans. Big ones. He listens in a silence so still I half expect him to explode. Instead, he just sits there, absorbing it. "I know I already signed your prenup," I continue, my voice softer now, "so you don't have to worry about me getting half of your trust fund. All I ask is you give me the house."

"Fine," he mutters.

That was surprisingly easy. "Okay, great. If you want to have your people serve my people the documentation, I'll sign on the dotted line as soon as possible." I can't help the small burst of enthusiasm that slips through.

He stands abruptly, moving toward the door. "Wow. You seem excited to divorce me," he says, a note of bitterness dripping from the words. I swallow my smile, forcing my face into something somber. "It is really a shame it didn't work out between us. I hope we can remain friends."

He nods, hand already on the doorknob.

"Oh, wait." I rush to the kitchen, pulling open a drawer until my fingers land on the laminated VIP backstage pass. I return and hold it out to him. "I would love for you to be there," I say with a polite smile.

He takes it without looking at me, the motion stiff, before slamming the door behind him.

That evening, Tom picks me up for dinner. This will be our last night together for a week. Tomorrow the girls and I head to Long Island for rehearsal to make it easier on Jonna. I've already taken an indefinite leave from work.

When I tell him about Damien's surprise visit and the divorce now in motion, he doesn't miss a beat before suggesting a celebration. We pull up to the gates of one of Newport Beach's grandest estate-converted restaurants. It looms like a modern White House, flanked by towering pillars and gardens bursting with white and blue hydrangeas. The name gleams on an engraved brass plaque: The Garden of Eden.

"How did you get us a reservation last minute?" I ask, my red lips curving into a grin.

He eases the car into valet. "I'm a Gallagher."

Right. I keep forgetting he is a quiet storm of influence. The drivers open our doors in unison, and we step into a lobby drenched in opulence. A spiraling chandelier cascades down from a ceiling two stories high, light shimmering off mirrored gold walls and white quartz floors. I've chosen my gold shimmer Valentino strapless dress, its fabric catching every flicker of light, paired with white gladiator heels laced high up my legs. Tom is in a tailored navy Louis Vuitton suit, crisp white shirt, and a gold tie to match me.

The hostess leads us to a secluded corner table, candlelight flickering from a candelabra of three slender tapers. White rose petals scatter across the linen like they have fallen from some other, softer world. A bottle of Opus One waits on display. "Good evening, Mr. Gallagher, Ms. Devon," the waiter greets with practiced elegance. "May I present our vintage reserve, Napa Valley, preserved in 1990."

He pours a sample into my glass. I swirl it, watching the wine cling to the sides before sliding down in slow, heavy streaks. The scent wraps around me, black currant, blackberry, cassis, underpinned by cedar and vanilla.

"Delectable," I say, letting the word drip with playful pretension.

Tom chuckles, lifting his glass. "Cheers to an amazing woman who makes my world spin. I am so proud of the person you are and the person you are still becoming. I hope to be part of every era of your life. As one chapter closes, another opens." The crystal chime of our glasses is followed by the first notes of Clair de Lune from a white grand piano nearby.

Dinner stretches into hours. We share two bottles of Opus, every bite exquisite, every glance lingering. Dessert arrives in a blaze, a flaming baked Alaska that bathes my face in golden firelight. Tom snaps a photo, smiling like he wants to bottle the moment forever. Then he excuses himself. When I glance up, he is at the piano, adjusting the microphone. "Can I get everyone's attention, please?" His voice carries, smooth and certain.

My heart jumps. "What are you doing?" I mouth, half laughing, half nervous.

He smiles. "Hi, I'm Tom Gallagher. Maybe you have seen me on a football field, or maybe I have been your attorney. But tonight, none of that matters. Do you see that drop-dead gorgeous woman in the sparkly gold dress?" Dozens of eyes turn to me. Heat floods my cheeks. I give a shy wave. "She is the love of my life. And I brought her here tonight to proclaim that loudly so all you fine people could be my witnesses." I press a hand to my mouth, heart thundering. "Clare Gabriella Devon, would you make me the luckiest man alive, and marry me?"

Gasps ripple through the room. He kneels before me, flipping open a ring box. The diamond catches the light, an oval solitaire, easily ten carats, set in platinum, each facet throwing off a dazzling spark.

"Yes," I whisper, still stunned.

"Did you say yes?" he teases, eyes glittering.

I nod, then shout it. "YES!"

He sweeps me into his arms, spinning me until my dress flares out like a golden wave. The applause swells around us as he slides the ring onto my finger.

"I cannot wait to become Mrs. Gallagher," I breathe before kissing him hard, sealing it in front of the whole room.

I arrive at MacArthur Airport still in a trance, my eyes constantly drawn to the diamond sparkling on my left hand. Every time the light catches it, it feels unreal, like I might wake up and find it gone. I haven't told the girls yet, and the thought of revealing it sends little surges of adrenaline through me.

The cab ride to Jonna's feels longer than it should. When we finally pull up to her driveway, I wheel my luggage over the smooth concrete, my sneakers crunching against a few scattered pebbles. The late morning sun is warm on my shoulders. I knock on the front door with my left hand, watching my ring flash like it has its own private spotlight. My stomach flutters with anticipation.

The door swings open to reveal Dexter. "Clare!" His gaze catches my hand. "That's a nice new ring," he says, his voice casual but his eyes curious.

I wiggle my fingers in front of him. "A nice new engagement ring," I correct, guiding him toward the obvious conclusion. His expression transforms instantly.

"Oh my God! Tom proposed?!" We both jump up and down in the entryway like kids who just got told school was canceled. Jonna appears from the hallway with Alissa balanced on her hip.

"What's all the fuss?" I shove my hand in her face, the diamond catching the light and throwing little rainbows across her cheek.

"What?!" she shrieks, eyes widening. "When?"

"Last night, in The Garden of Eden!" I say, my voice pitching high with excitement. We all jump together in a messy, happy cluster of hugs.

Alissa, apparently unimpressed, lets out a loud burp and promptly spits up all over Dexter's shirt. "Alissa!" Dexter yells, staring down at the mess like it personally betrayed him. Jonna and I dissolve into laughter.

"Go clean up, honey," she says, motioning him toward the stairs. She grabs my luggage with her free hand and sets Alissa down in her playpen.

"Am I the first to know?" she asks, shooting me a playful wink.

"Duh!" I grin.

"I better be," she says with a devilish smile. "Sabrina and Dani are going to meet us at rehearsals separately. I guess Sabrina wasn't feeling well this morning. She may not even show."

"I hope she's okay," I reply, my voice laced with concern, though my attention keeps drifting back to my ring.

Jonna and I drive just down the road to a private gym inside her neighborhood's country club. The place smells faintly of eucalyptus and freshly polished floors. We step inside wearing our tightest yoga pants and shortest sports bras, ready to sweat through a challenging rehearsal.

Dani is already there, stretching on a mat in the center of the mirrored room. "Hey guys!" she calls, flashing a bright smile.

"Hello, lovebird," Jonna teases, dropping onto the floor beside her.

"Hello, beautiful," I add, my voice syrupy and dramatic as I wave my hand in the air like I am fanning royalty.

Dani gasps, her eyes locking on the diamond. "Tom?" she asks, needing confirmation before she lets herself squeal.

"Who else would be able to afford a two-million-dollar diamond?" I scoff, grinning wildly.

Dani pulls me closer, turning my hand slightly to catch the light. "That's a perfect stone," she says, her voice almost hypnotized.

"Isn't she the prettiest?" I tease, glancing between the ring and Dani. We shift into a circle, each of us pulling the others into deep stretches, our laughter bouncing off the walls.

"Well, congratulations are in order," Dani says warmly.

"Where's Sabrina? I want to piss her off with my new rock," I say with a devilish grin.

"I don't know," Dani says, glancing toward the door as if Sabrina might materialize there out of thin air.

We all shrug, then turn our attention to the rehearsal. We pick our old classic to warm up, Runaway Summer. It's muscle memory now—light, bouncy footwork in the verses, playful hip sways and turns in the chorus, with a few hair-whips for drama. We hit the big ending pose in unison, arms outstretched and heads tilted up to the ceiling, our reflections in the mirror looking like the younger versions of ourselves we used to be, only sharper and stronger now.

We hold it for a beat before breaking into laughter, breathing hard and grinning like we just time-traveled back to the best summer of our lives. All we're missing is Sabrina and Nora.

Sabrina doesn't show to rehearsal until we are already finishing up for the day. She walks in wearing an oversized hoodie and sweats, her face pale, eyes heavy. She looks exhausted. Jonna, Dani, and I are sitting by the fan, trying to cool off, when she trudges toward us.

"I'm sorry I'm so late," she says, her voice strained.

"Are you ok?" I ask, stretching my arms behind my head.

It only takes one glance upward for her to break. She falls to her knees, sobbing so hard her shoulders shake. We all scurry over to her in panic.

"Brina, what's the matter?" Dani cries, trying to lift her up.

"I can't tell you guys, it's so bad. I don't know what to do." She sniffs into her palms.

The three of us exchange wide-eyed looks, fear and confusion thick in the air.

"Well, we can't help you unless you tell us," I say as gently as I can. She wipes her eyes and drags the back of her sleeve across her nose.

"Eric couldn't tell us at the bar, and I understand now why."

"You found out about Nora?" Jonna whispers. We all freeze in place, afraid of the answer.

"I still don't know if she killed herself or not," Sabrina says, trying to steady her breathing. "But I found something else out." She swallows hard, wipes her face, and takes a deep breath. "Robbie and I went to Walter's house and found Nora's high school journals."
The three of us look at each other, hearts pounding. "We skimmed through the pages. It was like a slow deterioration of her sanity. And in the end, she basically described Donovan raping her without even knowing that's what was happening."

We freeze. The room tilts. My mind blanks. Dani steps forward, her voice darkening. "Donovan did what?"

"He raped her! He called it coaching sessions. He would grab her diaphragm to 'help her breathing' so she wouldn't be so pitchy. He touched her inappropriately on multiple occasions. And then he raped her!" Sabrina sobs uncontrollably. Jonna drops to the floor, bawling. Dani grabs the bar on the wall to steady herself. I stand rooted in place, numb with shock.

"And Dani," Sabrina suddenly chokes out, her eyes flashing with fury, "we found Marlene and asked her questions. She told us she saw you and Donovan sucking face!" The words slam into the room. Jonna and I whip our heads toward Dani, waiting for an answer. Her face drains of color, like she's staring at a ghost. "I don't know what you're talking about," she says, her voice trembling.

"Don't you dare lie to me!" Sabrina shouts, standing and getting in Dani's face. I rush between them, holding my hands out. "Woah, woah, woah, let's all calm down. This is obviously very intense."

"Is it true, Dani?" Jonna asks, her hand pressed against her chest.

Dani stares at the ground as the truth claws its way out of her. "I always tried to bury it. I always told myself it didn't really happen, that I imagined it. But it did. He pushed himself on me. He told me it would be our secret, that what he was showing me would help me when we got famous. He said I couldn't be a prude as the lead singer of Five Heart, that he needed to give me pointers. He totally manipulated a sixteen-year-old me, and I fell for it."

"What did he do to you, Dani?" I whisper, my blood beginning to boil.

"We kissed. A lot. It was awful. His breath always smelled like tobacco. He touched me. Told me this is what other men I'd meet would do, and he was 'preparing me.' After the third time, I knew it wasn't right, and I distanced myself."

"Why didn't you tell us until now!" Sabrina cries.

"I was scared! I pretended it wasn't real. I don't know!"

Jonna grabs my hand and squeezes so tight it hurts.

"Did you know Nora was being abused?" Sabrina says flatly, her eyes narrowing at Dani.

"No, I swear," Dani pleads, her voice shaking. "I thought I was taking the brunt of it. I hoped he didn't manipulate any of you. I thought because I was the lead, I was the target."

Rage builds in my chest, hot and uncontainable. "We need to go."

"Where?" Jonna whispers, tears streaming down her face.

"To kill that motherfucker."

Chapter 24

Jonna

Clare storms out of the gym into the lobby of the country club. I run after her, catching her arm before she gets too far. A hush falls as clusters of people stop mid-step, their conversations suspended to watch the scene unfolding.

My voice trembles. "You can't go there, Clare." She jerks her hand free, fury written across every inch of her.

"I can, and I will!"

Dani and Sabrina come rushing out behind me.

"Clare, just wait!" Sabrina shouts.

Clare spins around, and the four of us form a tense circle in the middle of the lobby. Guests weave around us, whispering, pointing, eyes darting between us like they've stumbled onto a reality show in real time.

"Let's talk about our next course of action, together," Sabrina whispers, low enough that no stray ears can pick up. Clare crosses her arms, her chest still heaving, but she nods.

"The Grammys are in two weeks," Sabrina continues, "and then the concert a week after that. We don't have enough time to gather evidence and do a full takedown."

"What can we do, then?" I ask, my stomach turning.

"This is what we do," Dani cuts in, voice firm, acting like the true lead. "If my assumptions about Donovan being at the Grammys are right, we arrive together with our significant others. We stand united, wearing our colors, showing him we aren't backing down. We tell the interviewers and reporters how excited we are for the concert. That will rile him up. He'll lose his shit when he hears the concert is still on. Then, when we're back in the city, we go to his office together. We drop copies of the journals on his desk, and we threaten to expose him unless he drops the lawsuit. We might never know exactly what happened to Nora, but at least we can claim some justice."

We all glance at each other, silent agreement moving between us.

"Ok, it's settled," Dani says, forcing a half-smile. "Now let's talk Grammys."

Two weeks pass quickly, and Dani's private jet hums with restless anticipation the night before the show. The cabin is chaos in the best way. Clare and Tom are already clinking glasses of bubbly, Sabrina and Robbie are doubled over at an inside joke. Dani, Sam, and Stacy are talking about a future Europe expedition. Selma is dissecting fashion news with Eric and Ryan, while Dexter and I sit quietly, content to let it all buzz around us.

"This is such a nice jet," Dexter whispers. "If this concert takes off, maybe we can afford one." He chuckles at himself, and I shake my head, laughing softly.

By the time we land at LAX, we've already shifted into performance mode. Sunglasses on, hands linked with our partners, we strut through the airport like a wall of glamour. Phones fly into the air, flashes pop, gasps follow us through the terminal. People point, scream, chase. We keep our heads high but coy, feeding their frenzy just enough to remind them who we are.

A limo whisks us to an Airbnb mansion in the Hollywood Hills, the "HOLLYWOOD" sign gleaming proudly through the floor-to-ceiling windows. The place is something out of a glossy spread. Neutral tones, arched windows, it's like the inside of a Pottery Barn catalog.

"We call the master!" I shout as soon as we step inside.

"No, we want it!" Sabrina fires back.

"The last one there is a rotten egg!" Clare squeals, already racing toward the staircase with Tom close behind. We all take off running, shrieking and laughing like kids again, our heels clicking against the polished wood floors as we scramble up two flights to the eleven bedrooms sprawled across the upper levels. Of course, Clare's and Tom's nimble, athletic bodies beat us all.

"Not fair!" Dexter and I huff, collapsing against the doorframe of a chinoiserie-inspired room.

We drop our bags inside. Sunlight pours through arched windows, casting a golden glow over wide patterned wallpaper. I fall to the bed with a sigh. "This is gorgeous."

"*You* are gorgeous," Dexter murmurs, flopping down beside me.

"It's so nice to not have the kids," I say, though guilt stirs immediately. "I just miss them."

"I know." His guilt mirrors mine. "They're proud of you though," Dexter says. "DJ told me the other day he can't wait to see Mommy on TV. Harley drew a picture of you all from an old CD cover she found." He rummages through his satchel and pulls out the folded paper, smoothing it open. It's us, Five Heart, stick figures with sparkly outfits, my name scrawled "mommy" above my head. My heart twists.

"You brought this all the way from home?"

"I knew you'd have a breakdown or two, so I figured this would help." He rubs my shoulder, his touch grounding me.

I cradle the drawing to my chest, tears threatening, then turn back to him. His face is soft, open, waiting. I cup his cheek, and he closes his eyes, leaning into my palm. Heat surges between us. I lean closer, tasting the familiar sweetness of his lips.

We kiss slowly at first, tongues grazing, breath mixing. His hand trails over me, hesitant, as if rediscovering me after years of exhaustion and routine. The hesitation only fuels me. I grab his hand and press it harder against me, desperate for more.

That's all it takes. He growls low in his throat and pushes me back onto the bed, tearing his shirt over his head. I yank mine off, fumbling with the buttons of our jeans. He takes his length in his hand and guides himself inside me.

"Dexter," I gasp, my body arching as he fills me.

He thrusts hard, quick, both of us clawing at each other like we've been starving for this. The hunger overtakes us. It's messy, urgent, our laughter bubbling between moans as the bed creaks beneath us.

"God, I missed this," he groans against my neck.

"Don't stop," I beg, nails digging into his back. In seconds, we're both spiraling, our release hitting at the same time, warmth flooding me. We collapse together, breathless, laughing at the absurd speed of it.

"It's been so long," Dexter says, sprawled naked beside me.

"Yes, it has." I grin, pressing a kiss to his shoulder.

We tangle ourselves in the sheets, bodies slick with sweat, and drift off in each other's arms.

The next morning is Grammys Day. The boys head off for a round of golf while the girls stay back at the mansion, letting the glam squad work on us from dawn until dusk. Hair pinned, curled, airbrushed makeup brushed in layers, cocktails in hand and we gossip, reminisce, and sip between rounds of laughter.

By the time the boys come back, they're dressed in their "dad uniforms." Ball caps, polos tucked into khaki shorts, New Balance sneakers squeaking against the hardwood.

"Hello boys!" Clare calls out, waving like a queen, her engagement ring sparkling against the light.

"How was golf, sweetie?" I ask Dexter softly.

"Tom hit a sick birdie on hole two," he raves.

"It was nothing," Tom mutters, humbled, though his grin betrays him.

"I couldn't keep up with these two," Robbie admits, tugging at his gloves.

"Yeah, you sucked," Ryan teases, snickering with Eric.

Clare rolls her eyes, annoyed that Ryan is even here. "I'm proud of you, honey," she says sweetly, Tom leaning down to kiss her cheek.

"Bleh! Get a room!" Dani cackles with Sam, both sticking their tongues out.

"You're one to talk," Clare fires back. "Oh Sam, that's the spot!" She mimics Dani's moans from the night before.

"Yeah, the whole house heard that," Sabrina quips, sipping her drink without looking up.

"Sorry," Dani says with a devilish grin, fingers interlaced with Sam's.

We're all laughing when Selma strolls in, Donatella Versace gliding beside her like royalty. "Ladies, Donatella Versace. Donatella, the ladies of Five Heart," Selma announces proudly. We all stand, stunned.

"It's so nice to meet you," Clare gushes.

"Nice to see you again, D," Dani says, ever the insider.

"I'm honored to dress you all tonight," Donatella says with her dramatic flair. She gestures, and racks of gowns are wheeled in by assistants. One by one, the bags unzip to reveal glimmering masterpieces. "Each gown represents you. And for the men, a matching touch."

"Oh my god, they are stunning!" Clare shrieks.

"Wow," I whisper, hypnotized.

We are definitely making a statement tonight.

By the time the limo rolls to a stop at the red carpet, the outside world is already vibrating with energy. The barricades bow inward with the force of hundreds of fans pressed against them. Their screams crash like thunder, rolling across the boulevard. Camera flashes explode in rapid-fire bursts, strobing the night like lightning. Hands claw at the air, phones wave high above heads, every inch of space filled with bodies straining for a glimpse.

The sound is deafening. Our names chanted, sobs mixing with shrieks, some fans crying so hard they can barely hold their phones steady. It feels like standing at the center of a storm made of devotion.

Clare and Tom step out first. She looks like fire itself in a strappy fuchsia gown that catches every flash, Swarovski crystals dripping like stardust. Tom's tux and matching bow tie complete the look. Paparazzi bulbs explode in a frenzy. Clare raises her hand high, showing off her engagement ring, and the crowd screams so loud the air quivers. Tom dips her back for a kiss, and the world roars like a wave hitting shore.

Sabrina follows, emerald sequins wrapping her like a jewel. Robbie beams at her side, soaking up her shine.

Dexter squeezes my hand before we step out. My gown gleams silver under the lights, every angle dazzling like liquid metal. Dexter looks steady, grounded, bow tie matching mine, as we walk out together. "This is nuts," he murmurs.

"It's like riding a bicycle," I tell him, forcing my shoulders back and my smile wide. We wave. Fans shriek, sob, reach for us, as if touching us would mean touching their own youth again. The air is thick with hysteria, like we've stepped back into the peak of our fame.

Ryan and Eric emerge next, followed by Dani and Sam. Dani's golden gown is pure spotlight, her every step radiating control. Sam clings to her side, overwhelmed but unflinching.

Finally, all of us come together before the Grammys backdrop. We pose, laughing, kissing our partners, then join hands. We raise them high—four women once fractured, now whole again.

And then the air shifts. Black Escalades pull up. The door swings open. Donovan Blake steps out. His presence is oily, smug. He's flanked by models with practiced smiles, his assistant trailing behind, struggling to keep up. Fans shriek louder, some even reaching out for him. He tips his sunglasses down, squinting at us with the smirk of a man who still thinks he owns the world.

We step forward, our hands still raised. A declaration. We are unbreakable.

"Well, well, well," Donovan drawls, sauntering closer. "If it isn't Five Heart. Or should I say… Four Heart."

The jab lands like a slap. The crowd gasps.

"You have a lot of nerve," Sabrina spits, Robbie's hand tightening on her shoulder to hold her back.

Donovan chuckles. "Actually, you all have a lot of nerve. Showing up here like you're untouchable. You think a reunion concert saves you? I'll sue you into oblivion. You'll be blacklisted. Washed up has-beens chasing fifteen minutes." His voice drips venom. Cameras click. The crowd shifts uneasily, sensing the tension.

Dani's eyes blaze with tears she refuses to let fall. Her voice cracks, raw and guttural. "We're going on that stage in honor of Nora, our best friend, who you never gave two fucks about. You never gave a shit about any of us."

The words hang heavy, slicing through the noise. For a moment, even the fans quiet, as if the truth of her grief eclipses the spectacle.

Donovan only smiles, unbothered, and turns away. "Let's go, Sarah," he orders. His assistant jumps, startled. She hesitates just long enough to look back at us, her eyes wide, brimming with something like horror… or guilt. The apology in her stare lingers before she scurries after him.

"She knows something," Sabrina murmurs, her reporter instincts sparking.

"You saw that look too?" Dani asks.

"Yeah," I whisper, my stomach twisting. Maybe the key to taking Donovan down isn't just us. Maybe it's Sarah.

Chapter 25

Nora

My eyes fluttered open. The blur of a spinning ceiling fan and a trash bag taped to the window filled my vision. The pipe scorched my lungs last night. Somebody said it could have been laced, but I didn't care. I just wanted nothingness, even if it killed me.

The air reeked of piss and sweat. I slowly sat up, waking back into my nightmare of a life, and trudged out into the living room. Mattresses were scattered across the floor like discarded bodies, people twitching and groaning in the corners. A single bulb flickered overhead in the hallway.

I staggered into the bathroom, gripping the sink. The cracked mirror stared back at me, grimy and streaked. The girl in it was pale, hollow-eyed, dull onyx hair tangled, lips dry. She looked like a ghost. "What the hell am I doing?" My voice was raspy, cracking with the hoarseness left over from the night before. I barely sounded like myself anymore.

I felt like death. A living corpse. That was the first time I'd smoked from a crack pipe. This was the lowest of lows. I pressed my palms into the porcelain, stomach lurching. I'd been running too long, crashing on couches, singing in shitty bars where no one listened, numbing myself with poison. Every night was borrowed time.

Tears welled hot as I stared at this stranger in the mirror. I didn't want to die like this. I wanted a bed of my own. A life of my own. Peace. The only way forward was to get clean. And the only way to get clean was to shed the poison I'd carried for half my life.

Donovan Blake.

Whenever I had these revelations about sobering up, I grasped for anything to distract me from the memories that forced themselves into my brain like a photo collage. An intrusive scrapbook of every awful thing that had ever happened to me, creating an inner slideshow I couldn't shut off.

Over the years, I'd crashed at each of the girls' places. My most recent refuge was Jonna and Dexter's house a couple of years ago. That was the longest I stayed clean. If it wasn't for her kids, I probably would've fallen off the wagon much sooner. Those kids were my life for a little over a month. But the lounge I was singing at brought in a few old dealers from the city. Temptation won. I didn't want to corrupt the kids with my non-lucid behavior, so I disappeared one day.

In the past, I'd stayed with Clare—that was a disaster. And when Sabrina first moved to the city, I crashed with her, but she kicked me out instantly. I left. I didn't want to compromise her new internship.

The only person I could stay with now until I sobered up was Dani. But we barely spoke. She was a global superstar now. I was so proud of the woman she'd become. I just don't know if she has time for me.

She was playing in Denver next weekend. I could scrounge enough money for a concert ticket to see her in person, to make things right. I pulled out my phone and texted her. She and I had always kept in touch, but the life she led was untouchable, and she was always on the road. Hard to track down.

I walked out of the rundown house, backpack slung over my shoulder. The sun's rays blinded me as I adjusted from the unlit corridors I'd resided in for the last couple of days. I checked my phone to see if she'd written back. Nothing yet.

"Who can I call," I mumbled, scrolling through my contacts. I couldn't call Dad. He was a bad influence whenever I was trying to get sober. One drink from him led to a smoke, then to the pills. A disaster waiting to happen.

I tried calling Dani, just to see if she answered. She didn't. I scrolled to Eric's name next. My heart dropped. Eric and I talked every now and then. We still loved each other but knew we couldn't be together. I was too broken for him. But he'd gotten me out of some sketchy situations. Maybe he'd help me out one last time.

This time, I was ready.

I'd been in Colorado the last couple of years. Weed was legal, so that'd been my vice. I wandered into a nearby bookstore. Silent readers tilted their heads up from their novels with wide eyes. Did I look that terrible?

I called Eric and, finally, he picked up. He told me he was coming to Denver for Dani's upcoming show with the other guys. They'd be in the city in four days. I needed to stay sober and lay low for just under a week until I could see him, until I could tell him everything.

I gave him the cliff notes over the phone. I told him how Donovan had a hold over me for the last decade, since I was a teenager. I told him about scarring all my relationships with the girls from Five Heart. I told him I still think about him always. About us. He seemed eager to meet me after that.

He also mentioned the letters he's received from me over the last five years. He kept them all. I smiled, knowing he'd read my thoughts. I'd always escaped through writing, whether in my journals as a teenager or lyrically through songwriting. A pen and paper were my salvation.

I cleaned myself up in the bookstore bathroom, taking the wheelchair-accessible stall with an adjacent sink. Once my face was clean and my hair pulled back into two buns, I slid to the floor. My eyes felt heavy. Exhaustion crashed over me like a tidal wave.

I rubbed my eyes and awoke in a pitch-black room. Panic jolted me upright. I glided my hand across the wall until I found the latch of the door and pushed it open, still dragging my fingers along the surface until I felt a switch. Got it. I flipped the light and revealed the same bookstore bathroom.

What the heck, was I still here? The drugs from the night before must have left me in a daze. I passed out. I snuck out of the bathroom and wandered into the dim aisles of crisp new books. The store was empty. I made my way to the front and looked out the windows. The sky was pitch black, the moonlight slipping through the crevices of the blinds.

"Shit," I muttered, dropping down on the leather couch by the coffee counter. At least it was a place to sleep tonight. The old structure creaked, and the occasional zoom of a passing car had me wired. I stared wide-eyed at the vaulted ceiling of the bookstore, my thoughts all-consuming. The intrusive memories began their crawl.

My explosive breakup with Eric when I was nineteen. Our rekindling five years later, when I was twenty-four. We gave our relationship another try, secretly. But that was when cocaine entered my life. I couldn't go an hour without a bump. He found my stash, confronted me about my erratic behavior, and left me, again. Typical. Everyone leaves.

My mother's face flickered before me, shadowed by sadness and disappointment, telling me in her soft voice, "I never wanted this for you."

Tears stung. My father appeared. I was fifteen, newly accepted into Five Heart. He came home so drunk I could smell it before he entered the room. I told him the news, and he slapped me so hard across the face that I went flying into the kitchen. My hand rose to my cheek as if the sting remained.

Then Donovan.

The monster under my bed. The devil who whispered in my sleep. He ruined me. And nobody knew. Not really. Eric sensed something was wrong, but I could never tell him what happened. I didn't even understand the magnitude myself until I was older and the pieces began to click. By then the drug abuse had become unstoppable.

I closed my eyes, tears streaming, as my mind drags me back to the "coaching sessions." The way his clammy fingers touched me. A shiver ran down my spine. He promised he was helping me. I knew it was wrong, but I couldn't let the girls down. He would have destroyed the band before it even began.

And then that night.

The worst night of my existence. The band broke up, everyone had scattered, and I was left alone with him. His eyes gleamed with something monstrous as he grabbed me by the shirt.

"This is your fault." His voice was guttural, dripping with rage. He lifted me off my feet like I was weightless and slammed me onto the couch.

"You have cost me everything." He pinned me so hard against the leather I could barely breathe. My sternum felt like it might crack under the pressure. I turned my face to the side, desperate for air. Then I felt the cold rush of exposure as my shorts tore away.

And it was too late. The wrenching pain of him forcing his way inside me flooded my memory.

I hugged myself into a tight ball on the bookstore couch, body trembling. Then the rage set in. I sat up abruptly, my breath sharp. I marched to the register, pried it open, and pulled out the cash inside. Seven hundred and fifty dollars. My hands shook, but I didn't hesitate. I unlocked the door and darted into the night.

At an ATM, I deposited the money onto my debit card. I turned down a narrow alley and, with trembling fingers, grabbed my phone and bought a plane ticket for Manhattan on the first flight out. Five a.m. from Denver.

I called a rideshare and climbed inside. No second-guessing. No turning back. It was time to meet my maker.

I bought new clothes at the airport. A simple "I Love Denver" sweater and matching navy shorts. Five hours later, I arrived at JFK.

The city was worse than when I left it. Litter lined the streets, the smell of urine lingering under my nose at every corner I turned.

I took the subway to the Upper East Side, where Kaleidoscope Records stood like a monument. The contrast made me dizzy. His office building gleamed, marble floors polished to glass, fresh-cut flowers arranged with precision. My boots scuffed across the tiles, each step too loud, reminding me that I don't belong.

The receptionist froze when she saw me. She's younger, polished, her pencil skirt pressed sharp against trembling hands.

"I need to see Donovan."

Her expression hardened. "Mr. Blake is in a meeting. You can't just—"

"Tell him his past just walked in the door," I cut in. "He'll know what it means."

She stepped from behind the desk, trying to block me. "You don't want to do this. Please. Just leave." She knew who I was. Of course she did. I had been part of his only successful girl group. He had only signed solo artists ever since Five Heart's demise.

And that's when I saw what was in her eyes. A flicker of recognition. Of shame. Of fear. The same hollow place I had carried for years. My throat tightened. "You too," I whispered. Her lashes fluttered, and she looked away. But I wasn't running anymore. I shoved past her and yanked open the door to his office.

Donovan Blake sat behind his mahogany desk, suit sharp, expression smug. He leaned back, a predator assessing prey. Our manager, Steve, was sitting in the chair across, stunned to see me.

"Well, well. Nora Hayes." Donovan smirks. "To what do I owe the pleasure? Out of bar gigs already?"

My fists curled at my sides. "I'm not here for your money. I'm here because I'm done being quiet."

His smile faltered. "Careful, now."

"You ruined me," I said, my voice shaking but steady. "You touched me. Used me. Raped me. You turned me into a shell, and I carried your secret until it nearly killed me. But I'm sober now. And I remember everything."

The air dropped ten degrees. The assistant hovered in the doorway, clutching a file, eyes darting between us. Donovan forced a laugh, leaning back further. "Sober? That'll last a week. You think anyone will believe you? A washed-up addict blaming her failures on me?"

I stepped closer. "I wrote it all down. Every detail. If you don't come clean yourself, I'll make sure the world knows." Donovan and Steve exchange worried glances.

Donovan's jaw tightened, the smirk gone. "Shut your mouth, Nora. You don't know what kind of fire you're playing with."

"I'm not afraid of you anymore," I said. "If anything happens to me, they'll know it was you. I've made sure of it."

He slammed his fist on the desk. The assistant jumped, nearly dropping the folder. His eyes cut to her like blades. "And you," he snarled. "Why did you let her in here, Sarah?"

Her face went white. "I—I tried to stop her, Mr. Blake, I—"

"Enough," he snapped.

I turned, fury burning through me. "Don't you dare blame her. This isn't her shame to carry. It's yours."

Sarah's eyes glistened, her lips trembling. She didn't speak, but I knew. I saw it. She was living it, too.

Donovan leaned forward, voice low, final. "Then I guess we have nothing left to discuss."

The weight of it pressed against my chest like a knife. But I stood tall, holding his gaze one last time. Then I walked out, brushing past Sarah.

As I passed, I whispered for her alone: "Someday, you'll tell the truth too. And expose this man for the monster he is." The door closed behind me.

My heart thundered, but for the first time in years, I felt light. Free.

I hesitated to reach out to Sabrina or Jonna. I knew they were still living in New York, but I decided to fly back to Denver instead. Dani's show was coming up, and I needed to tell Eric everything. I needed someone to stand with me when I released all my journals to the world. I was done being scared and hiding behind Novocain.

On the plane ride home, two men in suits stared at me the entire flight. I tucked my head down and ignored them. They probably recognized me from the band. Over the years, I've dealt with a few fans who sought me out for selfies or an autograph or two. I still carried a girlish look despite the dryness of my skin from cigarettes. God, I could use one right now.

My arms began to itch. The sensation grew unbearable. By the time we landed, I was an irritable mess, restless and twitching. I spent the night in the airport, curled in one of the terminals, mind buzzing with withdrawal. I scrolled through my phone, texting anyone I could think of, begging for a couch to crash on. Nothing. The irritability grew catastrophic. My body screamed for relief. I needed a distraction.

I wandered into a duty-free shop and bought a pack of Marlboros with a lighter. Outside, in the short-term parking lot, I lit one and pressed the filter to my lips. The smoke slid down my throat, filling my lungs with its sharp embrace. The nicotine worked fast, melting the tension in my muscles, quieting the itch crawling across my skin.

I smoked until all that was left was a stub of burnt tobacco. The buzz was heavy, almost comforting. Leaning against the elevators, engulfed in the haze, I saw them, those two men from the plane, in my peripheral vision. They were on the other end of the garage, walking toward me.

My heart lurched. My gut screamed: *run*. I stabbed at the elevator button with frantic fingers. When the doors opened, I darted inside, jamming the "close" button repeatedly. The men quickened their pace, nearly reaching me, but the doors slid shut just in time.

I trembled as the elevator carried me back inside. When it opened, I shoved through the crowd and bolted, sprinting down the terminal.

I rushed down the escalator into ticketing, then burst through the revolving doors onto the arrivals drive. A line of yellow taxis stretched in front of me. I dove into the nearest one.

"Where can I take you?" the driver asked, his accent thick, his eyes catching mine in the mirror.

"Anywhere but here!" I gasped, peeking out the window. The men spilled out of the revolving doors, their heads turning, scanning. I slouched low, melting into the seat. "Drive!"

My pulse throbbed, stomach churning. One of my friends I had done molly with a few times finally texted me back, saying I could stay the night in her studio apartment. I told the driver to drop me off there and slipped him a fifty-dollar tip. I only had a hundred and fifty dollars left on my debit card from the bookstore. I needed to be careful until the show. I walked up to Jane's apartment, number 104. As soon as she opened the door, I slipped inside and deadbolted the frame.

"Are you ok?" she asked, looking just as rough as I felt.

"Can I smoke?" I pulled a cigarette from the pack. She nodded, motioning for me to give her one too. I passed her a stick and lit hers first, a small act of courtesy for letting me crash. She tilted the end of her lit cigarette to mine. I inhaled deeply, the medicine filling my lungs, relief spreading fast.

I crept toward the window, scanning the street below, trying to spot those men. Who were they? Why were they following me? Jane and I eventually passed out on her bed, totally platonic. She was the kind of friend who didn't say much, but she was always there. Consistent. Reliable, in her own broken way.

Jane was hooked on opioids. She often tried to get me back on them, but I stayed away. The highs were too good, the crashes too deadly. "I'm clean now," I whispered into the dark, almost like a spell, trying to manifest it. "I'm clean. And I actually threatened Donovan."

Jane was out cold, her shallow breathing filling the room. I stared at the ceiling, replaying New York. The look on Donovan's face when he saw me. Sharp, rattled. Frightening, but in that moment I'd felt powerful. Like he was shrinking into the pathetic shell of Voldemort at the end of Harry Potter. Then I thought of his assistant.

She was being abused by him, just like I had been. I knew it. And she had heard everything I said. She was a witness. If those men chasing me were Donovan's dogs, then Sarah could be the one person to stand as an eyewitness if he tried to silence me.

My heart began to palpitate. I reached for my phone, desperate to distract myself, and saw two missed calls from Dani. My chest squeezed. She had tried to call back. I sat up abruptly, hurried into the bathroom, and dialed her. She answered right away, voice low and tired. "Nora, it's like two in the morning."

"Dani!" I shouted, relief pouring out at the sound of her voice. "I'm sorry I didn't see your missed call until now, I was in a situation…" My words trailed off. Silence.

Then her voice again, edged with concern, maybe even sarcasm. "What situation are you in now?"

I couldn't tell her, like this. Not over the phone. "I'll have to tell you in person," I whispered, hearing Jane stir in the other room. "I have to go." I hung up.

The bathroom door cracked open. Jane stood in her underwear; makeup smudged beneath her eyes like a raccoon.

"I gotta pee," she said flatly. I squeezed past her and left her to it, the heavy smoke and exhaustion of the night pressing down on me.

The next morning, Eric texted me, telling me to meet him at the hotel bar where he was staying. I asked Jane if I could shower and borrow one of her dresses. She laughed. "I have never owned a dress in my life."

"Okay, then what's your nicest top and skirt?" I pressed. I wanted to look cute for Eric.

She rummaged through her closet and pulled out a red plaid mini skirt with a chain hanging from belt loop to belt loop, and a sheer black lace long sleeve top.

"Do you have a black bra or something I can wear? You can literally see my nipples in this," I said, staring at my reflection. I looked like Hot Topic had just held a clearance sale. She tossed me a studded black leather bralette. "This should work."

I slipped it on beneath the lace, tugged the skirt into place, and pulled on my charcoal combat boots. It would do. Then I headed downtown.

Eric sat at the curved barstools, sipping coffee from a mug.

"Hi," I said awkwardly. What do you say to the man you will forever have feelings for, the one who will never give you another chance?

He spun around in his stool, smiling. A true smile. The kind he used to give me in the old days. "Nora," he said warmly, and pulled me into a soft embrace. I melted into his grasp like butter, his long dark hair brushing against me.

"Where's Robbie and Ryan?" I asked, glancing over his shoulder.

"Um… I don't know. I think they went out for breakfast?" His tone wavered.

"They don't know I'm here, do they?" I chuckled, calling him out. Eric had always been the worst liar, every white lie etched across his face before the words even left his lips.

"I'm sorry," he says, embarrassed.

"Don't be sorry. I get it. Blast from the past, always showing up when she needs something," I joked, though there was more truth in it than I wanted to admit.

He shrugged. "What do you need this time?" That one stung. Before I could answer, something caught my eye. The familiar figures of the two men from the airport appeared at the front of the lobby.

"Oh my lord," I gasped, quickly turning Eric to block their view of me.

"What's the matter?" he asked, glancing back to see what I had seen.

"I promise I'll explain if you just guard me and take me up to your hotel room," I whispered urgently. I had never been so eager to go to a man's hotel room.

Eric used his height to shield me as we slipped into the elevator. When we reached his floor, we hurried inside his room. I shut the door and deadbolted it, my hands shaking.

"What the hell, Nora?" he asked, out of breath.

I pressed my back against the door, struggling to slow my heartbeat. "I don't know what came over me," I said, words broken between breaths. "But I went to New York the other day. I went to Kaleidoscope. I cornered Donovan, and I threatened to finally expose what he did to me."

Eric's eyebrow arched sharply. "You never exactly told me what he did to you. You've only given me riddles over the years. But I never liked the way he looked at you. And your face always looked strained after I picked you up from the studio when we were dating."

A wave of courage washes over me. "He raped me, Eric. After abusing me for years. When the band broke up, when the girls left, he blamed me, and he raped me in anger."

The words sounded foreign rolling off my tongue, as if they belonged to someone else.

Eric stumbled two steps back, catching himself on the edge of the bed. "What?" His voice cracked.

I felt stronger than ever in this moment. I sat him down, anchoring myself in the truth. "That night you picked me up, and I was bawling over the band breaking up… He'd just raped me. He was so angry." I said it again, and again. Each time the words left me, it felt like a release. A weight peeling away.

Tears welled in Eric's eyes, spilling fast. "Nora, why didn't you ever tell me? I could have protected you."

"I don't know," I admitted. "I was so young. Five Heart was all I had. When the abuse started, I knew if I said anything, it would all be over. But then the band broke up anyway, after the flop of the second album. I knew it was finished. And in a way, I felt relief. At least I had a reason to walk away. But then—"

Eric's phone pinged. He glanced down, face tightening. "It's Ryan and Robbie. They're coming back up. I'm so sorry, Nora. But you need to leave."

The strain in his voice gutted me. I hadn't even told him about the men following me, or Donovan's threats, before he was pushing me toward the door.

"I promise we'll continue this, but the guys can't see you here." His words tumbled out desperately. "Meet me outside Dani's show tomorrow night. I'll send you a ticket." Then the door closed behind me, and I was alone in the sterile hallway. My pulse hammered as I glanced back and forth down the endless maze. Somewhere nearby, I heard Ryan and Robbie laughing, their voices bouncing off the walls. I darted in the opposite direction, slipping into an open room before the maid noticed.

At the window, I peered down. There they were. The two men. Lingering outside. Waiting for me.

"Excuse me, ma'am, you're not supposed to be in here," the maid said sharply.

"Sorry!" My voice broke. "Is there an exit in the back?"

She hesitated, then nodded. "Yes. Ground floor. Left at the elevator corridor. Pool area. Gate leads to parking lot." Her English was clipped, but it was enough.

"Thank you," I muttered, rushing past her. I moved with purpose out the back of the hotel and called a rideshare straight to Jane's apartment.

When I finally reached the studio, my breath tore from my chest. "What the actual fuck, Eric!" I shrieked, slamming the door behind me.

Jane shuffled out of the kitchen, her stomach spilling over the edge of her too-tight shorts. "You good?" she asked casually.

"No," I muttered, locking myself in the bathroom with my phone. Eric had texted me. A general admission ticket link for Dani's festival. His message followed: *That was awful timing, and you didn't deserve me pushing you out like that after revealing... everything. The guys would never let me hear the end of it if they knew we met up. I promise tomorrow I'll get away from them and meet you in the crowd. Please don't be mad at me.*

I wrote back: *I could never be mad at you.*

The next day, I woke up and got ready for the show. I had to tell Eric everything. And I needed to tell Dani. She had to know too.

I dressed in one of Jane's Metallica tees, black skinny jeans, and my combat boots. My hair pulled back, I let Jane drop me off at the fairgrounds.

Crowds stretched across the lawns and parking lots like ocean waves. The woman at the ticket booth scanned my code and waved me through. I bought a Diet Coke from a stand and found a spot on the lawn. From where I stood, I was a speck in a sea of thousands, but close enough to see the stage.

I texted Eric: *I'm here.*

No response. Then the lights flared. Two pillars of fire shot upward, and Dani rose from beneath the stage on a pedestal. "Good evening, Denver!" she shouted into the mic. The fans screamed back, a wall of sound. She was radiant in a black sparkly mini dress with fringe that shimmered with each movement. She strummed her guitar and smiled. "Are you ready for a killer show tonight?"

"Yes!" the crowd thundered.

She launched into her first song. I didn't know her solo catalog, but it didn't matter. She was flawless. Every chord, every lyric, every flick of her hair. She owned the stage like she was born on it. A pang of envy mixed with pride rose inside me. She was my friend. And she was everything I wanted to be again.

Near the end of the show, Dani's eyes swept the crowd. They landed on me. Her face faltered, as though she had seen a ghost. She raised her hand, flashing me the number five against her wrist, then motioned for me to come to her after.

"Thank you, Denver! I love you! Have a great night!" she yelled, waving as the crowd roared. As fans poured out, I edged my way to the stage. Security blocked me, but Dani pushed through. "It's okay, boys. She's my friend. She's also a celebrity. Nora Hayes from Five Heart." I smiled faintly as the guards stepped aside. Dani pulled me backstage, where I met her band. She wiped sweat from her brow, chugged water, and sank into a chair. "Long time no see," she said, grinning. "Did you like the show?"

"It was amazing," I admitted, my throat tight. I wanted to tell her right then.

"I'm starving. Want to grab a bite?"

"Yeah," I said, checking my phone. Ten texts and a missed call from Eric blinked on the screen. My heart sank, but I stayed quiet. Dani came first.

The diner she picked was chaos. Neon signs buzzing, trays clattering, fans crowding Dani with cameras raised like weapons of adoration. The air was hot, thick with grease and perfume. I laughed weakly when someone gasped, "Is that Nora Hayes? Are you guys getting the band back together?"

But then I saw them. Through the glass doors, just beyond the swarm of bodies outside of the diner, the two men stood. Donovan's men. Their eyes locked on me. My pulse spiked.

Instinct took over. I ducked low, weaving between fans and waitresses, heart in my throat. Dani's hand brushed my shoulder, grounding me, guiding me toward a booth. We dropped into the hard vinyl seats.

"So, what do you want? My treat," Dani said brightly, sweat still glistening at her temples. She chugged more water, smiling wide. "I can't wait to catch up."

Her voice felt far away. My hands shook under the table. "Dani, I have to tell you something," I whispered, but she leaned closer, brows furrowed.

"Was it whatever you tried to tell me on the phone the other night? You hung up so abruptly."

"Partly," I said, swallowing hard. "But this is about what happened to me, back when we were in Five Heart—"

"Dani Rose!" a fan squealed, shoving forward with a phone. Dani smiled, slipping into autopilot, posing for a selfie.

"Order me a burger, will you? I'll be right back," she whispered, sliding out of the booth toward the restroom. And then she was gone.

The noise of the diner swelled again, too loud, too close. My eyes darted toward the entrance. They were inside now. Suits cutting through the sea of bodies. Scanning left, then right, hungry.

My breath came fast, chest tight. The walls pressed in.

I shot to my feet, nearly toppling the table, pushing through the crowd, squeezing between chairs, ignoring the curses and stares. The kitchen doors slammed against my shoulder as I barreled through them, into the stench of frying oil. Then out the back door, cold metal against my palms, bursting open into the alley.

The night air hit like a slap. Damp. Heavy. Reeking of rot and dumpsters. "Where is everyone?" I gasped, stumbling, voice cracking into the darkness. I ran blindly, shoes slapping wet pavement, until I turned a corner. Dead end. A wall of brick. Footsteps behind me appear, calm and certain.

"Nora Hayes." The voice was deep, final.

I spun, chest heaving. They stepped into the pale light, shadows stretching long against the walls.

"Dani!" I screamed, my voice ripping from my throat.

"Donovan sends his best," one said. The syringe flashed before I could move.

The sting bit deep into my arm. A rush of liquid fire surged through my veins. My knees buckled. Fentanyl.

I knew the feeling. The seduction of it. But this was too much. Far too much. Warmth spread, flooding me, then numbing me. The alley wavered, walls tilting like a funhouse. My heartbeat slowed, heavy, like drums underwater.

For a moment, it was bliss. Floating, untethered, the pain gone, the fear gone, everything soft and quiet. I was light, I was air. I almost let myself surrender. But then the bliss turned sharp.

My chest clamped shut, vision tunneling, sounds were muffled like cotton stuffed in my ears. My limbs wouldn't move. My body was no longer mine.

The men vanished into the night, leaving me crumpled against the cold brick. The high was still there, pulling me higher, sweeter, deadlier. *And then, everything went black.*

Chapter 26

Dani

Eight days. That's all we have left. Our tribute show is so close I can feel it tightening in my chest every time I think about it.

After the Grammys altercation with Donovan, the girls and I pulled together every single one of Nora's journals. We scanned the entries and mailed them as an urgent delivery straight to Kaleidoscope Records. On the back of the envelope, we sealed it with a kiss in red lipstick. It was our silent blackmail, our way of telling Donovan that we are not afraid, and that his time is running out.

Tonight is Christmas Eve. Friendsgiving ended in chaos, so we decided to try again, this time at my penthouse in the city. No secrets. No hidden daggers in the air.

Clare flew in yesterday with Tom, and today Sam is arriving. Her flight was delayed in the holiday storm, so I told her I would keep Christmas warm and waiting for her.

Before dinner, I made us all hit the thrift store and pick out the ugliest sweaters we could find. The four of us now stand in front of my floor-length mirror, clutching our stomachs as we laugh.

"These are repulsive," Clare gasps, doubled over.

"I think it's iconic," Jonna declares, striking a pose with her hand on her hip, as if the hideous thing were couture.

Sabrina lifts her phone, framing us in the reflection. "Christmas selfie!" she shouts. We arrange ourselves like a messy staircase, each throwing a different facial expression. The camera clicks. Laughter erupts again, spilling into the air and echoing across the polished marble floors.

"The boys should be back from the store soon with everything," Clare says, checking her texts. She's glowing, curled in the corner of my sectional with Tom's name lighting up her phone.

The plan is simple. A glazed ham. All the comfort food sides. Something heavy and familiar to soak up the stress of the last few weeks. We all know these next days are going to be brutal rehearsals, every second carved into muscle memory. This meal is our last indulgence before the grind.

The door swings open. Cold air and holiday noise rush in. The boys file through, arms overflowing with brown paper bags.

"Baby!" Clare squeals, throwing herself into Tom's arms. He kisses her lightly on the cheek. Robbie grunts as he drops his haul onto the dining table.

Dexter lifts a box of wine bottles over his head like a trophy. "We are stocked!" he sings, his voice booming.

We swarm the kitchen, unwrapping bag after bag, spreading the groceries across the counter like treasure. "What temperature does the ham need to cook on?" I ask, instinctively turning to Jonna, the one who always knows.

"Usually three-fifty. But check the package, it might have its own directions."

FIVE HEART

I shuffle through the groceries, moving aside bags of green beans, potatoes, rolls. My stomach sinks. No ham.

"I don't see it," I say.

"Oh fuck!" Robbie smacks his forehead with his palm. "That's on me."

Every pair of eyes lands on him, sharp as knives.

"I'm sorry, alright? The guy at the counter was packaging it, but Tom called me over about the wine. I forgot to go back."

"The whole point of Christmas Eve dinner is to serve a ham!" Sabrina's voice cuts like glass. "Someone probably scooped it up by now." She looks at me apologetically.

"I'll go," I say quickly. "I need a distraction while I wait for Sam anyway. Who's coming?"

Clare is already tucked against Tom on the couch. Jonna's in my apron, sleeves rolled, already prepping the sides. I turn to the others.

Sabrina raises her hand half-heartedly. "I'll go. I guess."

"That's the spirit." I grin. I ping Rolf to pull the Rover around front, tug my beanie over my head, and slide on sunglasses for disguise.

Whole Foods is chaos. Shelves stripped bare. The air smells like cinnamon candles and exhaustion. Shopping carts crash and weave like bumper cars. I grab one and steer through the madness, Sabrina trailing beside me.

"Think we'll even find one?" I mutter.

"I'm sorry my boyfriend's an idiot," she says, rolling her eyes.

"He's just a man," I laugh, and the tension breaks.

We reach the butcher's counter. Empty. Not a single ham in sight. "Aw, man," I groan. A man in a tall white chef's hat approaches, tugging on gloves. His name tag reads *Joe*. "What can I do for you ladies?"

"We need a ham. But it looks like you're out," I say.

"You had to be here first thing for those. Sorry."

My eyes flicker past him. There. A single packaged ham sits on the counter behind.

"Our friend Robbie was supposed to pick one up earlier," I explain. "He said the butcher was wrapping it up. He…forgot."

Joe's face lights up. "That Asian guy? He left it under the name Dani Rose. Unless you're her."

"Well," I smirk, tipping my sunglasses down just enough for him to see my face. "You're in luck."

His jaw drops. "Oh wow, you really are—"

"Shh." I pull the beanie lower over my forehead. No need for a crowd.

Joe slides the ham across the counter. "Score," I whisper. "Thanks, Joe. I'll put in a good word for you."

We turn down the next aisle, laughing under our breath. The laughter cuts short as our cart slams into another. "Oh, shoot, sorry!" I blurt out, instinctive. But Sabrina's sharp intake of breath makes me freeze.

Standing on the other side is Sarah. Donovan's assistant. The blood drains from her face the moment she recognizes us. Her knuckles whiten around her cart, her eyes darting left and right as if searching for an escape.

"Sarah, is it?" Sabrina says, her tone dripping with mock sweetness.

Sarah swallows, her throat bobbing. "Hi."

I push our cart forward, closing the space until the metal bars pin against hers. Sabrina steps behind her, boxing her in. Shoppers pass by, carts squeaking, but here in this aisle it feels like the air has been sucked out.

"Let's drop the niceties," Sabrina mutters, low enough so only we can hear.

"Yeah," I add, my pulse hammering. "We know who you're working for."

Sarah shakes her head, eyes wide. "I—I don't know what you mean."

"You know what happened to Nora," Sabrina presses, her voice steady, almost too calm. "And it wasn't a suicide."

Sarah's lips part, but nothing comes out. Her hands tremble on the cart handle, squeezing, releasing, squeezing again. I can practically see the panic crawling under her skin.

"Nora wouldn't kill herself," I whisper, leaning closer.

The words cut through her denial. Her eyes flick upward to the ceiling. A tiny, jerky movement. Force of habit, from cameras always watching.

"You're scared," Sabrina says softly, her tone shifting, coaxing now. "That tells me everything I need to know."

"I can't," Sarah stammers, shaking her head, her hair falling into her face. "You don't understand what he'll do to me."

"Oh, we understand." My voice drops lower. "We've lived it. We've felt it. And Nora…" I stop, my throat tightening. "Nora's gone because of him."

The silence stretches. The hum of the refrigerator cases fills the gap, loud and buzzing. Sarah presses her lips together, fighting herself.

"You know something," Sabrina pushes gently, stepping around until she's nearly face to face with her. "And you've been carrying it alone. Let it out."

Sarah's jaw trembles. She hugs herself tight, as if trying to hold her body together. "I shouldn't."

"You should," I counter. "You owe it to Nora."

Her shoulders sag. Her voice is barely audible. "She came to see him this past summer."

The world seems to tilt.

"She…barged into his office," Sarah continues, halting, shaky. "I tried to stop her, but she pushed past me. She was desperate. Furious. She wanted to expose him. Said she couldn't keep living with what he did to her." She stops again, choking on the words. Her eyes dart nervously to the end of the aisle. A couple wanders past, oblivious.

"What did he say?" I demand, but softly, to try not to spook her.

Sarah's voice cracks. "He told her she was playing with fire. The look in his eyes…" She shivers. "I knew then he would destroy her if she kept pushing."

Sabrina's hand brushes Sarah's arm, grounding her. "What happened after?"

Sarah's breath hitches. She looks at the linoleum floor, at the fluorescent lights flickering above. Finally, she raises her eyes, filled with tears. "He punished me. For letting her through. The way he does when he's angry."

The words hang in the air, heavier than lead.

"And then?" I whisper.

Sarah wipes her face roughly, as if trying to scrub the memory away. "He called in his hench men. Steve Bishop was there as well. I listened at the wall in the next room. I heard him… rattle something. Told them to follow her. Not to lose sight. To stick her with it." Her voice breaks. "He said, 'Tell the addict Donovan sends his best.'"

My heart lurches. Sabrina's hand flies to her chest.

"So he had her killed," I say, my throat dry.

Sarah closes her eyes and nods, one slow, painful movement, tears falling now. She tells us about her rape. The abuse. The others before her. She speaks with the ferocity of someone who has finally ripped the gag from her mouth. "I'm ready to bring him down," she says, voice trembling, yet louder now.

Sabrina pulls her to the side, already in journalist mode, pressing for details, for evidence, for the statement that will break this wide open.

I glance down at my phone. A text from Sam glows on the screen. *Just got to your place. Everyone's here.*

FIVE HEART

Christmas Eve dinner is officially postponed, indefinitely.

Chapter 27

Jonna

The dining table looks perfect. Too perfect, considering the mood. I was able to set up Christmas Eve dinner by myself. Candles glow in glass holders, their light flickering against polished silverware. Steam curls up from the roasted vegetables, and cranberry glaze catches the shine of the chandelier. Sam even pulled out a plate of cinnamon rolls she brought, the sugar glaze softening under the warmth of the kitchen. We all sit impatiently at the dining table, waiting for the missing centerpiece of the meal to arrive.

"The ham," Dexter mutters, checking the empty platter again. His tone is playful, but his shoulders are tight. "Can't have Christmas Eve without it."

"They'll be back," I tell him, though my eyes are on the clock. Dani and Sabrina left ages ago.

Clare twirls the stem of her wine glass, tapping it nervously. "They didn't forget, right? The store had it, didn't it?"

"They'll manage," Tom murmurs, pulling her closer.

Robbie swirls his wine. "We should've ordered Chinese," he mutters.

Sam gives a small laugh, brushing crumbs from her lap. "My first Christmas with all of you, and we're stalled by a ham." She tilts her head. "Honestly, it's sweet. Feels like family."

Dexter finally sits down, shaking his head. "Feels like waiting for detention." And then the door slams open.

The sound cracks through the silence. Dani and Sabrina step inside, grocery bag swinging from Sabrina's hand. Their faces are pale, set, carrying something heavier than a missing ham. Dexter starts, "Finally. What the hell took you—"

"Don't," says Dani. The room freezes.

Sabrina sets the bag down on the counter like it weighs a thousand pounds. "We saw Sarah," she says quietly.

"Sarah?" Robbie frowned. "Who's—"

"Donovan's assistant," Dani spits.

The name alone drains the warmth from the room. Clare bolts upright in her chair, her glass clinking against the table as she sets it down too fast. Tom stiffens beside her.

"She told us the truth." Dani's voice cracks. "Nora didn't kill herself. Donovan's men did. Steve was a part of the plan. Sarah heard them."

Clare's gasps so sharp I flinch. "No— No, that—"

"It's true," Sabrina whispers, her eyes wet. "She knows. She's been carrying it alone, but she finally said it."

Sam crosses the room, wrapping her arm around Dani's waist. Dani leans into her, her jaw trembling.

Robbie leans forward, incredulous. "Wait, you're telling me she just gave you that information? Out of nowhere? Why would she just tell you that?" Dani and Sabrina exchange a soft, heavy glance toward each other.

"She didn't tell us easily," Sabrina says at last, her voice low. "But she's lived it, too."

The table goes silent again.

Dani's voice breaks the stillness, quiet but steady: "Donovan hurt her. The same way he hurt Nora. The same way he tried with me, with all of us back then. She said Nora gave her courage… the last time she saw her, Nora begged her not to let him keep winning. Tonight was the first time she felt brave enough to speak."

The weight of it sits like lead over the table.

Dexter finally mutters, "Jesus Christ."

Clare presses shaking fingers to her mouth. "That's why Steve attacked me," she mumbles. Tom pulls her closer, rubbing her arm. Robbie shakes his head, whispering something that sounds like a prayer.

I swallow, my chest burning. Nora's ghost is everywhere, even in Sarah's voice.

"That's why she told us," says Dani, firmer now. "She's ready to leave Kaleidoscope for good. And she's ready to tell the truth."

The silence is broken only by the ticking clock until Dani reaches into her coat pocket. She unfolds a creased envelope and slides it across the table. It's a Kaleidoscope Records letterhead.

My stomach drops before I even read it.

If you continue with this so-called tribute show, I'll be there in person. I want to see your faces when I serve you with the lawsuit of your lifetime.

Signed: Donovan Blake.

Clare recoils like she touched fire. "Oh my God."

Robbie curses. Tom's jaw tightens, his eyes scanning the page again.

"Why didn't you tell us this sooner?" I ask carefully.

Dani's throat works. "Because I didn't want to ruin tonight without knowing for sure. I thought, maybe it was just another empty threat. But after what Sarah told us? He's not bluffing. He'll be there."

Sabrina straightens suddenly, resolve flashing in her eyes. "Then we don't waste time. I have her number. She gave it to me when I pulled her aside at the store. I can reach out tonight, ask her to come here, now. Get her statement on video while it's still fresh."

"You think she'll come?" Tom asks.

"She might," says Sabrina. "She doesn't want to carry this around anymore. If we give her a safe space, she'll do it. I know she will."

Dani nods. "And when we have that video? We don't hand it over quietly. We put it on the LED screens at Madison Square Garden. In front of everyone."

Clare's eyes widened. "You serious?"

"Yes." Fire sparks in her eyes. "We'll roll her statement during the show. Let the world hear it straight from her mouth. And when the camera pans to Donovan sitting in the audience, every lens will be on him. No spin. No escape."

Robbie whistles low. "That's very bold."

"It's justice," Dani snaps.

Sabrina leans forward, her hands clasped. "And if we coordinate with the police, have them waiting in the wings, he won't walk out of that arena free. Not this time."

Sam's voice is soft but certain. "He'll walk out in handcuffs."

The room falls silent once more, but this time, it isn't out of fear. It's resolve.

I raise my glass, steady now. "Then that's the plan. We finish the show for Nora, and Donovan Blake ends the night going straight to prison."

Chapter 28

Sabrina

Christmas morning is quiet in the city. The streets outside Dani's penthouse are nearly empty, a rare stillness over Manhattan. No car horns, no rushing footsteps, just the faint ringing of church bells in the distance and the muffled sound of children squealing somewhere down the block. Inside, though, my head is anything but quiet. I barely slept. After everything last night, the images keep replaying in my mind.

Sarah agreed to come over. Her trembling hands, her cracked voice. The way she kept flinching at shadows even though we locked the doors and shut the curtains.

She only let herself relax when Dani and I sat with her. Around the others, she was too shaken. I had to ask Jonna, Clare, Tom, Robbie, and Dexter to step out into the living room while I set up the camera.

She sat across from me at the kitchen table, a lamp pulled close for light. Her mascara was smudged from crying even before I pressed record. Her fingers twisted the hem of her sweater until the thread unraveled. But when she began to speak, her voice steadied with each word.

She told the truth. Every piece of it.

That Donovan had his men handle Nora. That she had heard them, seen enough to know. That he had hurt her too, used his power over her, broken her down the same way he had tried to break us. She confessed that she had been too scared to come forward until now. She said Nora had looked at her once, right before the end, and begged her not to let him win, to expose the monster within. Those words stayed with her, haunting her, until last night when she finally decided to let them out.

By the time she finished, her cheeks were streaked with tears. But she was free.

I shut the camera off and promised her she would be protected. Tom and Clare both swore to cover her as attorneys once the story went public, and Dani made her sit down with us until the police could be looped in. She would not have to stand alone. She would be under the police department's protection.

Now, this morning, I'm staring at my laptop with Sarah's video file saved and my article drafted. I titled it "Nora Hayes: Silenced Star, Silenced No More." The words look stark against the white screen, like they're waiting to explode. I poured everything into it. Every quote from Sarah. Every reference from Nora's journals. Every timeline detail. It's a puzzle, and the edges finally fit.

I set it to run on a timer, scheduled to go live the second our concert ends on January 1. My name will be at the top under the byline. I'll be the first reporter to break the truth.

I'm doing this for Nora, yes. But I would be lying if I said the ambition didn't spark in me too. This is the story of my lifetime, the kind of piece that will make headlines across the world. It will be dangerous, it will be messy, but it will change everything.

FIVE HEART

I close the laptop and look around Dani's penthouse. Christmas morning with no tree, no stockings, no family chatter. Just me, my sneakers, and the thought of rehearsal. The rest of the girls are already at the gym. The boys are out together to see the lit tree at Rockefeller. We don't have the luxury of anything so leisurely. The show is in one week.

The studio smells like old wood and lemon cleaner. The mirrors lining the walls fog up with each breath as we dance. The sound system blasts the first notes of "Just a Daydream," one of our oldest songs, a track that still makes fans scream like it was released yesterday.

Clare takes her place beside me, her hair tied back, determination written across her face. Dani steps forward, counting us in. Jonna takes the backline, her movements controlled and precise.

The beat drops, and we move as one.

Step, cross, pivot. Hands hit sharp angles. My lungs burn but my voice pushes through the chorus, singing while my body obeys the choreography. Clare glances at me in the mirror, grinning despite her sweat. Dani calls out corrections, pushing us harder, demanding we give everything even though it's Christmas Day.

"Again," she says, replaying the track.

We do it again, sharper this time.

"Again."

The third time, the moves sink into our bones. My arms ache, my legs feel heavy, but the music carries me. For a moment, I forget everything. Forget Donovan. Forget Sarah's trembling voice. Forget the weight of the article waiting in my laptop. I just feel the beat, the four of us in sync, like we never stopped being Five Heart.

When the song ends, we collapse against the mirrors, gasping for air.

"We still have it," Jonna says, smiling for the first time in days.

"Of course we do," Clare pants, tossing her ponytail back. "And wait until the fans hear us live again."

Dani nods, sweat glistening on her forehead. "We're ready. One more week."

That night, instead of a Christmas feast, we end up at a greasy burger joint off Seventh Avenue. The kind with torn vinyl booths, sticky menus, and neon signs buzzing in the window. Christmas lights dangle crookedly along the walls, half of them burned out.

We squeeze into a booth, shoulders pressed together. The table fills with fries, milkshakes, and burgers stacked high. The smell of grease and grilled onions clings to the air. We decided tonight's meal will be our last hoorah before the concert, since dinner was, yet again, interrupted last night.

"This is the best thing I've eaten in forever," Dani says with a full mouth, dunking fries into ketchup.

"You said that about the rehearsal snacks too," Clare teases, but she is laughing.

Jonna raises her soda cup, lifting it like champagne. "To Nora. To the concert. To all of us." We clinked our paper cups together, the fizz bubbling over the rims.

"I just wish she were here," Clare murmurs, staring down at her food.

"She is," I say quickly, firm enough that she looks up. "Every time we sing, every time we hit a note, she's with us. She always will be."

Clare smiles faintly, eyes shining with tears.

Dani leans back, stretching her arms over the booth. "We're ready. Our vocals are solid, our choreography's locked. The fans are going to lose their minds. And Donovan? He has no idea what's coming."

Jonna smirks. "He's walking into a trap."

"And walking out in cuffs," Clare adds, determination cutting through the softness.

I look at the three of them, my throat tightening. "No matter what happens, I love you guys."

Jonna reaches across the table, sliding her hand into mine. Clare follows. Dani sets hers on top. Four hands stacked together over greasy wrappers and ketchup stains, the kind of moment that feels stronger than any contract, stronger than any threat.

"For Nora," Jonna whispers.

"For us," I add.

"For the takedown," Dani says with a grin.

We laugh, loud and messy, and for a little while the weight lifts. It's a Christmas for the books. In that tiny burger joint, surrounded by the smell of grease and festive lights strung crooked, we feel untouchable.

And in seven days, the world will know why.

Chapter 29

Dani

The streets are alive again, back to their bustling tendencies. Taxi horns blast in sharp bursts, delivery bikes weave through lanes like restless fish in a current, and the smell of roasted nuts from a corner cart drifts into the cold air. Sam and I jog side by side, our strides syncing naturally with each block we pass. The chill nips at my cheeks, but the warmth of her presence keeps me steady. She glances around wide-eyed, taking in the noise and rhythm of the city. She is a Tennessee girl through and through, and the rush of New York still feels like an entirely different planet for her.

"Let's stop at this smoothie shop coming up, it's delicious," I say between breaths.

She nods, her ponytail swishing behind her, and together we round the corner. The bright awning greets us, and we push the glass door open. Immediately the sound of industrial blenders drowns out the street noise, the heavy scent of spinach, kale, and citrus hitting me all at once. It's sharp, earthy, and overwhelming in a strangely refreshing way.

We plop down at a small wooden table near the door, the chill clinging to us as we peel off our gloves. I tug my ball cap lower over my forehead. With luck, no one will recognize me here. The shop is nearly empty, just a barista humming off-key and two college kids sharing a laptop in the back.

I order us two Purple Flamingos, the kind that leave your tongue stained violet. When they arrive, condensation slides down the plastic cups and we sip through the straws, smiling over the rims at one another.

"Good call coming here," she says, laughter bubbling up between her sips.

I reach for her hand, her skin soft and warm in mine, and I lace our fingers together.

"Thank you for being here," I say, my voice dropping low, weighted with more than casual gratitude.

"Of course. It's the holidays and regardless of the concert, I want to spend my first holiday season with my girlfriend," she replies sheepishly.

My smile takes over my whole face, stretching wide, refusing to be tamed. "I mean really being here. For me. For my friends. With everything that we've found out about… Nora." Saying her name aloud cracks something inside me. A heavy wave of sorrow rolls over, tightening my chest.

"She is going to get her justice. And so are you, Dani. He hurt you, too." Sam's eyes are wide, full of a fire I both admire and lean into.

I nod slowly. My mind drifts unwillingly to the dark corners I have tried to board up. I see Donovan again. The way he leaned close, whispering that he would show me how to kiss a boy. I had already been confused about who I was, unsure of what my feelings meant, and I thought maybe he was helping me. Maybe this was guidance. I never realized the predator lurking beneath his smile.

Another memory, sharp and cruel. His hands on me as he explained what second base meant, an excuse to touch where his fingers never should have been. The recollection makes me shudder, my entire body stiffening at the thought.

Sam squeezes my hand tighter. "We are going to get that son of a bitch."

"I just hope our plan works," I whisper, tilting my gaze upward, sending a small prayer to anyone, anything that might be listening.

"It will. And when it does, I'll be in VIP watching first row." She grins wickedly, her expression equal parts love and vengeance. The thought steadies me.

After our smoothies, we jog back through the crowded sidewalks, the city buzzing louder as evening approaches. When we finally reach my building, the guard greets us warmly and ushers us into the private elevator. It hums as it carries us to the top floor, my sanctuary above the chaos.

Inside the penthouse, the air is cooler and still, scented faintly of lavender from the diffuser by the window. I head straight for the kitchen, pulling a glass pitcher of lemon water from the fridge. The slices float lazily inside, tiny bubbles clinging to the rind. I fill two glasses, the cold stinging my fingers as I hand one to Sam. She settles onto a stool at the island, watching me with curiosity while I stand and chug, feeling the water run sharp and clean down my throat.

"You know what," I say, setting the glass down with a small thud.

She arches a brow. "What?"

"We should throw Clare an engagement party." The thought makes me smile instantly, already spinning into plans.

"You don't think that's adding too much to your plate? The concert's in four days," Sam says, her brow creased with concern.

"I just feel bad. Every time we get together to celebrate something, something crazy happens. Poor Clare and Tom haven't been celebrated properly. I feel awful."

"So, what are you thinking?" she asks, leaning in.

"Let's surprise the both of them. I want Tom to feel welcomed into the family completely. Tomorrow, I have to go to the venue all day to help lay out the stage map, lighting, and our special effects with the manager, but the next day is kind of a lull day. Let's invite all our friends to Club Macanudo. I know the owners and it's totally up Clare's alley there. Luxury lounge, expensive wines, open cigar bar, completely her speed." I unlock my phone, already picturing the setting.

"That sounds so fun. I'll help with whatever you need," Sam says, her smile matching mine.

Within minutes, I design an elegant e-invite, soft gold script on a black background, and send it off to our circle. One by one, the names confirm in my head. Our friends, family, the people who will stand with us through the storm.

I head over to my sectional and plop down. Sam joins me, curling her legs under herself, sipping her water. Her eyes flick toward the laptop I left open on the coffee table, papers stacked neatly beside it. "What's all this? Don't tell me you're working right before the biggest show of your life."

I smirk, dragging the laptop closer. "Maybe. Or maybe I'm just setting us up for something bigger."

Sam raises an eyebrow, intrigued. "Bigger than a sold-out tribute concert?"

I glance at her, lips twitching into a grin. "Look what just got approved."

I tilt the screen so she can see, only for a second. Her eyes widen, and she gasps, clapping her hand over her mouth. "Dani. You didn't."

"Oh, I did." I snap the laptop shut, sliding it out of reach like it's a secret too hot to touch.

She leans in, excitement bubbling. "This is huge. Do the girls know?"

"Not yet," I say, smirking at her reaction. "They'll find out when the time is right. And trust me, they're gonna flip."

Sam laughs, bouncing on the couch cushion, practically glowing with pride. "You're out of your mind. But in the best way."

"Guilty," I say, sinking back with a satisfied sigh. "Let's just keep this between us until after the engagement party and the show. No spoilers."

She squeezes my hand, eyes sparkling. "Deal. But Dani? This changes everything."

I grin, letting the weight of her words settle in. Exactly what I was going for.

Chapter 30

Clare

Two days until the tribute show. Two days until we see our fans again. Two more days until I get to see the look on Donovan's scum face when Sarah's statement blasts across the stadium for everyone to hear. I play it out in my head like a movie as I sit wrapped in a cotton ivory robe on the terrace of our hotel suite, watching the sun crawl its way over the Manhattan skyline. The city hums beneath us, quiet for now, but full of promise. I lift my latte to my lips, the steam brushing my nose, warming me against the chill of dawn.

The glass door slides open and Tom sinks into the wicker chair beside me, his own mug steaming in his hands. His hair is messy from sleep, his grin lazy.

"Good morning," I say with a devilish smile, still gazing out at the horizon, still savoring the thought of Donovan being dragged away in handcuffs.

"Good morning, beautiful," Tom answers, tilting his head to catch what's stealing my focus.

We decided to stay at this hotel the rest of the week, close to the venue, no interruptions. Just us. I've been soaking up every second of this one-on-one time with him, every stolen kiss and whispered secret in between rehearsals.

"Damien was served the papers yesterday," Tom says suddenly, his tone low but firm.

My head snaps toward him, curiosity flashing in my eyes. "And?"

"And he signed them. My team got the fax this morning." His eyes light up.

My lips curl into a smile, teasing it out slow. "What does that mean?"

"It means… you are officially divorced!" He opens his arms wide like the words themselves are champagne bubbles.

I don't hesitate. I climb across the table and launch myself into his lap, my robe flying open behind me. "Do you mean it?" I ask, cupping his handsome face in my palms, searching those glimmering crystal eyes that catch the sunrise like glass.

"I absolutely do," he says, sealing his answer with a kiss.

"Oh my god!" I pull back, my voice sharp with delight. "The house is mine!"

"Speaking of that," he says smoothly, stroking my cheek, voice dipped in something secretive. "I have somewhere I want to take you today."

"As long as it's before three o'clock. We've got rehearsal and a venue walk-through to set the stage," I remind him as I rise from his lap. I pause at the sliding door, fingers tugging at the tie of my robe. Then I let it drop to the floor, bare skin flashing to the city below. I glance back at him over my shoulder, giving him the *look*.

He growls low in his throat, tears his own robe off, scoops me into his arms like I'm nothing but a feather, and throws me down onto the bed.

Tom rented an Aston Martin for the week, sleek black with a low growl, though the poor man barely fits inside with his build. The car roars low through the winter streets until he pulls up in front of a row of gorgeous historic townhomes in Greenwich Village. The December wind bites at my cheeks, teasing my scarf into my face.

"What do you think?" Tom asks, pointing toward the street.

I wrestle with my scarf, hair flying across my eyes. He steps behind me, gentle, tucking the fabric into my Bouclé coat, sweeping my hair out of my face with that easy touch of his.

I finally see it. A white brick townhome draped in ivy vines, the edges softened by nature. The front door is stained glass that glimmers like jewels in the weak sun. A tiny garden of red roses lines the stoop, stubbornly blooming against the cold.

"This is stunning," I breathe.

"Come on," Tom says, tugging me forward with boyish impatience.

"We can't just go in someone's house!" I hiss, giggling as he pulls me up the stoop.

The front door gives under his hand, unlocked. My eyes widen. "Tom, we can't just break into someone's house," I grit between my teeth, glancing around, praying no one saw us.

He doesn't answer, just pulls me deeper inside, and suddenly I forget how to breathe. Sunlight floods through massive windows, dancing across linen-colored walls framed with alabaster molding. Vintage brass sconces glow faintly even in daylight, as if holding the house's history in their light.

He pulls me into the kitchen, where stark white cabinetry gleams, crystal knobs catching the light like diamonds. Black and white quartz counters stretch wide, and a matte black mosaic backsplash snakes across the walls.

Before I can catch my breath, we're running upstairs, laughter bouncing off the walls. The loft opens wide, bigger than my California living room, with a bed facing a bay window that frames the skyline like a painting.

"This is the prettiest townhome I've ever seen," I say, mesmerized.

"Do you love it?" he asks, voice edged with something more.

I spin to him, eyes narrowed, finger pressed to his chest. "Don't fuck with me."

"It's ours," he says, slipping a golden key into my palm and curling my fingers tight around it.

My jaw drops. "What?"

"I was looking at this place the first time we came to the city together. The second time, I knew we needed something here. I closed on it yesterday while you were at rehearsal. And when the divorce papers became official, I knew it was time to tell you. It's ours, Clare. Our home away from home."

My heart leaps, a rush of heat exploding in my chest. I throw myself at him, pinning him down to the hardwood with a squeal. "You bought us a home just for when we come to New York?"

"I think we're going to be in New York a lot more than you think over this lifetime," he laughs, pulling me closer, hands gripping my hips.

"That's literally the sweetest thing anyone has ever done for me!" I say, voice pitched with disbelief and joy.

I soak in his face, every detail of him, the man I stumbled into but can't imagine life without. "I love you, Thomas Wayne Gallagher."

"I love you, Clare Gabriella Devon."

Clothes still tangled around us, I guide him out of his slacks and slide onto him, moving slow, deliberate. He fills me completely. His hands slide up my thighs, circling my hips, guiding me into a tempo that's more about connection than urgency. I move steady, rolling my hips, feeling every inch of him as I tilt my head back and let the moment wash over me.

He sits up, wrapping his arms around my back, holding me flush against him as though he needs my heartbeat pressed against his to believe this is real. His lips trail down my collarbone, and I thread my fingers through his hair, tugging, whispering his name in a way that makes him groan.

"This house is ours," he murmurs against my skin. "Every wall, every room. I wanted it to be the place we always come back to."

My chest tightens. We are writing ourselves into the walls, carving our story into the foundation. I kiss him deeply, slower this time, our bodies moving like two colliding waves.

When it builds and the pleasure curls sharp and hot inside me, I cup his face, needing him to see me. "I need you," I whisper, voice breaking.

He looks at me like I'm everything he's ever wanted. "You're all I've ever needed," he says, pulling me closer as we fall apart together, trembling in unison.

I collapse against his chest, his heartbeat steady under my ear, his breath warm in my hair. For a moment, I just let myself rest there, safe, claimed, exactly where I'm supposed to be. Then I lift my head, smirk tugging at my lips. "You know we can't just stop here, right?"

He raises a brow, amused. "Oh? And what exactly do you have in mind, Ms. Devon?"

I press a kiss to his jaw, still straddling him, my grin widening. "If this place is really ours, we're going to have to christen every single room."

He groans, tipping his head back with a laugh, already sliding his hands down my back again. "You're insatiable."

"I'm thorough," I correct, climbing off him and tugging at his hand. "Now, are you coming with me to the kitchen, or do I have to start without you?"

His laugh echoes through the townhouse as he scoops me up again, carrying me down the hall, both of us giddy with love, lust, and the promise of making this home ours in every possible way.

Dani texted me earlier during our christenings, telling me to meet her and the girls for a drink so we could go over the stadium layout. She added that Tom could come with, so he wouldn't have to sit in the hotel by himself.

Back in our room, we change and pack up to check out, ready to move into the townhouse for the rest of the stay. Tom tosses our bags into the trunk while I adjust the straps of my heels. We slip into the Aston Martin, the engine purring with that quiet confidence only expensive cars carry, and Tom pulls us into the city stream.

We cut through Midtown, weaving toward Central Park, the streets glowing with that golden New York dusk. The closer we get, the more butterflies stir in my stomach. I don't know why. It's supposed to be just drinks and planning, but something about Dani's message on the phone sounded mischievous.

When we pull up in front of Club Macanudo, the marquee lights glow like it belongs in a movie. The place has an old-world elegance. A cigar bar mixed with a wine lounge.

"This looks nice," I say as Tom rounds the car to open my door. He takes my hand and steadies me as I step out. I smooth the wrinkles in my cream silk dress, tugging my trench coat closed against the cool, biting breeze that whistles down the avenue.

Tom matched me without even trying, in a cream silk button-down with wooden buttons and dark jeans. We look like we coordinated our attire.

Inside, the burgundy interior wraps around us like velvet. Smoke curls lazily above leather chairs, and the clink of wine glasses fills the room. We stroll up to the hostess stand.

"Hi, we're meeting a few girls here." I give her my most polite smile.

She looks uncertain until I lean in and whisper, "Dani Rose."

That does it. Her whole face lights up. "Right this way."

We follow her down a narrow hall until the room opened up to a bar glowing under soft amber light.

"Surprise!"

The word explodes around me. For a second, I don't even process it. My eyes dart from face to face, so many familiar ones, until it all lands at once. There are balloons shaped like giant engagement rings, some spelling out 'Congratulations.' Bouquets of flowers spill across the bar, gift bags sparkle under the lights, and bottles of champagne sit with white bows tied neatly at their tops.

"Oh my!" I clasp my hands over my mouth.

"Congratulations, Clare and Tom!" Selma calls, rushing over to wrap us both up in her arms. She leans close to my ear. "I better be styling you in your wedding dress," she teases with a laugh.

I smile so wide my cheeks hurt and hug her tighter. "You already know you're hired."

"How the hell?" I reach Jonna, hugging her and then Dexter.

"It was all Dani," she says knowingly. "She pulled it together a couple days ago."

My mother appears next, as if she's materialized from thin air. "Mom!" I yelp, shocked. She lives all the way out in Buffalo, yet here she is.

She wraps her arms around me, her perfume overwhelming and sharp. "You have a lot of explaining to do," she mutters under her breath before plastering on her fakest smile for Tom.

Typical. My mother had always been like this. Growing up, everything revolved around her. Her moods. Her stories. Her needs. I was never the lead, only the extension. Until she decided I could be useful.

She shaped me carefully, deliberately, molding me into something loud, confident, undeniable. She taught me how to walk into a room and make people look. How to smile like I meant it. How to perform. Not so I could be happy, but so I could be chosen. By the right man. The rich one. The one who could take care of both of us.

When Five Heart happened, she lived through me without shame. Every headline felt like hers. Every spotlight belonged to her too. She is the reason I know how to command a room.

And she is the reason I never stop clawing for it.

Before I can spiral into those thoughts, Dani and Sam sweep me into their arms.

"So, were you surprised?" Dani asks, beaming so hard she could have lit the room herself.

"Yes! You are crazy for doing this right before our show," I say, half laughing, half scolding, and hugging her tight.

"With everything going on, we totally overlooked your moment. You deserve to be celebrated." Her eyes soften, and I have to press my hand against my chest to keep the emotions from bursting out of me.

I glance over and find Tom still held hostage by my mother's grip on his arm. "Let me save him," I mutter. I march over and wedge myself between them. "Mom, we have our rounds. Please don't overwhelm my fiancé."

Tom easily follows my tug, flexing those arms that had already won my mother's approval. We make our way toward Sabrina and the boys from No Reason, where I suddenly realize who else is there—the Gallaghers. The family people whisper about, like royalty. My pulse skips.

Not intimidating at all, I tell myself. Lie.

They congratulate us, and before I can blink, Tom's father hands us a check. For three million dollars.

"Congratulations to you both," he says warmly.

I stare at the check, blinking like I might have hallucinated it. His father is just as handsome as Tom, only polished silver at the temples. And his mother could be my twin. Blonde, petite, curves in all the same places.

"Tom has always had great taste in women," she says with a laugh, kissing me on both cheeks.

"Clare, this is Arnold and Melanie Gallagher, my parents," Tom says, his pride glowing as bright as his grin. He holds the check tightly, like he doesn't quite trust me not to drop it.

"It's so lovely to finally meet you both," I say, shaking their hands. "I absolutely adore your son. Thank you so much for your generous gift."

"Tom has talked about you since you came to work for him three years ago," Melanie says, her eyes sparkling. "He told me one night, Mom, I met my wife today at work."

I snap my head toward Tom, stunned. "You said that?"

He grins. "I've always known. From the first day you introduced yourself as Clare Devon, my competition."

I giggle, remembering that very first day. "I was always after your job," I tease.

Arnold pulls me into a strong embrace. "Welcome to the family." He grabs his wine glass from the bar and taps it with a knife. The chatter dies.

"Good evening, everyone. I would like to thank Danielle and Samantha for calling us and holding this special event for our wonderful son and soon-to-be daughter-in-law. We are over the moon that our boy has found the love of his life, and we wish them many years of good health and happiness."

My eyes sting with tears as glasses clink around the room.

Dani lifts her glass next. "I would also like to thank everyone who has helped make our upcoming show in T-minus thirty-six hours possible. We couldn't have done it without you!"

Everyone raises their glasses again, voices overlapping in cheers.

A wave of warmth, or maybe just champagne, gives me the push to speak. "Last but not least, I want to toast to friendship. Dani, Sabrina, Jonna and I haven't been this close since we originally started Five Heart. I never realized how lonely my life has been until these girls came back into it. And I want to thank Nora for that. I know she is here with us and has been showing us her truth. I hope she is proud of us, and I know she will get the justice she deserves very soon."

The girls and I lock eyes, tears glittering.

"Here, here!" Sabrina shouts. We all recite it together, our voices uniting like the chords of an old familiar song.

I hold onto the moment, reluctant to let it go, then blurt out, "Oh, and before I forget. Tom bought us a townhouse here in the city. So, you'll be seeing a lot more of me."

Dani gasps. "Wait, what? You're moving here?"

"Not moving permanently, but I'll be splitting my time," I say, beaming. "We'll finally have a real place to crash in New York instead of hotels or Dani's place. And obviously you three have keys. I expect constant visits."

Jonna smirks. "Clare, you're basically forcing us to reunite the band for good."

"Exactly," I say proudly. "Five Heart, back in business."

Dani smiles devilishly at the statement.

The girls crack up, clinking their glasses against mine again. The champagne fizzes over the rim, and for the first time in a long time, I feel like everything is aligning exactly how it's meant to.

Chapter 31

Jonna

"Three… two… one… HAPPY NEW YEAR!"
The countdown echoes across the city, and the night sky erupts
in a dazzling storm of fireworks. From our hotel balcony,
Dexter and I watch as the glowing ball finally drops in Times
Square, the streets below erupting in cheers. The kids jump and
twirl beside us, their tiny hands clutching glittery party
streamers.

Dexter leans down and kisses me softly as Frank
Sinatra's "New York, New York" roars across the blocks,
carried up to us by the cold winter air. DJ and Harley squeal
with laughter, running little circles around us until they're
breathless. Behind the sliding glass doors, Finn and Alissa are
curled up safe and sound in the adjoining suite, oblivious to the
chaos of celebration below.

I scoop DJ up in one arm and Harley in the other,
planting kisses on their cheeks. "Happy New Year, my babies!"

I beam, my heart swelling.

"Happy New Year, Mommy!" Harley shouts back, her tiny voice competing with the orchestra of fireworks.

Dexter pulls us all into a warm, tangled group hug, his arms closing around our little circle. For a moment it feels like nothing else exists but the four of us, wrapped in the golden glow of the city lights.

He ruffles DJ's hair, then points to the two of them with mock sternness. "It's past midnight. Which means it's way past your bedtime."

The kids groan dramatically, arms crossed in perfect unison. "But we aren't tired!" Harley whines, dragging out the last word as if it might convince him.

I laugh, stifling a yawn. "Well, Mommy's tired. And Mommy has to wake up extra early tomorrow for her concert." Just the thought of it makes my chest flutter.

I let myself picture it again: standing on that massive heart-shaped stage, looking out at row after row of seats. All 19,500 of them filled. Yesterday Dani walked us through the arena, her voice steady but her eyes brimming with pride. Seeing the layout from backstage, the lights glittering across the crimson velvet seats, was almost too much to take in. We rehearsed until our legs went weak, until the four of us could move and sing as one heartbeat. It was surreal.

Once the fireworks fade, we herd the kids back inside, tucking DJ and Harley into the third bedroom with their blankets and stuffed animals. Finn and Alissa are already dreaming peacefully in the second bedroom, their little chests rising and falling in rhythm. The quiet hush of the suite feels like a protective cocoon after the roar of the city.

Dexter and I slip into the master bedroom. The sheets are cool against my skin, the lights dim. I roll onto my side, propping one hand beneath my pillow. Our eyes meet in the silence, searching each other for something unspoken.

He finally exhales, a quiet sigh that carries both weight and relief. "Today's the day," he murmurs. "Are you nervous?"

I nod, vulnerable. "We have it all down. We sound amazing. But… it's not the same without Nora." The truth slips out before I can stop it. "She made the group."

A tear escapes, trailing down my cheek. Dexter catches it with the pad of his thumb, brushing it away as though it were fragile. "She is so proud of you," he says, his lips curving into a gentle smile. "I'm so proud of you." His words make my throat tighten. "I just want you to know how grateful I am to have you," he continues. "Not only are you gorgeous, an amazing performer, and a super mom, you are the best wife I could ever imagine being married to. I am so sorry if I haven't been the best husband for you."

I blink, startled. "What do you mean? You are the most amazing husband."

He looks down, his hands fidgeting in the sheets. "Because, I wasn't supportive of the tribute show at first. I worried it would wedge itself between us, between our family. I see now that it hasn't. Even with the cease-and-desist, you weren't named. I just feel bad I didn't support you fully."

I reach out and graze his cheek with the back of my palm. His skin is warm beneath my touch. "You being here with me now, and tomorrow is support. Your concerns were valid. It's awful to say, but I never had any run-ins with Donovan or Steve. I always slipped into the background of the group. And my parents were always there. Picking me up from the studio, from the label. Always watching. Maybe their presence shielded me from what the others faced."

My chest aches as the images resurface. Nora, left waiting after practice, her eyes wide and hollow while the rest of us climbed into cars with our families. The way she forced a smile when her ride was late. The shadows she carried that we never noticed.

"I can't believe we didn't see it," I whisper, shaking my head. "I can't believe Dani never said anything, either. I wish it had been me. I could have been the strong one for everyone. I could have protected them."

Dexter's hand finds mine. "You are going to protect future girls in the industry in less than twenty-four hours. I promise, justice will be served."

His words settle in me like a bomb. My eyes grow heavy, the exhaustion of rehearsal, of emotion, of longing pulling me under. I fall asleep face to face with my husband, wrapped in the steady beat of his breath. He is my comfort. My home.

"Mommy."

My eyes flutter open abruptly to find Finn perched on top of me, his little nose pressed against mine. His grin is wide and mischievous, his breath warm in the cool room.

"Good morning," I mumble, my voice still thick with sleep as I grab him gently and swing him over between Dexter and me. The clock on the nightstand reads 4:55 a.m., five minutes before the alarm was even set to ring. At this point, I don't really need an alarm anymore. My nerves have already taken over.

"I'm hungry," Finn whispers, his voice growing impatient, as though the day itself has not quite started yet.

Dexter stirs at the sound, rolling over to face us, his hair sticking up in soft tufts. He stretches, a yawn escaping his lips. "Hey, bud," he says warmly. "Why don't you go back into bed for a little while? We'll order some room service for breakfast."

Finn nods obediently and hops off the bed, his little feet pattering across the floor as he disappears into his room.

I sit up, rubbing my eyes, and a yawn pulls through me. But then it hits me, the jolt, the spark. Today is not just another

233

morning. It is *the* morning. Our tribute show. My heart races as the weight of it lands in my chest.

I grab my phone and open our Five Heart Lives group chat. My screen glows in the darkness, and at the very top is a new message from Dani:

Some updates, girls. On the way to the venue. Hair and makeup arriving in two hours. No singing until the show, save your voices. Police have Sarah's video statement and Nora's journal evidence. Eric has come forward as a witness to her sexual abuse. Police are on stand by for Donovan's arrival at the venue. They are complying with our terms to arrest Donovan when we show the video live. Let's get this fucker.

Clare and Sabrina have already liked the message. I tap the little heart to join them, my thumb trembling with adrenaline. A surge of electricity floods through me, and in an instant I am wide awake.

I spring out of bed and head into the shower. The hot water hits my skin in a rush, loosening my muscles and washing away the haze of sleep. By the time I step out, Dexter is in the other room on the phone with the lobby, placing our breakfast order. His voice is low and calm, grounding me even as my nerves buzz like static.

Twenty minutes pass, and I throw on my black zip-up jacket and matching yoga pants, pulling my black sparkly ball cap snug over my damp hair. When I step into the suite's living area, the kids are already gathered around the table, tiny mouths full, Dexter dishing pancakes onto their plates. The smell of maple syrup lingers in the air.

I swipe a piece of toast from the tray and take a bite, then steal Harley's apple juice to wash it down.

"Hey!" she protests, glaring at me with wide eyes as though I have committed the ultimate betrayal.

I smirk, bending down to kiss the tops of their heads. "Mommy has to go to the venue with Auntie Clare, Sabrina, and Dani. I can't wait to see your little faces tonight, front row at the show." My smile stretches wider with each word.

I lean toward Dexter and cup his cheeks, which are stuffed full of pancakes, before crushing my lips to his. The taste of warm syrup lingers against my mouth. "I love you," I whisper, my eyes locking onto his.

"I love you too," he replies, muffled through his mouthful of food, his eyes twinkling.
I linger in the doorway, holding the moment in my chest like a photograph. Their faces, their laughter, the hum of the city outside. It is all fuel for what I have to do tonight.

"Make sure to scream louder than you have ever screamed when you see me on stage," I tease, pointing playfully at the kids.

"Yay!" they squeal, clapping their syrupy hands together in unison.

Downstairs, Sabrina and Robbie are waiting for me in her burgundy Jaguar, parked out front the hotel. She honks as soon as she sees me, her fiery red hair swept into a high ponytail. Robbie leans casually in the passenger seat, a navy Yankees beanie pulled low over his ears.

I climb into the back, sinking into the cool leather and leaning forward between them. "Good morning," I say, grinning. "You dyed your hair back?"

Sabrina glances at me, her lips pulling into a sly smirk that mirrors the energy coursing through my veins. "I can't be Sabrina Daniel of Five Heart without my signature red hair. You ready for the return of a century?"

"Let's do this!" I shout, pumping a fist into the air.

Robbie lets out a triumphant "Woohoo!" just as Sabrina revs the engine. The Jaguar growls to life, and in a blur of motion and laughter, she floors it down 31st Street, the city lights streaking past us.

We arrive at the arena through the quiet back entrance, the world outside sealed away behind heavy steel doors. The air is cool and sterile, carrying the faint echo of our footsteps as we walk down the endless hall lined with closed concession stands and freshly polished floors that gleam beneath the fluorescent lights. Every sound bounces back at us in the emptiness, making the silence feel heavier, more dramatic.

Turning the corner, the space suddenly opens, and there it is—the heart-shaped stage, towering in front of us like a monument waiting to breathe. My chest tightens at the sight. In ten short hours, this stage will belong to us. Our voices, our history, our story will pour out into the cavernous arena, and nearly twenty thousand people will be listening.

"This is insane," I whisper, my eyes wide, unable to contain the awe.

Sabrina slips her hand into mine and gives it a squeeze, her face glowing. "It's just like the old days." She giggles and throws her arms around Robbie, hugging him tightly with a burst of girlish excitement.

"A little birdie told me you're our guest artist tonight on stage," I say sheepishly, watching their affection with a knowing smile. Robbie and Sabrina glance at one another, their cheeks lighting up, their expressions soft and full of pride.

"We wrote a song together," Sabrina admits. "Think of it as an acoustic surprise song. No choreography, just us with our guitars and a microphone." Robbie leans over and kisses her cheek gently, their closeness radiating warmth.

"I think that's great. It will be a good transition for us to change into our next costume," I say, already arranging the night's sequence in my head, trying to balance the logistics with the magic.

We continue down the length of the stage, our footsteps light, almost skipping, until we reach the entryway lined with dressing rooms. The energy here is buzzing. Hair and makeup stations are already being set up, counters filled with rows of hot tools, bottles of hairspray, and eyeshadow palettes that shimmer in every shade of the rainbow.

Inside, Dani and Clare are already in their sparkly robes, each reflecting their signature colors. Clare glows in fuchsia, her robe glittering under the bright bulbs, while Dani shines in gold. Dani's hair is half in rollers, the other half hanging flat against her shoulders. Clare has only her eyeshadow applied, the shimmer catching the light as she spins around.

The second they spot us, they leap out of their seats.

"Ahhhh!" Clare screams, her voice shrill with joy as she rushes forward. My best friend of twenty years. My partner in every crime worth remembering. I catch her in my arms, squeezing her tightly.

"Jon! We are really doing this," she squeals, crushing me even harder.

I kiss her cheek with exaggerated force, unable to release my excitement in any other way. She turns and plants a kiss on my lips, both of us laughing through the sheer chaos of it.

"I love you!" she screams.

"I love you!" I echo, and soon we are bouncing together, arms locked, unable to contain the flood of nerves and excitement.

Dani and Sabrina watch us with wide smiles before pulling me into their own hugs. For a moment, the four of us stand in a circle of pure joy.

"Put your robes on, and when you're ready I have to show you all something," Dani says, her eyes glinting with anticipation. She gestures toward the rack where silver and emerald robes hang neatly, waiting for us.

Robbie kisses Sabrina goodbye, promising to return in a few hours with the rest of the boys from No Reason.

Sabrina and I slip into our robes, the fabric cool and heavy against our skin. We join Clare and Dani on the leather couch, the four of us lined up under the glow of the ring light. The sparkles from our robes catch and scatter the brightness, each of us glowing in our iconic colors.

"We're just missing violet sparkle for Nora," Clare says softly, her lips curving into a pout. The room grows still. We bow our heads for a moment, letting the silence honor her, the fifth heart that will always belong to us.

"I have something big to tell you girls," Dani finally says. Her lips twist into a mischievous smile. We all glance at one another, confused but leaning in, curiosity brimming.

"I wanted to surprise you with this sooner, but I figured the day of the show would be the best way. Tonight, instead of introducing ourselves as Five Heart, we introduce ourselves as our new entity, The Hearts!" she exclaims. She unlocks her phone and flashes the glowing screen, displaying the official PDF document.

"What!" Clare shrieks, snatching the phone from Dani's hands and scanning the text with wide eyes. Sabrina grasps it next, then passes it to me. My chest tightens as the reality sinks in. We all glance at one another before bursting into tears. "How did you do this?" I choke out through my tears.

"I needed a backup plan so Donovan couldn't sue us for using the Five Heart name," Dani explains, dabbing at her eyes with the sleeve of her robe. "Do you like it?"

"Like it? We love it!" Clare answers for all of us.

Sabrina and I nod, still wiping our cheeks, still trying to process the enormity of what Dani has done.

"Well, I'm so glad. Since you love it so much, I was hoping maybe it could be our permanent name, for the rest of our career together." Dani's eyes glitter with something deeper, her smile widening into a grin.

"What do you mean?" I ask cautiously, my heart beating faster.

"If you girls would do me the courtesy of joining The Hearts permanently. I already talked to my label this week, and they will sign us. No more solo Dani. I want to be with my girls. We will re-record our old singles as The Hearts with different beats, and create an entirely new catalog. What do you say?" Her voice is breathless, eager, waiting for our answer.

My head spins. In my mind, flashes of my children's faces appear. Their laughter, their little voices. To commit to this would mean time away from them. I shake my head, torn. Being a mother always comes first.

Before I can find the words, Dani reaches for my hands and holds them firmly. "Jonna, I know your kids are priority. That's why we'll record at the studio around the corner from your house, Violet Hayes Records."

I blink, trying to recall a studio by that name near my home. Dani chuckles at my confusion.

"I bought the building yesterday," she says, her grin widening. "The studio is ours. We control the inflow and outflow. We control what we record. And it is all at the convenience of being close to you. Since we are all in the city, it's only an hour's drive. It is worth it to know you will be part of it all." My heart swells, my chest heavy with love for these women.

"Dani, this is the most special thing," I whisper, overcome.

"I want to be part of The Hearts," Clare says, her eyes shining.

"Me too," Sabrina adds, sniffling.

"Count me in," I breathe, the explosion of emotion too much to contain.

We collapse into a hug.

"I know you have your lives. I know I am asking a lot of you, walking away from that," Dani says fiercely, her voice carrying conviction. "But I promise this time will be different. We make the rules. We hold the cards. I want The Hearts to change the way of the industry. We can be a beacon to new artists everywhere. They can come to us to feel safe. We'll pave the path to a new era in music and the industry."

Her words swell like an anthem, filling every corner of the room. We weep tears of joy, clinging to one another, and in that moment a warmth spreads around us, almost tangible. It feels as though Nora herself has wrapped her arms around us from beyond, guiding us into this new beginning.

Chapter 32

Clare

I stare longingly into the mirror, hardly recognizing the woman looking back at me. The reflection is dazzling, a vision sculpted out of light and sparkle. My blonde hair falls in big, bouncy curls that cascade over my shoulders, the kind of curls that belong on a movie screen. On one side, a rhinestone clip grips the waves, glimmering under the dressing room lights. Every tilt of my head sets it ablaze, a small crown announcing that tonight is mine.

My eye shadow gleams like crushed jewels, shimmering with each blink, while my lips, painted a vivid pink, glow against my flawless skin. I can almost hear the echo of my teenage self in this exact moment eleven years ago at our last concert.

My gaze drops down to my body suit. Fuchsia sequins cling tightly to my frame, hugging every curve with unapologetic confidence. The fabric reflects the glow of the ring light, tossing flecks of hot pink fire across the walls. Around my waist, sparkly tassels sway like a skirt, brushing against my thighs every time I shift my weight. My legs look endless in sheer nude tights, tapering down into white leather knee-high boots encrusted with glitter that sparkles like frost with every tiny movement.

Then I see it, winking at me from my finger. My engagement ring. Its diamond catches the glow of my costume, glistening in perfect harmony with the sequins. The sight floods me with warmth and pride.

"I'm like a human-cut diamond!" I shriek, the excitement bubbling out of me in a laugh I cannot hold back.

I spin around to face the others, my girls, my sisters, The Hearts. They stand in front of me like goddesses in armor, each one a beacon of strength and beauty, each in their own shining color.

Sabrina is a vision in emerald. Her newly dyed red hair blazes beneath the lights, slicked into a high ponytail that cascades in thick curls down her back. A fierce red lip matches the fire of her hair, while her black sparkly boots anchor her like a warrior ready for battle.

Jonna glimmers in silver, her body suit flashing like liquid moonlight. Her boots mirror mine, white leather kissed with glitter, and her mocha-colored lips soften her striking look. Her dark hair flows straight and sleek, every strand glossy as though it has been spun from satin.

Then there's Dani. My breath catches. She looks like fire and royalty combined. Her golden sequins cling to her form, radiant as the sun itself. Black sparkly knee-high boots give her a grounding strength, while her lips, painted in a bold violet, honor Nora in the most heartbreaking and beautiful way. Violet extensions peek out beneath her chestnut curls, and tiny braids, each laced with gold hoops, weave throughout her hair. Her head is a crown of art and rebellion, her whole being a tribute.

"We look hot!" I squeal, my voice rising above the pounding of my heartbeat.

The girls erupt into screams, joy spilling over like champagne. In a blur of sequins and glitter, we grab hands and spin, laughing, dancing together in the circle we have always known.

After we put our ear pieces in, the atmosphere backstage becomes a whirlwind. Stage managers and crew members dart around us, shouting instructions into their headsets, wires coiling across the floor like snakes. Techs rush from one station to another, testing cables, adjusting lights, setting monitors into place. The dressing room doors slam open and shut as runners deliver last minute items. It is chaos, yet a controlled chaos, the kind that hums with anticipation.

"Guests have just started arriving to the venue. They'll begin letting them into their seats shortly," one of the crew announces, his clipboard tucked beneath his arm as he speeds past.

We sip from our water bottles, saving our voices, centering our nerves. Sabrina warms up, singing scales again and again, her voice stretching across the octaves. "Do re mi fa sol la ti do!" she repeats, focused and determined. Dani crouches low, tuning her guitar, strumming and twisting the pegs until the sound matches perfectly. Jonna sits with her bass across her lap, plucking the strings with slow precision.

I don't sing or play just yet. Instead, I take a breath and simply look around. I watch it all unfold, imprinting the sight of my sisters, the staff, the set pieces, the instruments. I want to remember this exact moment forever, the hum of energy before everything changes.

Time slips forward without me realizing it. I finally grab my guitar and tune it carefully to match Dani's. The sound vibrates through my chest, calming my nerves and sharpening my focus.

Suddenly Robbie strides backstage, a burst of glamour in his black sparkly suit. He carries a bouquet of a dozen red roses in one arm. The blooms are vivid and alive, a stark contrast to the steel-gray chaos of cords and gear.

"Robbie!" Sabrina's entire body lifts as she throws herself into his arms. Their kiss is fiery, their tongues tangled shamelessly in front of us.

I laugh and turn away dramatically. "You're making me horny!" I joke, shaking my head.

The other girls burst into laughter, the tension cracking just enough for us to breathe.

Robbie finally lets Sabrina down, his grin wide. He gives each of us a hug in turn. "You girls look great," he says, his eyes scanning us with admiration.

"So do you!" Jonna replies warmly.

"Thank you for being a part of the show," Dani adds, pulling him into a quick half hug.

"Sam is on her way with Ryan and Eric," Robbie tells us, still smiling.

Dani flushes instantly, her cheeks turning pink as she smooths out the sequined tassels on her costume. "I can't wait to see her in the crowd," she admits, her excitement barely contained.

Before we can tease her, the stage manager cuts in abruptly. "Guests are scanning their tickets and beginning to make their way into the arena."

We nod, instinctively straightening, every muscle snapping into readiness. I can't resist slipping to the side of the stage and peering through the curtain. At first, only the farthest rows begin to fill, shadows moving like waves. The faint sound of chatter rises, a murmur that grows stronger by the second.

"They're starting to trickle in!" I dart back into the room. We all smile at one another, the adrenaline bubbling higher.

"Ok, don't forget," Dani says, her voice breathless. "I'll introduce us as The Hearts. And we will turn our attention to the two LED screens on each side of the stage." Her eyes search ours until we nod in agreement.

The voice of the stage crew crackles into our ears.

"Thirty minutes to show time."

Those thirty minutes vanish like smoke. It feels like seconds. We're ushered beneath the stage, into the cavern where our pedestals wait like guardians. One for each of us, placed in perfect alignment. Dani in the center, Sabrina to her left, Jonna beside Sabrina, and me to Dani's right. Our instruments are strapped across our bodies, heavy but grounding. The machinery whirls beneath our feet as the platform prepares to lift.

The muffled hum of the crowd seeps through the floor. At first it is only a dull roar, then it swells into thunder.

The stage begins to rise. Slowly. Deliberately. Like the heavens splitting open. The darkness breaks into a flood of blinding light as the crowd erupts. Drums pound, the opening beat of our anthem rolling like thunder. Snippets of our melody cut through the noise. The fans scream, their voices colliding into one deafening sound that rattles my bones.

I glance sideways at the girls. We lock eyes and smile knowingly. This is it.

The platform locks into place. Lights swing in our direction, beams exploding across us like a sunrise. Our sequins ignite, refracting into the crowd like a thousand shooting stars. Sparkle bursts through the air, casting rays into the audience.

The arena goes wild. The fans scream, wave, jump up and down in colors that mirror ours. From this distance, they blur into a sea of pulsing light, like little fireflies buzzing in the night. Signs lift into the air: We Love U. Nora's Watching.

It's overwhelming. My chest tightens, but I push through. Routine takes over. Dani leans forward, her microphone attached to her ear.

"Good evening, New York City!" she shouts in her most dazzling performer voice. The crowd answers with a roar so loud it makes the arena shake. "We are The Hearts! And we are so happy to share the stage once again after a decade!" She gestures toward us, her smile radiant.

We wave, each of us glowing beneath the storm of cheers.

Jonna steps forward, her silver body suit glimmering. "We have a jam-packed night for all of you!" she declares, her voice strong.

My turn. I lean toward the crowd, lowering my voice into a sultry growl. "So, get ready—for the night of your lives!"

The cheers double, the energy surging back toward us like a tidal wave.

"But before we get started, we wanted to have a moment of silence for our fifth Heart, Nora," Sabrina says, her voice faltering only slightly. She points to the LED screens. Instant silence falls across the arena.

The screens flicker to life. An AI rendering of Nora appears, dressed in a matching violet body suit, descending gently from above on her pedestal. She sits childlike on a stool, her face lighting with the sweetest smile. She waves to the crowd and to us, her presence so lifelike that my throat closes.

I can't believe how real she looks. My chest aches. Beside me, Jonna wipes at her eyes quickly, struggling to hold it together.

The silence breaks. The crowd erupts into applause, chants swelling into the rafters. "We miss Nora! We miss Nora!" Over and over, thousands of voices uniting in grief and love.

The girls and I exchange looks of awe, hearts swelling at the sound.

"We miss our Nora, too. So much, it hurts!" Dani shouts into her mic, her voice breaking.

"In honor of Nora, we came here tonight to celebrate her. We brought the band back together, for good!" Dani adds, fierce with conviction.

It is not scripted, but I blurt out my own line, the words clawing to be heard. "So get used to seeing us on stage!"

Dani glances at me, a flicker of surprise in her eyes, but then she smiles.

The opening chords of "Runaway Summer" strike through the speakers. Dani and I strum in unison, our guitars ringing across the arena. Jonna's bass pulses beneath us, Sabrina blending with her harmony. The drummer pounds the beat like a war cry.

Our voices lift, weaving together, the notes entwining into something angelic. For a moment, I nearly black out, lost in the harmony, the light, the thunder of thousands of voices singing back.

The song ends. The crowd explodes into pure chaos.

In my ear, a voice crackles. Donovan has just arrived. Club level seating.

I glance at the others. Our eyes lock. Our smiles curve, sharp and knowing. The game has begun.

We launch into our next set. The opening chords of "Just a Daydream" ripple out across the arena, and the crowd erupts before we even move. The four of us step into position, our bodies falling into the rhythm we know by heart. The choreography takes over, hips swaying in perfect unison, hands carving through the air as the sequins on our costumes scatter sparks beneath the spotlights.

The beat thunders from the drums, and the bass line pulses through my chest like a second heartbeat. Dani's voice cuts through first, bold and fiery, and we follow her lead, layering harmonies until the sound blooms like fire across the stage. Sabrina flips her red hair with every beat, Jonna glimmers like a silver blade, and Dani is molten gold. I pour every ounce of myself into the song, my guitar vibrating against me as if it is alive.

The crowd is a storm of color and motion, swaying and shouting every lyric back to us. They are on their feet, thousands of them, a sea of green, fuchsia, gold, and silver, all flashing beneath the lights. It feels like the earth itself is moving, like we are standing on the center of something bigger than ourselves.

When we hit the final chorus, our voices rise together, one last explosion of harmony that fills every inch of the arena. The lights flare with us, bursting across the crowd in a blaze of brilliance. The final note crashes into silence for a split second, then breaks apart as the audience erupts.

The sound is deafening. Screams, applause, chants that roll like thunder. I clutch my guitar against me, my chest heaving with exhilaration. My face hurts from smiling, but I can't stop. I glance at the others, and the joy mirrored on their faces tells me they feel it too.

We bow quickly, still breathless, and slip off toward the wings. The roar of the arena follows us as the house lights dim in preparation for the next set. Adrenaline hums in my blood, but already my mind is shifting to what comes next.

Backstage waits for us. A change of costumes. And then the truth. Sarah's video testimony.

Chapter 33

Sabrina

The chaos backstage is the kind of chaos that feels like home. Crew members rush around us, applauding, clapping our shoulders, congratulating us for the opening set. Their voices are full of adrenaline as they usher us toward the racks of costumes. Hands tug at zippers, lace up boots, and pass us bottles of water as if every second matters. The air smells faintly of hairspray and sweat, mixed with the metallic tang of stage lights burning overhead.

We slip into our next outfits: matching violet leather two-piece sets that bare our navels, each of us wrapped with a glinting gold chain around the waist. Our boots are violet leather, rising high and sharp with shine. Violet. Nora's color.

I feel my throat tighten as I fasten the chain across my stomach. This is not just a costume change. This is a declaration. This is war paint. Tonight, Donovan will see us glowing in Nora's shade, and he will know exactly who this performance belongs to. This is for her.

We stand in a circle, hair down and free, tumbling in waves over our shoulders. There is no time for mirrors, so we glance at one another, eyes shining, and nod in silent approval. We are each other's reflection now.

The opening beat of our next song pulses faintly through the monitors. Nora's song. "Never."

We step back onto the stage as one. The crowd recognizes it instantly. A slower tempo. Haunting. The air shifts, a hush rippling across the sea of people before the applause crashes down like a wave. Their screams carry grief and devotion.

I sling my bass over my shoulder, fingers trembling, and glance to Dani. She grips her electric guitar like a weapon, then strums the opening chords. Her voice follows, low and raw, scraping at the edges of pain.

"Deep in the trenches, along the ravines, I travel the world in a soul flying dream."

The sound slices straight through me. The fans cry out, their flashlights swaying like hundreds of small stars.

Dani strikes a heavy chord, then snarls into the mic again, voice rising. "I search for the meanings, fight perilous fiends. I'm chewed up and spit out, but still sparkle and sing."

Our cue arrives. The three of us join her, our voices locked in a harmony that feels ripped from the heavens.

"Never grow up, never be wise, I choose ignorance every damn time."

Our voices are desperate, the words laced with truth. We belt harder, tears stinging the corners of our eyes.

"Never stand true, never act used, because in the end, you're left bound and bruised!"

The crowd screams along, their voices breaking, thousands singing Nora's words back to us. The stadium becomes a choir of grief and rebellion. Flashlights swing in unison, white fireflies shimmering in the dark.

I force my gaze upward, my chest pounding. At club level, his figure is clear enough. Donovan Blake. He is unmistakable. He sits in his box seat like a king surveying his kingdom, his smile smug, his eyes locked on us. He thinks he is untouchable.

Not tonight.

The final solo wails from Dani's guitar, piercing, haunting, dragging the last threads of the song into silence. We hum softly into the microphones, weaving a ghostly echo across the crowd.

When the final note fades, the arena erupts in thunderous applause. And then, from the darkness above, Nora appears again.

Her AI rendering descends slowly on her stool, her body glowing violet. She waves, her smile bright, her pedestal lifting her back toward the rafters. The sight nearly steals my breath. It looks so real, so heartbreakingly real, as if heaven itself is reclaiming her. My chest aches, my throat locks.

Dani steps forward, her voice steady but low. "As most of you know, Nora Hayes wrote this song and it appeared on our first studio album, *Our Summer.* This song means a lot to us, as it depicts the pain she suffered in her life during the process of that album."

Clare's voice follows, soft but sharp with grief. "What we didn't know was how deep that pain struck. All that time, come to find out, Nora was being abused."

Jonna inhales, her voice nearly trembling. "She endured abuse of every kind from the man that signed us. A man we entrusted with our safety and girlhood."

The arena falls silent, every soul waiting. My turn.

I grip the microphone with steady hands and let the fury ignite in my chest. "Donovan Blake raped Nora Hayes. She endured the shame and painful memories for years until she had enough. And when she threatened to expose him, he sent his goons to kill her." My voice cuts through the arena, calm but louder than thunder.

The audience gasps in unison, thousands of breaths caught in horror.

In our ear, the crew's voice crackles. "Steve came forward to the police an hour ago after questioning. Playing Sarah's testimony now."

We glance at each other, stunned. Relief flashes across Dani's face. Steve confessed. The walls are closing in on Donovan.

Sarah's face appears on the screens. Her eyes are wet, her voice shaking, as she delivers her testimony. The arena is silent, listening to every word, hanging on her truth. Each syllable slices like a blade, exposing years of rot.

When her video ends, the feed switches to a live shot of Donovan. His face fills the jumbotrons, enormous above us. The crowd explodes in fury. Booing, screaming, throwing food at the glass. His smile has vanished. He looks stricken, pale, like a ghost caught in the spotlight.

Then the cops appear. A line of them, suited in dark uniforms, climbing the stairs toward the box seat. Dozens of them. Their boots pound in unison, an army rising toward him.

Dani's voice booms. "Donovan Blake. We have served under your control for too long. We hope that no one else ever feels the wrath of your abuse. We have proof now. You are a monster, and you deserve to rot in prison for what you did to Nora. For what you did to all of us!" Her words crackle with rage, every syllable a strike.

The camera remains on him, zoomed in so the world can see his downfall. At first, his eyes are wide with panic. Fear rolls off him in waves. But then, something changes.

As the police break into the box and snap the cuffs around his wrists, his terror curdles. His lips twist into a slow, terrible grin. He looks straight into the camera, straight at us, and smiles. Not a smile of confidence, not even of arrogance. It is a demon's smile, cold and hungry, as if he carries the shadows of hell behind his teeth.

Dani meets his gaze, unflinching. No words are exchanged, but the air between them is heavy with defiance. She does not look away, and neither does he.

The officers drag him out of the box, forcing him down the stairs. The crowd continues to roar, screaming for his downfall. My knees weaken with relief, my chest finally exhaling the breath I had been holding for years.

Our plan worked. For the first time, it feels like justice is real.

Chapter 34

Dani

The sound of the audience is a storm. Applause crashes against sobs, weeping collides with screams of relief and fury. It is so loud that I can barely hear the sound of my own breath. Yet beneath it all, my heartbeat pounds like a drum, steady, insistent, louder than the chaos around me.

A strange stillness lives inside that rhythm. Justice. It flows through me like an electric current, every nerve alive with tingling approval, as though the universe itself is acknowledging what just happened.

I look down, scanning the endless sea of faces, until I find her. My Sam.

She stands in the crowd as if a spotlight belongs only to her. She is radiant, wearing a sparkly gold dress that mirrors my own signature color. Her black shaggy hair tumbles in soft curls, her lips painted bright red, glistening beneath the lights. Tears streak her cheeks as she looks up at me, nodding with pride.

My breath catches. The butterflies in my stomach scatter wildly, but beneath the flutter is a profound confirmation. This happened. We did it. We exposed him. And the plan worked flawlessly.

On the jumbotrons, the feed of Donovan vanishes. The camera is cut, his face erased as he is escorted out of the venue. The overhead lights swing back toward us, bathing our violet leather costumes in a glow so fierce it feels like Nora is shining down.

I reach for my microphone, adjusting it with a trembling hand. My lungs burn as I drag in a deep breath. "Justice was served today," I begin, my voice carrying into the rafters. "We want to thank the NYPD for complying with our approach to honor Nora, and for catching her predator, her murderer."

The word murderer tastes like ash on my tongue. My stomach twists, but I push forward. "May no one else get abused like Nora and me."

For a moment, I hesitate. The arena is silent except for the faint rustle of bodies shifting. I glance at the girls beside me, searching for their eyes, needing their strength. They nod, their faces open, loving, accepting. Permission to continue.

"Or like Sarah. Or anyone who ever came into contact with Donovan Blake." My voice rises. "The music industry doesn't have to be evil. You should not have to sign a deal with the devil. It can be a place of beauty, where artists come together to create with passion, in peace, and in love."

The last word breaks from my chest in a shout, filled with everything I have left.

The crowd explodes. Cheers shake the arena so hard it feels as if the earth itself is moving. A rumble of unity. A sound that will never leave me.

I lift my chin, tears stinging my eyes, and keep going. "That is why we are bringing the band back together. At our own recording label. Violet Hayes Records. A safe and creative space where no one will ever fear again. We will come back stronger. We will come back united. We are… The Hearts!"

The girls' hands slide into mine, warm and strong.

Together we lift our arms high into the air. Four women. Four survivors. Bonded. Unbroken.

The audience becomes a sea of stars, phone flashlights lifted, swaying in time with their chants. The moment is holy, a cathedral built not of walls but of light and voices. It will live in me forever.

The beat drops for our next song, "The Boy Next Door." Without hesitation we grip our instruments and dive into the sound, playing with every ounce of fire, soul, and love that still burns inside us.

Sabrina and Robbie finish the second-to-last song of the night with their duet, their voices weaving together so effortlessly it sends the arena into a frenzy. The roar of the crowd is deafening at the sight of his cameo, fans screaming his name as if he were one of us.

Clare, Jonna, and I slip backstage while they perform, crew members already waiting with our last costumes of the night. Silk fabric glimmers under the vanity lights as we step into gowns the color of moonlight. Flowing white dresses cling and sway, slit high at the thighs, each of us lifted by gold stilettos that gleam like molten metal. The effect is ethereal. We look like Greek goddesses summoned to the stage.

"That was ELECTRIC," Clare squeals, her voice bubbling with adrenaline.

"Did you see the LOOK on his face?" Jonna shouts as a stylist zips her dress and brushes her hair back into place.

I purse my lips as a makeup artist sweeps fresh color across them, sealing me for the finale. "May he rot in prison for life," I whisper, tilting my gaze upward as though the ceiling might part and carry my words straight to Nora. My smile softens. I can almost feel her presence, watching us.

"'Free for the Season' is our last song," I remind the girls, my tone shifting into command. "When Sabrina comes back, she's quickly going to change and we are going out with a bang!"

Both nod, focused now, adrenaline turned into readiness.

Sabrina bursts through the curtains, still glowing from her duet, her cheeks flushed, hair slightly undone. "Did you hear it? The crowd absolutely adored us!" she squeals, her excitement infectious.

The crew strips her down in a practiced blur, sliding her into her flowing silk gown, the fabric falling into place like water. She steps into her gold stilettos, transformed in seconds.

"You sounded amazing," I tell her, my words firm and grounding. She catches my look, and I can see the silent approval she needed in my eyes.

"You ready?" I ask, glancing at each of them.

The girls nod in unison, a sisterhood of light.

We step onto the stage together. The arena answers with fire. Pillars ignite on either side, shooting flames into the air, their heat rushing across the floorboards as I strum the opening chords of "Free for the Season."

The crowd erupts instantly, their voices already catching the rhythm. Clare spins forward, her white dress flowing like wings. "Sun on my skin, hair in the wind!" she belts, her curls bouncing under the strobe lights.

Jonna steps into her line, her silver shimmer long gone, replaced by alabaster silk that glows like starlight. "No rules tonight, let the summer begin!" she sings, her voice smooth and rich.

The four of us converge, our harmonies slamming into the pre-chorus as sparks rain from the ceiling.

"We don't need love, we don't need plans,
Just a little freedom in our hands."

The floor beneath us trembles with the chants of the crowd, hands flying into the air as if they too have been unchained. The chorus hits like an explosion.

"We're free, free for the season!
Living wild, don't need a reason!

Hands up, hearts on fire,
Girls together, taking it higher!"

The fans are a tidal wave, every word thrown back at us, echoing louder than the speakers. Thousands of phone flashlights swing like stars, turning the arena into a galaxy orbiting us.

Sabrina flips her hair and struts across the stage, her emerald replaced by white silk, but her fire unchanged. "Drinks on the beach, glow in the dark!" she shouts into the mic, the crowd shrieking back.

I close my eyes as I strum, my guitar vibrating through my ribs. This is what freedom sounds like. This is what survival feels like.

We launch into the bridge, the crowd screaming the "oh-ohs" with us, their voices rising into the rafters. Then the music cuts. Silence. The spotlight burns hot, and the clapping begins.

I lean forward, my grin spreading across my face. "We're free!"

"Yeah!" the audience roars back.

"We're wild!"

"Yeah!"

"Living tonight!"

"Yeah!"

"In style!"

The chant repeats, louder each time, until the entire arena is pounding in rhythm, the sound rolling through my bones like thunder.

We slam into the final chorus, flames bursting in time with the beat, our arms raised, hair flying, silk dresses whipping in the smoke.

"We're free, free for the season! Free tonight, free for the season!"

The last note crashes into silence. The crowd explodes, their voices shaking the walls of Madison Square Garden. I turn to the girls, our eyes locking, our bodies trembling with exhaustion and joy. For a moment, I swear I feel Nora standing between us, smiling, free with us at last.

We strike our final pose, then bow together, a silent declaration that justice has been served. As the pedestals sink, the thunder of the crowd fades into a muffled blur, but the fire in my chest blazes strong.

Chapter 35

Clare

The girls and I stand in the darkness beneath the stage, our chests rising and falling, breaths sharp and heavy. The air smells of smoke, sweat, and confetti, but all I feel is the weight of the moment pressing down. My skin glistens, beads of sweat tracing my temples, my white silk dress clinging to me as though it, too, remembers the heat of the lights. I glance at my sisters. The glow from our gowns reflects faintly onto our flushed faces, our eyes shimmering with exhaustion and triumph. None of us speaks. We do not need to. The silence says everything.

We make our way down the corridor, back toward our dressing rooms, the muffled roar of the arena still echoing in our ears. The doors swing open and suddenly the quiet is gone, replaced by the flood of family and friends waiting for us.

Dani collides into Sam, their arms wrapping around each other in a desperate, joy-filled embrace. Dexter presses a soft kiss to Jonna's lips while the kids latch onto her legs, giggling and squealing. Baby Alissa has already been returned safely, tucked back into the care of Dexter's mom, likely waiting at the hotel for the night to be over.

In one corner, Sabrina and Robbie are locked together, kissing hungrily, while Ryan and Eric stride up to me, pulling me into a tight hug. Their pride radiates in their grip, but even as I thank them, my eyes search past their shoulders, scanning. My pulse races. I know who I am looking for.

And then I see him. Tom. My six-foot-five vision in white. He strides toward me in an immaculate suit, the sharp lines of the fabric making him look untouchable, like a god descending into my chaos. In his hands, he carries not one bouquet but four, an armful of wildflowers bursting with color.

"Baby," he says, shaking his head, utterly undone. His voice cracks with awe. "You were BREATHTAKING!" He shouts it with his whole chest, his eyes locked on me.

I cannot hold back. I leap into him, the flowers pressed between us, their scent flooding my senses as my legs wrap tight around his waist. Our mouths crash together, teeth grazing, tongues twisting. It is fire and ice, push and pull, a wrestling match we never want to end. His arms are iron around me, and for a moment, the entire room dissolves. There is no one else. Just us.

His lips break from mine, trailing hot against my cheek until they reach my ear. His voice drops to a growl. "I'm going to fuck you so hard tonight."

The words rip through me. A shiver explodes down my spine, my thighs tightening around him as my panties dampen instantly. My lips curl into a slow, devilish grin, a silent promise.

"Clare, honey!" The spell shatters with my mother's voice.

She waddles toward us, her hands outstretched. Tom eases me down, and I quickly smooth my hair before wrapping my arms around her.

"That was spectacular," she says, her tone almost

foreign. It takes me a moment to realize why it feels so strange. It is the first nice thing she has ever said to me.

An hour passes in a blur of celebration. Champagne corks pop, laughter fills the dressing rooms, flashes from phones and cameras catch us in the glow of victory. Normally, we would spill into the city after a show like this, ready to drink and dance until dawn. But tonight is different. Our bodies are drained, our hearts raw. We have given everything to the stage. None of us have the energy for after-parties.

Dani sends a text into our group chat while Tom and I ride in the back of the car, his hand resting on my thigh, warm and steady.

The Hearts are back with a vengeance! Tomorrow, brunch is on me!

She drops the pin to the restaurant, and one by one, little hearts light up in the thread. Our driver pulls up to the ivory brick tower, our new home in Greenwich Village. Tom slips his arm around me as we step out, the city lights gleaming against his white suit. I take a deep breath and look up at the tower, at the life waiting inside.

No longer just Clare Devon, the girl who once lost herself. Tonight, I walk inside as Clare Devon of The Hearts, reborn, reclaimed, unstoppable.

Chapter 36

Dani

THREE MONTHS LATER

Spring settles over Long Island, soft and insistent, as if the earth itself is reminding us to begin again. Dogwoods bloom pink and white along the streets, and the breeze carries the damp sweetness of thawed soil. For the first time in years, my chest feels light.

Three months have passed since the tribute show. Since Donovan Blake was dragged out of Madison Square Garden in cuffs while Sarah's testimony played on the giant screen for the world to see. His empire collapsed overnight, and the silence around Kaleidoscope shattered. One woman came forward, then another, and then dozens more. Their stories poured into the open, a tidal wave that could not be stopped. A *Me Too* reckoning inside the industry that once protected him. Their voices turned the whispers of survival into a roar of justice. Donovan's name is filth now, his legacy destroyed, his life confined to the walls of a prison cell.

And yet, even with justice served, Nora's absence is carved into us. We carry her in every note. In every lyric scratched out on paper at three in the morning. In the name we gave to the place that belongs to us now: **Violet Hayes Records**

All the money I have ever earned, every royalty, every deal, I poured it into this studio.

Around the corner from Jonna's house, our studio gleams like a second home. Polished floors, walls painted in warm earth tones, the hum of state-of-the-art equipment. Nora's name written across the sign outside, promising she'll never be forgotten.

Inside, joy fills the air like sunlight.

Clare perches on a stool, holding her left hand out so we can all admire the ring again. The diamond winks in the light. Tom watches her with soft eyes from across the room. Their Tuscan wedding is just weeks away, an intimate spring ceremony among vineyards and olive trees. Until then, they float between their Greenwich Village townhome and here, never missing a session.

Sabrina sprawls across the couch, Robbie's arm looped around her. She scribbles lyrics while he teases her about rhyming choices, their laughter spilling into every corner. Just last month, her editor Jerry at *The Times* offered her a major promotion after she released the story of Sarah being witness to Nora's murder. It's the kind of career step most reporters dream of, but she turned it down and resigned, choosing us instead. Choosing The Hearts.

Their loft in New York City has become their sanctuary. I've never seen her so steady, and so fearless in love.

Jonna and Dexter share the arm of a chair, fingers intertwined. Their marriage breathes new life now, no longer worn thin by routine and old wounds. The kids are thriving, loud and happy. Baby Alissa totters across the floor clutching her stuffed bunny, giggling at every step.

And Sam. My Sam. She sits close, her knee pressed against mine, her smile soft and sure. These months together have stitched something deep and lasting between us. Some nights, when she's asleep and I'm still wide awake, I picture what it would mean to make her mine forever.

We've given up everything else. Past careers, distractions, other lives and have become The Hearts. Together, full force.

Our notebooks are filled with half-finished verses, scraps of melodies, bursts of inspiration. We write until dawn, chasing the songs that belong to us alone.

I should feel complete. Whole.

The phone on the studio desk rings. The sound cuts through the warmth like glass breaking. The chatter in the room falls quiet.

I rise, every step toward the receiver heavy.

"Hello?"

"Danielle Richmond?" the operator's voice asks. "You have a collect call from New York State Penitentiary. Do you accept?"

My breath catches. My hand trembles. The world narrows to the phone in my palm.

"Yes."

A pause. A click.

Then, the voice. Smooth, cold, unmistakable.

"Hello, Dani."

My chest seizes. My fingers tighten until my knuckles burn. It feels like the air has been ripped out of the room.

"You and I both know," Donovan says, slow and deliberate, "I didn't write the suicide note."

The line goes dead.

I stand frozen, the receiver pressed to my ear. Around me, laughter resumes, faint and unknowing, as though nothing has changed. But my stomach twists, my heart pounding so loud I can barely hear them.

Because he knows.

And I pray the girls never find out the truth about what I did.

I hang up the phone. Forcing my lips into a smile, as I turn back toward the warmth of the studio. I let their laughter pull me in, weaving my own laugh into theirs.

On the surface, I am one of them again, our voices rising together, our future shining bright.

But deep down I know that if they ever uncovered my secret, I would lose them all over again. My best friends.

The silence of being utterly, unmistakably, alone again would completely destroy me, more than Donovan Blake ever could.

And sometimes, during the graveyard shift, my mind wanders—

How long can I keep the truth buried?

www.ingramcontent.com/pod-product-compliance
Lightning Source LLC
Chambersburg PA
CBHW071554110726
47908CB00007B/2097